SYMBOLISM

Printed in the United States of America

First Printing, 2019

ISBN 978-0578462219

Ingram Content Group Inc.
1 Ingram Boulevard, La Vergne, Tennessee 37086
(615) 793-5000
IngramContent.com

Preface

I would like to thank my friends and family that have helped me throughout my journey of finishing this story. This is the last installment of The Number Conspiracy, but I'm ending it with a more personal point of view. We live in a world filled with such overwhelming temptation, it can control us at any moment. We live in a world that's filled with many mysteries that are yet to be solved. In today's society, there are very few people that are credited for their good deeds, which most go unspoken. Despite the series being entirely fictional, every chapter that's read could teach a lesson.

Even heroes have their own weaknesses, whether it's from their past or from the outcomes of their actions. No matter what the outcome is, whether good or bad, there comes a point in life where you have to make hard decisions. With these decisions, they can either be life lessons or benefits. The last book of this series is called Symbolism for a reason. Because at one point or another, your actions may determine the symbolism of who you are.

In Loving Memory

Ralph William Giovannone (Saturday, August 26, 1950 – Wednesday, March 28, 2007)

Alberta "JoAnn" Heeter (Friday, January 15, 1926 – Sunday, January 19, 2014)

Sharon Sue Giovannone-Furbee (Saturday, September 1, 1951 – Wednesday, May 21, 2014)

Sierra Giovannone-Roberts (Saturday, October 6, 1990 – Friday, June 27, 2014)

Donald Leroy "Gio" Giovannone (Monday, February, 8, 1943 – Tuesday, November 18, 2014)

Megan Renee Grimsic (Thursday, April 11, 1997 – Saturday, November 4, 2017)

Deborah J. Stutler (Tuesday, March 27, 1956 – Saturday, May 19, 2018)

Ryan Scott Francis Jr. (Sunday, December 31, 1995 – Tuesday, July 17, 2018)

Introduction Part 1

March 21, 2021

Unknown Location, 0907 hours

"Seven months?" Darrell said in a weak tone. Darrell and Phoenix are in a room that looks like a hospital room. Phoenix looks around for objects, terrified. She shakes her head and says, "Alright, we have to find a way out of here. But first, we have to get your stuff together before they find out we're awake." All of Darrell's equipment is on a table that's neatly arranged near the door.

"Is this really happening?" Darrell said.

"Yes, this is. I have a feeling something's not right here."

Suddenly, Phoenix's communicator starts ringing. She whispers, "Who is this?"

"Take a wild guess," it was Russell.

"Russell?!" Russell laughs in an evil manner, "You got that right. It takes an army to just take two people in. How are you feeling?"

"It's only a matter of time. Where are you hiding, you coward? Show yourself!"

"Let's make this simple, we screw you over. That's how we do things in IFHR. How'd you like that glimpse of death near the Archives?" Russell laughs. Phoenix gets angry and grunts as she punches the table. "You're a sick bastard, you son of a bitch! Rose was right about you, you guys play it like a bloodsport." Darrell heavily breathes and tries to move his limbs, but struggles. Phoenix signals him to be quiet by putting her finger to her lips.

"I can hear you in the background. It'd be the best

intention for you to quit before you make it worse on yourself."

"DON'T tell me what to do!"

"Hmm, still stubborn from day one. You're never going to learn."

"I will find you and I will kill you!"

"Good luck doing that because I'm nowhere near where you're at."

"What are you talking about?"

Darrell regains some of his movement in his arms after moving them up and down. "The organization has its own way of doing things, now I'm in control, and you'll do what I say," Russell said.

"And what would that be? Your mind games are getting old. You've pulled enough tricks for me to know what you're capable of," Phoenix said.

"Wow, you read my mind!" Russell said sarcastically.

"Fortunately, that's what you guys will be participating in! You guys are my first test subjects."

Phoenix mouths out the words to Darrell, "Get up and try to walk." Darrell moves his legs up and down to regain some movement. "You're going to do things my way from now on. I call this the Game of Trials," Russell said. Darrell forces himself out of the hospital bed and falls hard to the ground. His legs were still numb from the side effects of his comatose stage. "This will last up to ten trials from whoever I choose and wherever I choose."

"And if we disobey?" Phoenix said.

"Then you will regret everything that you do during this. Your world of hell is just beginning." Russell dismisses.

Phoenix hears agents walking in the hallway. "She better be in there. She's on supervised watch," one of the agents said. They stop walking and look through the window of her door. "What the hell?!" one of the agents said, surprised.

One of them punches the door. "This is impossible! I thought she was in a fucking coma!"

"This isn't good, she could be hiding anywhere! Search the rooms and everything!" The agents split up and check in the vast number of rooms scattered across the hallways.

Phoenix walks up beside the door's window and panics, "Shit, they know I'm gone! I can't let them in!" She quickly moves her arm to the other side of the door and places her hand over the hand scanner. The screen read as ACCESS DENIED. Darrell grunts from his legs, "Son of a bitch!" Phoenix slams her foot on the ground in frustration, "Shit, I can't lock it, I don't have the code! It's no fucking use!"

Darrell was thinking about the scenario. He was going into a flashback of Russell using his communicator to override Base No. 00367's security system in New Idria, California to unlock the doors. "Use.. your.. communicator," Darrell said, grunting from the pain.

"How, Darrell? How do you know what to do?"

"Russell used his communicator in the training session. There might be something on the communicator that we haven't messed with yet." Phoenix looks around on the communicator to look for buttons they missed while searching for the Archives. "S and OVERRIDE?" Phoenix said. She presses OVERRIDE near the hand scanner. "No effect."

"Try pressing E, then OVERRIDE." She quickly places the communicator over the scanner and presses both buttons. The E button stands for emergency. The communicator releases powerful electrical energy, emitting a bright, blue light. She holds the buttons as the electrical energy is escaping the communicator, creating a noise similar to a circuit. "Come on! Go through!" Phoenix said. The energy was growing stronger as the circuit noise is getting more distorted. "This can't be good," Phoenix said, watching the light and almost feeling its energy. The screen read as ACCESS

After releasing the buttons, the light dissipates in a split-second as its energy was released, creating a loud, crackling sound. Some of its energy transferred to Phoenix, shocking her arm and giving her a temporarily immobilizing pinch. She reacts to the transfer and forcefully grabs hold of her arm. She grunts, "Oh, motherfucker!" Her arm starts shaking and she falls to the ground. She moves her body around as she reacts more to the pain. She starts to yank her arm around and slams it on the floor to reduce the numbness. Her arm starts tingling, "Damn, that hurt!"

Phoenix gets up and walks to Darrell, "Get up. Can you move?"

"Just partially, still need to take baby steps." Darrell attempts to get up, but is struggling from his legs. He tries to move his legs with all of his power, but that makes the pain worse. "Ow, FUCK!!" he yelled. Phoenix quickly crouches down towards Darrell and says in a soft tone, "Shh, be quiet! They know I'm up!" Darrell breathes heavily and panics. "Darrell, calm down. I'll help you move, we're going to be hiding beside the table. All of your stuff is on there."

Darrell and Phoenix begin to crawl away from the door and beside the table, but Darrell is struggling. Phoenix gets up and crawls back to Darrell, "Here, I'll help you. I'll take you over there myself." She wraps her arms around his chest and carefully drags him over to the far end of the table. "Try moving your legs," Phoenix said.

Darrell and Phoenix stop and approach the end of the table as Darrell gradually continues to move his legs around, regaining some of his movement. "First, you act like a bitch thirsty for blood for one moment, but then you're nice enough to suddenly care. What the fuck?" Darrell said.

"Who said we all can't have a soft spot? I still have a caring side in me when I was with Warren." Phoenix said, smiling. She quickly gets up and runs to the hand scanner to lock the door. "But, things are different now when it comes to *my* circumstances," she said, brazenly. She walks back to the table and grabs Darrell's pistol and hands it to him. "Stay low, I can hear them coming."

Two agents run up to the door of Darrell's room and look through the window. They don't see Darrell. "Shit, he's not there either!" one of the agents panicked.

"Open the door, maybe he's hiding. Also watch out for Phoenix, too." One of the agents attempt to budge open the door by charging himself into it, but no effect. The agents were surprised.

Phoenix was growing tense. The agents charge at the door again, but get the same result. The agents looked at each other. "They must've locked the door," one of them said.

"Let's find the alarm! We can't let them get away!"

"Shit!" Phoenix shouted quietly. The agents run away from the door before she could get up.

Phoenix panics and gets up, "Darrell, how far are you in regaining movement?"

"Not very far." Phoenix hesitates and briefly looks around the room, thinking of a solution. "I'll help you up if you're too weak to go long distances on your own," Phoenix said. "Try getting up." Darrell tries to use his legs to stand up, but he starts to tip over, reacting to the numbing effects of the coma. Phoenix catches him, "You're too weak." She smiles, "How about I help you up?"

Phoenix pulls Darrell up by putting his arm over her shoulder. Darrell was able to pull himself up, but just barely. He tries to get his weapons and supplies from the table, but struggles to do so as he picks up his daggers and knives. They walk to the door as Phoenix unlocks it with the hand scanner.

Phoenix opens the door ever so slightly and peeks her

head out to look for agents. There were no agents present.

"Alright, looks like the coast is clear," Phoenix said. She

quickly closes the door and approaches Darrell. She takes off

his hospital gown and goes to his business attire that's hung

by the hospital bed. "Hello? Anybody home?" Russell said.

"What the hell do you want?" Phoenix said.

"Surely, you would like to know. I'm only going to help

you this one more time. Remember in the organization for

when a new member is recruited? They call this the initiation.

But with my own little game, this is a special kind. There's

only one way out if you guys want to get out of there alive.

That's all I want to give. But after that, you're on your own.

Are you going to prepare for your deathbed or choose the

road to freedom? The choice is yours." Russell laughs and

dismisses.

Phoenix quickly grabs his attire and walks to Darrell as

they both put on his dress shirt and suit jacket. "I hope you're prepared for this," Phoenix said. Darrell cocks his pistol to check if it's in full capacity.

"Need to learn how to walk still," Darrell said.

"Well, we're moving out right now. You look like you're struggling a little bit, but you can manage through. Try not to make too much noise." Phoenix cocks her pistol and walks out of the door as Darrell follows her into the brightly lit hallways. He limps as Phoenix moves ahead. They turn and approach a long, straight hallway. She notices him falling behind, "Here, I'll slow down a little bit. Try keeping your posture straight." Darrell listens as he slightly straightens his back, but still limps.

There were security cameras that were equally separated and were close to ceiling level, which is about sixty feet high. Phoenix looks up in the cameras and says, "They've been keeping a watchful eye on us. Look at all of these damn cameras."

Darrell becomes paranoid, "Just what we need, cameras. They're everywhere, even in the outside world." Phoenix keeps shifting her head around, looking for a way out. "Maybe that could be our way out," she was referring to the cameras.

Suddenly, a loud alarm is sounded throughout the hallways, making Phoenix panic. "Shit!" she yelled. "Darrell, come on!" Phoenix starts to powerwalk towards the end of the hallway, approaching the door. Darrell regained most of his movement as he's almost catching up to Phoenix. "We have to get the fuck out of here!"

Phoenix sees agents' silhouettes fastly approaching the door. The agents budge through and aim at Darrell and Phoenix, showing expressions of anger and determination. Phoenix immediately pulls out her two gray pistols and aims at the six agents. "Get ready, Darrell!" Phoenix said. They charge at the agents as both parties start shooting. Phoenix fires in an alternating pattern and kills three of them, traveling through their necks and foreheads with blood gushing out profusely. Darrell shoots two rounds at the agents as the bullets split, killing them instantly. He suddenly trips and falls to the ground. Phoenix blows the smoke out of the barrel of her pistols. He struggles to get up as he still feels slightly numb. "Why in the hell does it this have to happen NOW?!" Darrell yelled.

Agents start emerging from the other side of the hallway as they are far away. The agents sprint towards them and shoot at them, barely missing them. "Darrell, get behind that wall! There's another hallway next to you!" Phoenix said. Darrell forcefully crawls over to the edge of the hallway and gets behind as the bullet ricochet on the floor past him. "Okay, I can play that game, too," Phoenix said towards the agents.

Phoenix jumps onto a wall and runs on it, going towards

the agents. As she jumps off of the wall, she shoots her dual

pistols with astonishing marksmanship, ending up with all

headshots on the four agents. She lands on the ground and

hoists her pistols.

More agents carrying pistols come from the door behind

Phoenix. They stop running and aim at her. "It's over,

Phoenix, just face it! You should've been dead by now!" one

of the agents said.

"*Hmm.*" Phoenix said, not expressing fear, but

determination. "How funny of you to say that." She slowly

pulls both of her swords out and turns around. "When you've

said it a million times before."

Phoenix walks to the agents as they fire a couple rounds.

She deflects them with split-second speed, causing them to

ricochet onto the walls. "You should take a better shot than

that," Phoenix taunted. While deflecting, one of the rounds

travelled through the center of one of the agents' chests.

"You've only failed yourselves." She notices one of the agents aiming at Darrell as he's still on the ground. She runs up to the agent and slashes him deep in the chest. She gets close in his face and says, "I wouldn't do that I were you." The agent collapses as he gurgles from the wound and dies. There are two of them left. She runs up to one of them. The agent was about to melee her with his pistol, but she executed a counter attack and strikes him in the diaphragm, making his eyes widen and redden from the pressure. "You should've thought twice before you decided to get involved in this shithole!" She takes her other sword and cuts through the center of his chest. Blood starts coming out of his mouth as he gurgles from the burning sensation. She quickly pulls the swords out of the agent as he collapses, giving way to the blood loss.

Phoenix focuses on the last agent, but the agent gets petrified and starts to run from her. He hyperventilates and turns his back while running and shoots a couple rounds, but she deflects them. She walks hastily after the agent, hunting him down. "Oh, no, not this time." He enters through the door the agents came in. "Just where do you think you're going?" She begins to run through the door.

As Phoenix enters the new room, it was gray and had a small flight of steps with a railing around it. The agent turns around again and shoots a round, but she deflects it, bouncing back and through his wrist. The agent screams in agonizing pain as he kneels and grips tightly on his bleeding wound. Phoenix widens her eyes in rage and vengeance that's quickly flowing through her. "PLEASE, DON'T KILL ME! I'm ashamed from what I've done! I'M SORRY!" the agent pleaded as he was crying. She walks up to the agent, "Oh, yeah?" She scrapes her sword across the floor as she walks down the steps. "You're SORRY?!" She walks off of the steps. She puts more fear in the agent's eyes as he backs away.

"Now you know how I feel when all of you pathetic excuses of WHAT we call humanity HAVE KILLED MY HUSBAND!" She walks closer to the agent. "Now, do you think it looks like that would a logical reason to apologize?" She smiles in disgust. "No, it doesn't, does it?" She said calmly, "Well, killing you won't solve the best of problems this time. It doesn't affect me as much."

"NO! PLEASE, NO!" the agent begged. She jerks one of her swords into his collarbone. He screams in excruciating pain as his whole body shakes. "This is only the beginning!" She yanks out the sword. "You have yet to experience what I'm FULLY capable of!" She jerks the sword into his leg.

Darrell is still laying on the floor as he listens to the agent's plead. Something popped in his head relating to all of the ordeals leading up to present day. "Wait a minute," he said. "Her psyche's getting worse! I need to stop her!" He grunts and attempts to get up. As he gets on his feet, he shakes his arms and kicks his legs to wake himself up.

Phoenix pulls out the sword from the agent's leg. She gets close in the agent's face, "Now, do you think I could get more sincere than that?!" The agent cries more as his eyes redden. She whispers in rage, "You don't know what I'm capable of, and you're just one of the very many on my list to experience it. You think I forgot about you? Think again!" She holds both swords and spreads them out. "I'm not finished spreading my message. The world needs to know for what you people did to them!" She jerks him in the diaphragm.

Darrell regains all of his movement, but his body feels slightly numb. "Son of a bitch," he said as he's running to the door Phoenix and the agent went in.

"Because my name is Phoenix Leyton! And I'm BACK with a VENGEANCE!"

"NO!" Darrell spots Phoenix and storms into the room, but it's too late. She jerks the other sword into the agent's heart, making him gargle by the blood coming from his

mouth. She pulls the swords out of his body, forming an X.

She disperses the swords and cuts deeply through more of

his chest as his eyes roll back and collapses to the ground.

"PHOENIX!" Darrell yelled. Phoenix could only see red as she

barely heard him. Darrell walks up to Phoenix and grabs her

by the arms, but not violently. "Phoenix, snap out of it!"

Darrell pleaded.

Phoenix wakes up and returns to reality, "What

happened?"

"Your psyche is getting worse, we need to get out of

here!"

"Don't you tell me what's getting worse! I already know

what's in my situation!" Darrell looks toward the door, "Well,

we have to get out of here. The alarm's still going off. We

need to find our car." Something snapped in his mind, "Wait

a minute, our car! Our car may be somewhere! Can you drive

for right now? My body's still a little numb."

"Yeah, I can do that."

Darrell and Phoenix exit the room and sprint into another hallway. As they budge through the door ahead of them, they enter a small corridor with cement walls and pipes with cages covering them. They budge through the door ahead of them and enter a large garage. The room was bright as there were dozens of vehicles to choose from, such as supercars, SUVs, and coupés arranged neatly. "There's a few Lamborghinis in here, look for an orange one that appears to be in elite form," Darrell said. They scour around the garage through the columns of vehicles. "And be on the lookout for agents. I'll try to find a way to get in the car if it's locked," Phoenix said.

Suddenly, agents come barging in from the door they entered in with assault rifles. "Shit! Phoenix we have company!" Darrell yelled. The agents start shooting in all directions as Darrell and Phoenix sprint around the vehicles. Phoenix runs around the Lamborghini to get to the driver's side. Darrell hides beside a midnight blue Porsche. The agents keep shooting as they create bullet holes on some of the vehicles. "You can't hide forever!" one of the agents said. The agents separate as they go after the vehicles they're hiding beside. Two agents come towards the Porsche as Darrell's hiding beside its wheel. Darrell quickly gets up and shoots one of them in the chest. He goes for the other agent and grabs him. He shoves the agent and pushes him with aggressive force against the hood of the Porsche. He then fires two scattershots into the agent's chest and neck, traveling through his skull.

Phoenix tries to open the door by bashing the window, but it doesn't work as its windows are bulletproof. Darrell runs toward the Lamborghini, "Here, let me help you." He pulls out one of his daggers and punctures the window after a couple blows, making the window look like snow. The remaining agents fire at the Lamborghini, making Darrell and Phoenix duck. Darrell gets out of cover and shoots rapidly at the agents in the chest, diaphragm, and head.

Phoenix budges through the window with her elbow as tiny fragments of glass hit the seat. She fumbles her hand around the door latch and unlocks the other side. They get in as Phoenix turns out of the parking spot and towards the garage door. As they stop at the garage door, they notice a security pad beside it.

Phoenix quickly gets out of the vehicle and runs to the garage door. She takes her communicator and releases energy onto the security pad to unlock it. The garage door slightly opens as Phoenix runs back to the vehicle. The garage door revealed a long, dark entrance with a small dim light in the distance.

Phoenix presses hard on the throttle and goes through

the entrance. As they approach closer to the light, they see the clear blue skies and trees. They drive onto the road and notice a large building behind them. As they make their way around the building, they notice that it was the same base they found the Archives in, Base No. 00113.

Darrell gasps, "Phoenix, look!" She looks at the base's establishment number, "Oh, my God! We're still in D.C.!"

Phoenix accelerates through the rubble and devastation of the small buildings surrounding them. She weaved around the damaged vehicles that are scattered around the road. Some of them were on fire, some were totaled.

Something was flashing in Phoenix's mind, which caught her off guard and made her head hurt. She was picturing a tall building that's as high as the Seattle Space Needle. The building was surrounded by barren desert. She shakes her head, "What the hell was that?"

"What's wrong?" Darrell said.

"Oh, it's nothing."

"There's something."

Phoenix hesitated, "Russell may be hiding somewhere that we don't know about."

"How do you know? What are you seeing in your head?"

"I don't know. I'm not even sure for myself. Do you remember what Rose said? Warren said they were building an army, but Rose told another part that we didn't know about at first. Read between the lines, Darrell. The key word is International. That's where the "I" comes from in IFHR. I should've seen it coming in the first place."

"What's next for us, then?"

"I have a feeling that something bad is going to happen. And if we don't do something about, the whole world will be under their control. Everyone will be the guinea pigs in their slaughterhouse."

They both look at the White House as President's Park

was decimated. Most of its trees were burned down and scattered around the park as there were also dead bodies from both factions. Some were alive, but just barely as they were laying on the ground dying. There were tanks and aerial fleets from IFHR and the United States militia continuing the battle. However, the White House still remains standing with minimal damage on its exterior.

Phoenix slows down as she enters the freeway. "I would lay low for right now to avoid detection. Try moving some more. It should get the numbness off," Phoenix said. "We need to get you back behind the wheel. We also need to find the jet, too. Do you think you'll be able to fly?"

"Why?"

"Because if you can feel more of anything by then, I want you to fly. I mean, you're a good wheelman, so, now you're going to have to learn how to be a pilot as well." Darrell moves his body around to get some of the numbness off.

About five minutes later, Phoenix arrives at the airport and sees the black Lockheed Martin still sitting in the middle of the runway. "Looks like our ride is here," Phoenix said. "How are you feeling?"

"I don't have any numbness."

"Alright, good." Phoenix enters the runway and stops beside the fighter jet. "Alright, get out of the car and climb on the ladder. We have to figure out how to use this damn thing before we get back in the fight." Darrell get out and runs to the ladder by the front hatch of the jet. He climbs on the ladder as Phoenix drives to the back hatch. The back hatch is still closed. "Great, now how In the hell do you get in this thing?" he said.

Something gave Darrell an idea. He looked down at his communicator, specifically the buttons. He pressed s and then OVERRIDE. s stands for security, which doesn't have as much power as the emergency function, but can still get the job done while not under pressure.

After a couple seconds, Darrell successfully unlocked the hatch without any harm done to his body. The hatch popped out, giving enough room for Darrell to lift it open.

"Come on, Darrell. Any minute now," Phoenix said, waiting for him to open the back hatch.

Darrell hops inside the jet and looks around the dashboard of the cockpit. "Holy shit, how the hell do you figure this out?!" he panicked. He finds a button that says BACK HATCH. The back hatch opens up and turns into an inclined plane, signaling Phoenix to pull into it. She notices the same mechanical bars that were in the trailers at Sheep Mountain back from Yellowstone. "Good work, Darrell," Phoenix said to herself while quickly getting out of the vehicle. As she jumps out of the hatch, the mechanical bars lower and mold into the shape of the vehicle, locking itself down to increase its rigidness during flight. This also increases protection of the vehicle and minimizes the chances of damaging.

Phoenix runs up to the front and climbs in the back seats of the jet. "Alright, we're good. Now all we have to do is figure out how to fly," Phoenix said. Darrell presses BACK LATCH again to close it. He presses FRONT HATCH and LOCK to secure themselves in the jet. As the hatch closes, it creates a clanging noise and releases air outside. They put on the flight suits that were provided for them in the past and connect their helmets' tubes to the oxygen masks. The suits were all black as there were jackets, boots, and gloves. Darrell looks at the flight controls and flips switches to wake up the turbines. Fumes and flames come out of the turbines as it whistles. In their points of view, there are heads-up displays that show statistics and the overall condition of the jet, such as fuel capacity, speed, and weapon capacity, similar to the monitors in front of them. "I think we're all ready to go, just need to activate the thrust," Darrell said.

Darrell activates the thrust and the weapon systems. He pushes a lever beside him forward to start accelerating on the small wheels below the jet. The jet climbs up to seventy knots. "Well, here goes nothing," Darrell said.

"Best prepare yourself, we're on our own, at least for right now," Phoenix said.

As the jet climbs up to two hundred knots, Darrell pulls the yolk down and leaves the ground. The jet drastically increases speed and altitude as it reaches the rate of almost fifteen hundred knots at cruising speed.

They notice three jets leaving the area of the White House on their screens. "Looks like a couple might retreat," Darrell said.

"I can't really say that for sure." The jets suddenly yaw into the direction of where Darrell's going and follow him. The jets draw in fast as they come closer. "Phoenix, ready your weapons," Darrell said.

"On it." Darrell accelerates and presses a button by the

yolk to activate his weapons. Darrell selects the rear machine

guns with armor-piercing ammunition. "Don't shoot, you

don't if it's them or not," Darrell said. Phoenix cautiously

locks on one of the jets. One of the jets start firing at the rear,

shocking Darrell and Phoenix. "I believe that would be IFHR,"

Phoenix said.

"Obviously." Darrell and Phoenix shoot at one of the jets.

The other two opposing jets come close to each other and

accelerate towards Darrell. "We're going higher!" he said.

Phoenix moves her machine guns higher and switches to

armor-piercing rounds. Darrell and Phoenix fire as Darrell

quickly pulls down the yoke and increases altitude. While

firing, the rounds pierced the glass of the jet's front hatch

they originally targeted, exposing the pilot to the swift,

unforgiving wind. The pilot's jet lost control and decreased

altitude, falling to the ground and exploding.

One of the two remaining jets fire at Darrell. Darrell and Phoenix lock onto that jet and fire at it, destroying it instantly. The last jet releases a Hellfire missile. Darrell panics, "Shit, where's the flares?!" He looks for the flares button by the yolk and activates them. The flares throw the missile off course.

Darrell pulls the yolk down further and makes a 360° flip, making him and Phoenix tighten their bodies up. The jet then straightens and levels itself as it is behind the pilot. The pilot fires its rear machine guns at Darrell.

Darrell activates the Hellfire missiles and locks on the jet. He repeatedly fires missiles, tracing it down like heat seekers. The missiles destroy most of the pilot's rear turbines and the jet explodes on impact. Darrell yaws out of the way to avoid impacting the debris. "That was actually pretty easy," Darrell said.

"This is only the beginning, Darrell. Don't get too

comfortable."

"Well, you won't have to wait any longer," a voice came through the jet's communication system.

"Who the hell is this?" Darrell said.

"Let's just say we've met in Los Angeles." They realized it was Adrian Wortham.

"Adrian?!" Phoenix yelled, surprised.

"You got that right," Adrian laughs.

"Surprised to hear your voice. How the hell did you survive?" Darrell said.

"We thought you were dead!" Phoenix said.

"It wasn't easy taking on those fuckers," Adrian said. "Still stubborn as they were before. The auto shop's still intact, they didn't manage to destroy anything."

"Are you there right now?" Phoenix said.

"Yes, this has been my home. Had to make use of it

somehow."

"We're just leaving Washington, D.C.," Darrell said.

"Russell got in contact with us. He betrayed us. Fucking

bastard," Phoenix said.

"Yeah, he's not a guy to trust."

"We all know that for sure. We're in a lot of trouble, do

you think you could help us find a way out?"

"Yeah, what's the situation? I could have what you're

looking for."

"Russell calls it the Game of Trials. IFHR's planning

something that's going to happen on a global scale."

"Just like what Rose said, right?" Phoenix hesitated in

fear, "I'm afraid so."

"Alright, we'll talk more about it when you get out of the

sky. Try pinpointing the location by the nearest airport of the

auto shop on your communications system. Do you

remember where the shop is?"

"We'll find our way around. I believe we got it from here. It'll probably take at least a couple of hours for us to get there, anyways," Darrell said.

"Alright, I'll see you guys in a little bit," Adrian dismisses.

Darrell sets up the coordinates near the auto shop as they make their way towards Los Angeles.

Introduction Part 2: Reunion

March 21, 2021

Los Angeles, California, United States, 1114 hours

Darrell and Phoenix turn onto a road and through a city block. The city of Los Angeles is devastated as most of the buildings had smoke coming out of them. Vehicles were on fire and scattered across the roads as papers and debris were rustling across the streets. Some buildings have also collapsed during their absence. Strangely, there were no signs of IFHR around. There were people on the ground that were crying from the devastation surrounding them.

Darrell slows down and stops by the auto shop. He honks

the horn, hopefully to get Adrian's attention. "I certainly hope

he's doing alright. Wonder what he's been up to all this

time," Phoenix said.

The garage door opens as it looks the same as before.

Darrell and Phoenix see Adrian in his white tank top, blue

denim jeans, and gray tennis shoes. Adrian realized right

away that it was them as he noticed the broken window. He

signals them to come in by bringing his arm to himself.

Darrell slowly pulls up inside the garage and parks it near

Adrian's white Audi, the same one he had before, unscathed.

Adrian lowers the garage door with the hand scanner beside

It before they could get out of the Lamborghini. They walk up

to Adrian. "Well, I'll be damned that they didn't wreck this

place. I don't how the hell you did it," Phoenix said, looking

around the garage.

"Like I said, it wasn't easy," Adrian said.

"Well, at least your alive, that's what matters right now,"

Darrell said.

"So it's called the Game of Trials, huh?" Adrian said.

"Yes, that's the situation," Phoenix said.

"Alright." Adrian pauses to think. "You know what? Follow me, guys. I might have what can help you guys along the way."

Adrian walks to the kitchen door as Darrell and Phoenix follow. "I bet you guys were wondering what that crack was in the hallway," Adrian said.

"What's behind there?" Phoenix said.

"Just follow me, trust me on this one." They enter the hallway and walk to the crack on the wall that's beside Russell's bedroom. "Does this look familiar?"

"How are we supposed to get in?"

"It's simple, but you're going to have to help me on this one. This is just a drywall. There's no technology involved. You guys get beside the wall. We're going to bash through it."

Darrell and Phoenix walk to the wall. "Alright, we're going to try to budge through it and hopefully break it down."

"How do you know this will work?" Phoenix said.

"It's a wall, Phoenix. There's a large spacing encompassing ahead of it. There's no protection. It was Russell that came up with the idea, but it was a waste of time and space if you ask me." They start to hit it with their shoulders, but the wall barely gives in. "It's not working, Adrian," Phoenix said. Adrian punches the wall in frustration, "Damn it!" He glances at Darrell's pistol. "Wait a minute. Darrell, use your pistol. Your scattershot should weaken it."

Darrell raises his weapon, "Stand back." He fires a couple rounds at the wall, easily penetrating through it. "Alright, that should do the trick," Adrian said. "Now hit it as hard as you can."

They continue to budge through the wall. The wall is weakening as it's bending and crumbling. They give one more forceful push and the wall gives in.

The wall revealed a large safe door. The safe door had a security pad next to it. "So, what made you get stuck with Russell?" Phoenix said.

"He's unpredictable, but I know him more than any of the other pieces of shit that work in that excuse of a place. It's pretty sad if you ask me."

"So, what else went on in IFHR?" Darrell said. Adrian puts in the combination to unlock the safe door. "A bunch," Adrian said. "More than what I could handle."

Adrian opens the safe door and reveals a staircase going downwards. After walking down the staircase, they enter a dark hallway that seems to be long in the distance. Adrian turns on the light by the wall and reveals glass walls. The walls display a vast arrangement of weapons to choose from, such as pistols and machine guns. There were also throwing weapons, such as knives and throwing daggers. The walls were lit up by cyan colored LED lights below them inside the wall. The hallway was also accompanied by bright white lights from the ceiling. Darrell and Phoenix were amazed. "And we all know that the organization is filled with lies," Adrian said as they start walking between the glass walls. "But there was a rumor that the president was involved with founding it."

"That's the same thing that Russell said," Darrell said.

"It's most likely true from my point of view. If that's the case, then he's in for a rude awakening. The organization was founded in 1990. I've been in the organization for at least four years." They stop walking. "I'd pick your weapons wisely for what you're in right now. Because if they're working at a global scale, they're not going to play lightly."

Darrell and Phoenix look at the pistols and assault rifles as they vary in a few different colors. Darrell picks up another white pistol and a white machine gun. The color classification also shares the same type of ammo with the type of firearm.

They walk further to look for the ammunition section. There were large boxes that were color coded to the color of the firearms. Phoenix just gets a couple boxes of ammunition as she already has two black assault rifles, two pistols, and two platinum swords. "You guys are also going to need some armor, too," Adrian said.

They walk out of the hallway and turn towards another room that reveals ballistic weapons, bulletproof vests, business attire, and leather suits. "Damn, Adrian. How did they not find this? Was it already here before it was abandoned?" Phoenix said.

"It's a long story. Let's just leave it at that, but here's a secret in today's world. With all of the security cameras installed on the grid, they'll document everything. There will be security cameras everywhere you go, even in the organization. There were even hidden security cameras in here. We need all of the evidence we can get because like I said before, the president may be involved in all of this as well."

"Wow, I've never thought of it that way." Darrell and Phoenix walk up to the vests.

"All of the vests are thin, lightweight and comfortable. The darker the color, the better your protection is. However, choose the one that's best for you because every situation's different." They both choose a midnight blue vest. "That's an excellent choice. That vest is at least five times stronger than steel. The vests should fit well with your weapons." The vests they chose were ergonomic in shape as there were compartments to put their weapons in.

Phoenix unloads her weapons and unzips the chestal part of her leather suit. She puts the vest around her chest and zips up her suit and puts her weapons back on. "Fits perfectly," Phoenix said, smiling boldly.

"Now it's your turn, Darrell. Take off your shirts and just

do the same thing she did," Adrian said. Darrell takes off his dress shirt, suit jacket and weapons to put on his vest. He then puts his clothes back on and hoists his weapons.

"Alright, you guys are all set to go, but there's one more thing that I need to get situated for you. Your communicators."

"What about them?" Phoenix said.

"I'm going to change the frequency on them, so that way I can help you guys along the way."

"Don't we have our cellphones?" Darrell said.

"Yes, but we need to stay off the grid while this is going on. Russell can't know about this."

"Well, thanks for the help, Adrian, we really appreciate it," Phoenix smiles and gives him a hug.

"No problem, just let me know what's going on. And when you're talking through the communicator, be careful with the frequencies. Every sender has a different frequency, so switch them when I'm talking. Keep in touch."

"Alright, we'll try," Phoenix said.

They work their way out of the hallway of weapons and into the garage as Adrian follows them. While Darrell and Phoenix get in the Lamborghini, Adrian puts his hand on the hand scanner by the garage door. The garage door slowly opens up. "There's nobody out there, so you're good," Adrian said. He points outside, signaling them to back up. While Darrell turns and straightens the vehicle, Adrian waves goodbye to them. They wave goodbye back.

As Darrell starts accelerating, Russell speaks through their communicator. "So, you guys still there?" Russell said.

"What do you want, Russell?" Phoenix said.

"You guys are done with the initiation. Now prepare for your first trial! The trial will take place in a deserted area with no vegetation someplace in South Africa. There will be a man-made town that's settling there. Your target will be an elite member of IFHR that has been active for four years. His name is Rashon Turay. Age: 28. Hair color: Black. Skin color:

Pallor-African. Weight: 197 pounds."

"Can you shut the hell up? You're testing my patience,"

Phoenix said.

"HEY! Do you want to get out alive or do you want to

suffer? We own you now, you're under our control. I'm giving

you information you need to know. I'm giving you a warning

right now. Either you stick with it or else suffer the

consequences in the future! You have NO idea what I'm

capable of!"

"Just do what he says," Darrell says quietly. Phoenix

gives an expression of anger and frustration, "Fine. Is there

any more information we need to know?"

"One more thing before I let you go. Put the coordinates

in your GPS system. But just remember this, you're still the

targets."

"Go ahead and test me. I'm ready for ANYTHING you'll

throw at me!" Phoenix yelled.

"We'll just have to see in due time. Good luck in the Trials." Russell laughs and dismisses.

As they work their way out of the city, they look back at the skyline as they arrive at the airport. The city is now a place for despair. The city was once a place of prosperity, but now the city's slowly falling into depression. Leaving the ruins of Los Angeles is just one of the warnings they witnessed.

As they exit the airport, they start their journey in order to achieve freedom, and a second chance. They will face multiple challenges that will test their abilities to move on or give up. But there's only one way out for them, and that's the Game of Trials.

SYMBOLISM

Chapter 1: Adjustment

March 22, 2021

An hour after landing in the Wonderboom Airport in Pretoria, Darrell and Phoenix travel through a poor district in the city. Most of the third-world countries are starting to enter the recovery stage in their economic status at this time. While driving, there were food stands and houses that were padded down and show signs of aging. There were some people that wore tathered clothing. Some people were skinny as their ribs were exposed. "Jeez, look at these poor people. They are starving," Darrell said.

Darrell stops and turns onto another street in between buildings, heading towards an empty parking lot exposed to the sizzling hot sun. Darrell stops the vehicle in the parking lot. "He's bald," Phoenix said, looking down at the communicator. "But Rashon's not anywhere near here, Russell said he's in a deserted area, and this doesn't look deserted to me. Just a little worn out, that's all."

"Let's get out of the vehi-"

"Guys, can you hear me?" They suddenly heard Adrian's voice, but it was muffled. "Change the frequencies, quick!" Darrell said.

"Where at?" Phoenix panics.

"Try finding it on its side," Darrell said. Phoenix looks at the communicator to find arrows with an F in the middle and a pair of arrows with VOL in the middle, indicating the volume. Russell's frequency is 115.025 MHz. Phoenix flips through the frequency numbers until she hears a clear and loud "Hello?"

from Adrian. Adrian's frequency is 126.000 MHz. "We're here," Phoenix said.

"Where are you guys at?" Adrian said.

"We're in a settlement in South Africa," Darrell said.

"What city?"

"Pretoria."

"Alright, what's the situation?"

"We have our first target assigned to us. Somebody named Rashon," Phoenix said.

"Hold on, let me look him up." Adrian is in the computer room where Russell used to work in back at the auto shop. "I'm surprised that he left the computers here. He's always in a rush." He scans through the database of all of the agents in IFHR. "Found him." He clicked on his profile and views his information. "Rashon Turay. intiated in 2017. He's bald and has mix of tan and black skin. Throughout his years, he's laid waste on a lot of things, specifically people. He's been known for extreme disregard to human life. He's definitely hiding out

in South Africa, though. There's people that you're going to

meet along the way."

"What do you mean by that?" Phoenix said.

"Because you're not the only ones that fought against

IFHR in the past. There's more people out there than what

you think." Adrian dismisses.

"Wait, what happened? Adrian, are you there?" Phoenix

said. She forgot to hold the button on the communicator. She

presses and holds down it, "Adrian, do you copy?" She lets

go.

"Yes, I'm still here, I'm trying to find information on this

guy. It'll take a while for me to get a result. I would get out of

the vehicle while you can. It's pretty hot down there, it's like

eighty-five degrees." Adrian dismisses.

"Come on, let's get out. Let's put our ear mics on and

take a walk," Darrell said. They get out of the vehicle and

work their way towards the street. They see some people wearing sandals and cloths over their heads. They see some children running around chasing each other, laughing and playing.

Darrell and Phoenix notice a man standing beside a modern black, armored muscle car in the distance. He is tan in skin color and has short black hair. He is wearing a black T-shirt, blue denim pants, black boots, and a golden cross necklace. They notice the man looking at them and walking towards them. This startles Phoenix, "Better prepare your weapons, Darrell." Phoenix gets tense as the man gets closer.

As they come face to face, Phoenix quickly draws one of her pistols and points it at his chest, startling the people around her. "You better step back and stay out of our way before I shoot you right here," Phoenix said, angrily. The man doesn't flinch. "I know who you are and I know just as much as you do," the man said.

"Well, who are you?!" Phoenix yells in fear and anger.

The man starts to get scared and breathes heavily, "Please, put the gun down, I wouldn't do that if I were you. I can help you guys out. I'm not from around here." Phoenix slowly and mercifully lets her gun down. "What is your name, sir?" Phoenix said. The man and Phoenix looks around to see the terrified people. "I'm sorry, everyone. We didn't come to hurt anybody. This is just a personal thing we need to take care of and fast," Phoenix said to the people. The people nodded and muttered to each other and carried on with their days. "We'll talk somewhere else. It's not safe to talk about it here. You guys want some coffee? There's a coffee shop beside my car," the man said.

"We'll stay for a cup or two," Darrell said.

"Alright, come on."

Darrell and Phoenix follow the man towards the coffee shop. The man holds the glass door open for them. "Thank you, sir," Phoenix said. The man didn't respond.

Inside the coffee shop were strong, wooden benches and tables. There were glass windows by the tables. There were some people occupying some of them. "Where do you want to sit?" the man said.

"Your choice," Darrell said. They walk to the counter and look at the menu showing the different kinds of coffee. They ask the clerk to make three small regular cups. "Is regular good with you guys?" the man asked.

"It's fine with us. We're not here for the delicacy," Phoenix said.

"I figured."

The clerk gives them their cups of coffee. The three go to a table by the window and sit down. "So, what is your name, sir?" Phoenix said.

"I'm Darien Summers. I'm actually from the United States. What brings you guys here?"

"You know Russell Arkwright?" Darien gets disgusted, "Don't even get me started with him."

"We're originally the targets."

"How did you guys get away without them killing you? That takes a lot of bravery."

"Not really." Phoenix looks down in despair. "We lost some people along the way."

"My situation's kind of the same as yours."

"What brings you here, then?" Darrell said. Darien hesitates, "So much to tell, so little time. Might as well say it now." Darien gets nervous and breathes heavily. "Take your time, Darien," Phoenix said.

"By the time Washington, D.C. was attacked, things got out of control. It was too overwhelming to me." Darien starts to shed a tear. "It all happened so fast in the blink of an eye. People were being shot down. Tanks were destroying the President's Park. Lafayette Square was affected and everything. Things got worst fast, I had to get out of there

quickly. We were too outnumbered." Darien shakes his head

negatively. "The United States is no longer what it is now.

People lost their homes, a couple well-known and populated

cities are now wastelands."

"Los Angeles is pretty much mostly ruins now," Darrell

said. "But the White House is still standing."

"Yeah, a lot of things have happened in the past seven

months."

"We just woke up from a coma yesterday. Woke up in

one of their bases. It looked like a hospital, but it was the

same base we found the Archives in by the time we escaped,"

Phoenix said.

"The Archives?"

"They're documents of all members of IFHR and records

of everyone that could be a potential target," Darrell said.

"I'm a smuggler according to IFHR."

"What does that mean?" Phoenix said.

"It's the pejorative term of a member that was once in IFHR, but later went against them in the end. But I went against them for a good reason. A couple other people went with me in an attempt to escape, and we did."

"Where are they at?" Darrell said.

"They're not here with me right now. They're hiding somewhere around a man-made settlement in the Kalahari Desert. But they're not there to hurt people. It actually used to be an abandoned base, too."

"Are there people down there?" Phoenix said.

"Yes, but the area's completely isolated. There's somebody from IFHR that's hiding around this country."

"Rashon Turay," Darrell said. Darien was shocked, "Yes, that's his name. How did you know?"

"Because that's the target we have to kill. We're in something called the Game of Trials that Russell organized.

He's a mad man, but I'll do anything to kick his fucking head

in after what he did. And if we don't do something, things will

get worse real quick," Phoenix said.

"Well, let's hope you break free and take him down,"

Darien said.

"My name's Phoenix, Phoenix Leyton."

"And my name's Darrell Friegman," Darrell said.

"It was nice meeting you guys. Good luck to you."

Darrell and Phoenix get up from the table and walk out

of the coffee shop. As they get in the Lamborghini, they head

into an unknown settlement in the Kalahari Desert.

Chapter 2: The Town

March 23, 2021

Kalahari Desert, South Africa, 1114 hours

Darrell and Phoenix are traveling on a road that's made of mostly dry dirt. "I see the town," Darrell said. The town looked strange in appearance as there were was a gray square perimeter that's rusted around it. The perimeter appeared to be lower than the town as nature is taking over it. "Hey, how are you guys doing?" Adrian said.

"We're just about to head into a town that appears desolate from here, but we met a guy that said it also used to be a base," Phoenix said.

"I'd be careful on this one. It appears that you're in the Kalahari Desert."

"How do you know where we're at?"

"I put a tracking device on your vehicle when you guys were sleeping one day, that is before you guys were knocked out for seven months. And speaking of the base, there was actually a base that was established there, but was last active in 2003."

"Hmm, never expected that," Darrell said.

"Oh, and before I forget, elite vehicles also have some offroad capabilities, so don't wonder why you're still going at high speed on rough terrain."

"Looks like we're drawing in close, we'll have to dismiss you."

"Alright, let me know what's going on. Adrian out," Adrian dismisses.

Darrell turns away from the road and heads toward the

entrance of the town. There is a slightly descending hill that leads down to the entrance.

As they enter the town, they see several black, rusted steel storage units and worn down houses. There were also shacks and farmhouses in various sizes, visualizing some elements from the Western days. There were people sitting under the shacks and houses as they catch their eye on the Lamborghini. There were mostly dirt roads that were in the town.

Darrell stops the vehicle as they both get out, readying their weapons. "Looks like there's nothing here but people indigenous to this place," Phoenix said.

"I guess Darien was right. Maybe there is someone that's watching these people," Darrell said. The people around looked terrified. "You're... not.... supposed... to... be... here...," a woman in tathered clothing said. Her voice was weak.

"Why, what's going on?" Phoenix said.

"Phoenix, behind you!" Darrell said. Phoenix is startled and looks behind her. She sees a strong man emerge from the side of a farmhouse. He has a mix of tan and black skin and has a hard face. He was wearing a black T-shirt and pants with boots. He was carrying an ammo belt around his shoulder blade with an assault rifle. The man matched the description Russell said. "Rashon!" Phoenix said, angrily.

"Phoenix, haven't seen you two in a long time!" Rashon said in his native accent. He started walking towards them.

"Is that supposed to be a warm welcome? You're first in line for what we have to do." Phoenix quickly draws one of her pistols and aims it at him. "Don't you make another fucking step!

"Oh, what good is that going to do? I have you right in my tracks. Some of us have been training hard just for this day!"

"Oh, really? Then how was it easy to kill everyone else in the past, huh? It was because they didn't expect somebody like me! You may look strong, but you can't always judge a book by its cover! There's some pretty 'strong' looking men that I've killed in the past!"

"I already know what you guys have to do. This is the first trial, there's a whole lot more than what you have to do after this one. Even if you kill me today, it won't matter, because we're everywhere! Darrell was originally the target, but now we have to go after you, too, which is twice the fun for us!"

"I did for a multitude of reasons!"

"They're... coming.... back!" the woman said.

"Who's coming back?! Is it IFHR?" Darrell yelled.

"I don't... know..., but they... look like... they have... the same type... of vehicles... as you...."

"We're not here to hurt you! We're the good guys!"

Darrell said.

"I wouldn't get too cocky now, Phoenix! Your hell's just beginning!" Rashon said.

Suddenly, a group of high-pitched engine sounds are heard in the distance. Darrell and Phoenix put their hand over their heads to locate the vehicles. They see six vehicles driving at high speed as they leave trails of dust behind them.

Rashon suddenly runs back into the farmhouse. "HEY!" Where do you think you're going?!" Phoenix yells. "Stand your ground, Darrell." She yells at everybody around her, "Quick, everybody hide! These may be the people you're talking about!" Everybody runs into the nearest building by them and hide in there. The vehicles are approaching the entrance. "Shit! Darrell, let's get in the car!"

Three of the vehicles fly in the air and land in the base. They were supercars that had black armor plates on them with netted windshields and windows. Darrell makes a hard drift and drives with the opposing vehicles, engaging in vehicular combat. One of the vehicles have spikes spinning around their rims.

Darrell and the agents drive in all directions and start shooting at each other. "We can't take these guys by ourselves! They have too much armor!" Darrell said. One of the vehicles, which was maroon, comes from behind him. The vehicle pursuing him has a spiked ram that's twice as thick as its front bumper.

Darrell activates the rear machine guns with armor-piercing rounds and fires. The maroon vehicle fires back with a shotgun blast, leaving a dent in the rear of the Lamborghini. The three other vehicles drive into the town and fire in all directions, already killing a couple people with no remorse.

As Darrell drifts beside a farmhouse, the maroon vehicle is still behind them and switches to machine guns, resuming fire. Darrell drifts again, but he surprisingly hears the tone of a classic muscle car in the distance. "Phoenix, did you hear that?" Darrell said, surprised.

"Yes, I did actually."

Three two-toned, red and black classic muscle cars emerge from the storage units and roll out. All three of the muscle cars were icons from the 1960s and 1970s. They had armor plating and rams on their front bumpers. "SHIT! We are FUCKED!" Darrell panicked.

One of the muscle cars chases after one of the supercars and shoots a small missile at its chassis, destroying it instantly. The action surprised Darrell and Phoenix. "No, we're not!" Phoenix said.

"Holy shit!" Darrell said.

Darrell and Phoenix get back into the fight and join with the muscle cars. He gets beside one of the muscle cars and pursues one of the agents. Darrell activates the magnetism and fires the machine guns at the rear of the agent's vehicle.

While firing, the muscle car fires a couple missiles and incinerates it, making it fly in the air and impacting the perimeter's wall.

Suddenly, three modern muscle cars emerge from the air and into the entrance. Darrell notices the same black muscle car Darien drove as there were two navy blue vehicles between him. "Darien?" Darrell said, looking in his rear view mirror.

"Looks like the muscle cars are with us," Phoenix said. Darien's team split up as caught up with the classic muscle cars. Darien follows one of the agents into the farmhouse. There were no animals inside. He activates a twenty millimeter cannon and shoots repeatedly at the agent. The vehicle was useless at it ignites and enters a series of barrell rolls, chipping off part of the roof of a shack.

Darien drives past Darrell and Phoenix and immediately pursues another agent and takes him down. Two of the classic muscle cars drive beside each other and accelerate towards two agents. The agents fire their machine guns, but no effect. The classic muscle cars fire their missiles and decimate the agents, ramming their useless vehicles to the wall.

Darrell and Darien drive beside each other and pursue the last agent. Darrell accelerates and rams his rear bumper, making the agent lose control and drifting to its side. Darien accelerates and fires a missile under its chassis, making the agent tip over. Darien accelerates further and rams the agent, puncturing its gas chamber and making it fly forward. The agent impacts the perimeter's wall as the vehicle's roof flattens, squishing the agent inside.

Darrell and everyone else stop their vehicles and they all get out. "I think that's everybody!" Darien yells.

"No, it's not! There's one more person!" Phoenix yelled. Darien paused for a moment to think, "Alright, take care of

Rashon! We're all going to hide inside inside one of the shacks!"

"Come on, Darrell, he could still be in the farmhouse!" Phoenix said.

Darrell and Phoenix run up to the farmhouse. As they enter inside, the building was dark as there were bales of hay. "You can't hide forever!" Phoenix said. They split up and slowly walk towards the bales of hay.

They hear a gunshot beside the back entrance of the farmhouse, startling them. "Take cover!" Phoenix yelled. Rashon emerges from the bale of hay he's hiding in and shoots at Darrell in the heel of his foot. Darrell yells in agonizing pain as the bullet pierced through his shoe, making him fall to the ground. He holds onto his leg and rocks his body around as he reacts more to the pain. Phoenix was enraged by this and runs after Rashon.

Phoenix tackles him and fiercely pins him down. She

pulls out her pistol and shoots Rashon in the collarbone.

Rashon yells from the burn as blood quickly oozes out. "So,

what are your leads on the organization?!" Phoenix

questioned.

"I'm.... not... telling.... you.. anything!" Phoenix grabs his

neck and puts a choking grip on it. She gets close in his face,

"You are going to tell me something. What do you KNOW?!"

Rashon starts gagging and coughing from her grip, making

Phoenix let go.

"Don't be.... stupid, Phoenix. You already know what

we're doing. But once you... kill me, it' won't.... matter how

many others you kill. We'll still... find ways.... to take you

down!"

Phoenix pulls out one of her daggers, "You know what?

It won't matter." She stabs him in the diaphragm. "But I'm

not doing this just because of freedom." She stabs him in the

diaphragm again. "I'm doing this because of what you did.

Disregard towards human life, how pathetic is that?" She

stabs him in the heart, making him gargle from his blood.

"But once I'm done with you, my message will spread,

and you'll be the first of many to experience what I'm

capable of!" She raises the dagger in the air and lifts Rashon's

head up. She performs one last blow by cutting through his

neck and into his mouth, killing him instantly as his eyes roll

back.

Darrell is still yelling in pain as he still rolls around from

his injury. Phoenix runs to Darrell's aid and says, "Let's get

you to the shack. Are you alright?" Darrell tries to stand up,

but he limps. He trips, but Phoenix catches him. "Here, let me

help you. Let's get you by the shack." Phoenix puts her arm

over Darrell's shoulders and lifts him up and walk out of the

farmhouse. They head towards the large shack where the

men are hiding out in the center of town.

Chapter 3: Smugglers

1205 hours

Darrell feels weak as he kneels down to the ground beside one of the muscle cars. He yells and groans from the pain in the heel of his foot. Blood keeps dripping down from his shoe. "Come on, Darrell! Don't give up on me now!" Phoenix said.

"Damn it! Just woke up from a coma, too! Son of a bitch that hurts!" Darrell yells.

The doors of the entrance of the shack bust open as it shows Darien wearing a black durag and a black leather cut-off jacket. "Bring him in here, come on!" Darien said.

"Come on, Darrell, I got you," Phoenix said, pulling Darrell back up. They walk up the wooden step on the front mahogany porch and towards the doors. "Come in, guys. Men, take care of him immediately," Darien said.

Two of the men surprise Darrell and Phoenix as they grab Darrell and pull him towards a chair. The shack's interior was rather convenient as there were countertops, tables, chairs, and separate rooms, similar to what a house would have. The room they were in appeared to be a dining room. Phoenix looks around to see people native to the town making a circle around a table, watching the men place Darrell onto the chair. "Don't move. Just sit tight," said one of the men. The men in the muscle cars wore black leather cut-off jackets, torn jeans, and steel toe boots. Some of the men have scars on their faces and arms. "Who are these people?" Phoenix asks Darien.

"Right now, there's no time to play meet and greet. Men, find some scissors. We're going to need tequila to get the bullet out!" Some of the men exit the room. "Excuse us," said one of the men, talking to the people around them. The men enter the living room and run upstairs. Darien walks up to Darrell, "Listen, Darrell. We're going to take the bullet out." Darrell is panicking as he hyperventilates. "Stop it, Darrell! We've done this before. We've taken shots for each other before. Just take a deep breath." Darrell takes a couple deep breaths to clam down, but still feels the pain.

The men come back downstairs carrying a small box, a first aid kit, and a rod of tempered steel that's already burnt as it's red on its end. The people move out of the way as they quickly set the supplies on the table. In the box were a couple wet towels and a large bottle of yellow tequila. One of the men open the first aid kit to reveal several surgical tools, such as a pair of surgical scissors, gauze bandaging, and a syringe beside a bottle of anesthetics. One of the men takes Darrell's shoe and sock off, revealing his foot. Darrell was shaking as his heel is extremely swollen and reddened from the bullet lodged into it. Phoenix panics, "Darien, what are they doing?!"

"They're going to take the bullet out. It's the best option for your friend to start walking again." One of the men take the syringe and crouches down to inject Darrell with the anesthetic, dulling some of the pain. One of the men takes the surgical scissors and digs it into his heel as another takes a wet towel and puts it in Darrell's mouth. Darrell cringes as he feels the sharpness of the scissors moving around in his body. Some of the people watching looked away while the surgery's being performed. The sharpness in Darrell's heel intensifies, assuming they found the bullet. "The bullet's deep in there, " says the man with the scissors.

The man grips tighter on the scissors to get a hold of the

bullet. He slowly pulls it out, but it gets stuck. "Damn it, it's stuck!" yells the man with the scissors.

"Pull it out more quickly, it may be in the thickest layer in his skin," Darien says.

The man with the scissors takes a deep breath and yanks the bullet out. This caused Darrell to scream at the top of his lungs, reacting to the burning sensation of the wound, "FUCK!" The blood in his heel starts to come out again, but not as much. Some of the people gasped as they witnessed the ordeal. One of the men takes the bottle of tequila and pours it on his foot. Darrell yells again from the stinging of the tequila. They stop pouring and grab the tempered steel. They gently place the steel on the wound as the rod makes a hissing sound and leaves steam. Darrell screams one last time from the pain, "Please, make it stop!" The last step the men take is grabbing the gauze bandaging and gently, but tightly wrapping around Darrell's foot. The men put his sock and shoe back on and step away from him.

"Why the hell are you stepping back?" Darrell said.

"We're done treating you, there's nothing more we can do," Darien said.

"Who are these men?"

Darien looks around at his men, "These are the men I recruited back with me when the nation was under attack. They can definitely drive, that's for sure." He lets his hand out to introduce them, "The men that treated your wound were Hannibal Keighley and Barry Goleman."

Hannibal has a hard voice and is bald. He has a scar on his cheek and was muscular in body shape. He is also tan in skin color. "Don't worry, we got you covered," Hannibal said to Darrell, smiling.

"How did they learn to treat a wound like that?" Phoenix said.

"We were pretty much on our own since the civil war

broke out in 2020," Darien said.

Barry has a Southern accent and has a black goatee. "It's all fun and games until someone gets hurt. Bastards got what was coming to him. We all kicked their asses back there!" Barry said, laughing about the entire situation.

"Barry, this isn't funny!" Darien yelled. Barry's smile went away. "Two people just fucking died! They showed no remorse, and you're laughing because you were thrilled to kill the people invading the town?! It's not all fun and games, Barry, and this goes to all of the other men, too!"

Darien starts explaining his story leading to the civil war, "We once had a code of ethics, a chance for freedom, but that's not where we seem to be anymore." Darien takes off his jacket and reveals a medal on his neck, showing it to everybody. "Do you see this?" This is the Humanitarian Service Medal." The medal's strap was purple, white, cyan, and navy blue towards the center with a bronze medallion. "I used to wear this with pride, with honor and dignity. But now, I can't after what happened. A couple of us used to be sergeants, sergeants that were proud to serve our country. I've failed to protect even my own country." He takes the medal off and sets it on the table. "IFHR didn't start showing up until 2019. The organization was no longer a secret since then. It's been in hiding for almost thirty years."

Darien enters a flashback of a series of events leading up to his initiation in IFHR, "I was a medical doctor working in the Middle East at the time. I was being sent back to the United States on June 29, 2017. I had a wife and two kids. She was a beautiful wife. My children were very lively, they never had to worry about anything. Or so I thought." He starts to shed a tear as he visualizes himself parking in his driveway and walking up to the porch of his house. The front door of the porch was completely shattered as the doorknob was broken. "I knew there was something wrong when I walked up my front porch. A lot of scenarios were going through my head. I wasn't sure if it was a home invasion or what else it was." He pushes open the door in his flashback. "When I went inside my house, I immediately looked for my family." He went through the kitchen and into the living room. "My family was being held hostage. My wife and children were tied up and they were crying." His eyes showed expressions of terror, "IFHR was there. They held them at gunpoint." The agents at Darien's house were in black ops suits with helmets that appeared to be advanced in technology, showing lighted heads up displays inside them. The helmets had glass in the front of their faces. Their suits were all in black as their chestal region molded the shape of a body that's made for fitness. They were all carrying modified assault rifles.

"Maddie!" Darien panicked, referring to his wife. She had tan skin with brown hair and wore a white shirt and pants.

Darien attempts to walk towards his family, but one of the agents block him and grabs him forcefully. The agent aims his assault rifle at his chest, putting a laser point towards his heart. The agent speaks in a distorted tone due to the helmet, "If you make another move, I will fill you up with lead! You belong to us now!"

"Please don't kill my family! They mean the world to me!" Darien pleaded.

"We all know that family means everything to a hard working man in the military, but it's too late for you now!

"Let them go, you son of a bitch!" Darien pushes the agent and attempts to lunge after the other agents, but two of the agents run after him and grab him, keeping him from making any more movements. One of the agents takes the butt of his assault rifle and jabs Darien hard in the diaphragm. Darien puffs his cheeks and kneels to the ground, coughing from the bruising.

One of the agents slowly walks up to Darien's wife, son and daughter and points the assault rifle at them. "Now, time to end things my way!

"NOOOO!" Darien yells.

The men slowly raise their weapons and aim them all at Darien's family, making them cry and yell. "It doesn't have to be this way! Please don't kill my family!" Darien cried. "Maddie, I love you and the children very much!"

"Please help us, daddy!" his daughter cries out as his son just cries.

"It's what we do, Darien. Agents, eliminate them," said one of the agents.

All of them fire their assault rifles at point blank range, killing them as the sofa gets splattered with blood.

"MADDIE!" Darien cries, putting his head down towards the ground. "Agents, grab him. We're taking him in for initiation," one of the agents said. "Prepare to get initiated,

Mr. Summers. You're one of us now."

All of the agents picked him up and push him out through the rooms of his house

Darien exits his flashback, "Ever since they initiated me, they abused me mentally. It worsened my post-traumatic stress disorder at the time. It was pure hell while working there. It'll brainwash you in the end."

"What was one of the agent's names?" Phoenix said.

"They didn't give names. But there are a few ways that you can get out. If you know it's morally wrong, you have a slim chance of getting out. It's difficult, but there's a chance. That's their weakness, they have no morals."

"We all know that for sure. They have no regard for human life," Phoenix said.

"If you form a group with fellow members in the organization and develop a plot against them, your chances are better, but escaping them is difficult. You have to develop an exit strategy to fight back and regain your freedom. You have to stay ahead of their game."

"I know there's one more way after that one," Phoenix said. "And I know you know the answer as well."

"I know what you mean, Phoenix."

"Then tell me the third way. Do you need a hint?"

Darien hesitates and takes a deep breath, "Some of the agents in IFHR were forcefully initiated. But most of the initiations took place after they immediately lost a loved one. If you still have enough in your heart to love, you can find a way out."

"But I wasn't initiated, though."

"I know your story about that part. You lost a loved one."

"But he was taken away from me when they initiated him. I've killed too many to know enough about what's going on."

"You avenged your husband."

"Yes, but not fully ever since I stepped back into the fight. They remind me of my self-loathing every time I see their faces."

"That's why we're called smugglers."

"That word means nothing if you have a heart, Darien. At least you have one. You and your men are not like them."

"I disagree with that sometimes. There's a civil war that going on, and I feel that we're to blame because of it."

"Darien, we escaped and that's what matters. We have something to protect now," Hannibal said.

"Darien, let me tell you this. I don't see coldness in your eyes, but I can see pain, sadness, and regret. That's not what an IFHR agent feels. So if you think you're still an IFHR agent, then why are feeling those emotions? You're not a true agent if you have feelings for someone that passed away," Phoenix said.

"All of us try to work together and get along. We all feel

something, we hate each other and we love each other. It's natural in all of us, but you have to believe what's right in your heart. If you don't feel any morals, then your mind will take you over."

"You have a good point, Darien. I respect that."

"Hey, guys, is everything alright?" Adrian speaks through Darrell's communicator, startling the men and the native people in the circle.

"Yes, we're alright, Adrian. Bastard shot me in the foot, though. We've ran into some former members of IFHR. There's a couple sergeants in here, too."

"Wait a minute, let me speak to him for a moment," Darien said. He walks to Darrell and takes his communicator. "Is this Adrian?"

"Yes, this is. Who am I speaking to?"

"I heard about you. My name is Darien Summers. My men have escaped from their trap, too. It wasn't easy, I was just telling them about my story."

"I heard about you, too. I heard that you used to be a sergeant in the military and you got a medal for humanitarianism. Congratulations."

"I'm hard on myself on that one. At least, since my initiation happened."

"I'm terribly sorry about your loss, though. I know how it feels. I have a brother that's fleeing from the organization."

"Smugglers alike," Darien chuckled.

"How long has Darrell and Phoenix have been down there?"

"A couple of days to my estimate."

"They have to be out of there as soon as possible. They're back in the fight. They're both targets against the organization. They're in something called the Game of Trials."

"They already notified me on that beforehand. That bastard, Arkwright went rogue, didn't he?"

"Yeah, guy's a fucking psycho. He can't be trustworthy.

He's the one that organized the Trials," Phoenix said.

"We'll get them out of here, but they're both going to

have to stay here for a couple of days in order for Darrell to

walk again. He got shot in the foot, and it's a pretty nasty

wound he was going on. We just treated it. He might show

progress within that time."

"Hurt like a motherfucker!" Darrell yelled. The men

smiled. Adrian laughed, "Don't worry, Darrell. At least you

didn't cry over a BB."

"Hey, at least you're not in a wheelchair, otherwise you'd

drive like a pro that way," Phoenix said. Everyone laughed in

the room, but Darrell smiled and was a good sport about it.

"Adrian, I want you to do me one last favor for now,"

Darien said.

"What would that be?"

"Are you able to get in contact with the United States

military?"

"I could try, I heard that IFHR was originally established by the president."

"Try getting in contact with anything that flies, preferably helicopters or cargo planes, but secretly. We can't let President Lavensa know about this. Call them out and ask a request for a search and rescue in the Kalahari Desert in South Africa. Tell them to look for an abandoned base with weathered perimeters, they shouldn't miss the buildings inside it."

"Alright, I'll try to get in contact with them. Never really attempted hacking, but this may be my first time working with a computer like this. If this works, they should arrive within a couple of days."

"Good. That should be just in time for Darrell and Phoenix. That's good for most of the people here, too. A lot of them need medical attention. There's not many supplies here. We'll be able to fix their car up, too, we have enough tools and parts to spare. They have partially snowed windows and some dents on the bodywork. We'll care of them from here."

"Alright. This goes for Darrell and Phoenix. When the air support comes, I want you drive out of there as soon as possible. You need all the time you can get to prepare for your next trial before Russell knows you're absent."

"It was nice talking to you again, Adrian."

"You, too." Adrian dismisses.

Darien gives back Darrell's communicator. "Didn't have to introduce myself," Darrell said.

"I kind of figured. I heard your name before when IFHR was looking for you guys," Darien said. "Alright, here's the deal. We're going to find a place for you guys to sleep here. You're going to get fed, we'll supply water, and we'll fix your car within that time frame. But for the food, we'll have to ration it between you guys, even with my men. I hope you're okay with that."

"We're fine with that," Phoenix said.

"Good, because look at all of these people. These people need more than we do."

"Just as long as there's water."

"Oh, don't worry, we have plenty of that. Things are going to be different for a couple days, kind of like the dark ages. We're out in the desert and we're in an isolated settlement."

"We found out how to survive one way or another," Phoenix said.

"Alright. Men, find him a walking stick or something. Get him out of the chair."

Hannibal and a couple of the men walk towards Darrell. "Can you get up?" Hannibal said.

"Let's give it a shot," Darrell said. Darrell slowly, but

carefully lifts his unaffected foot to stand up. As he moves his bandaged foot, he grunted and limps, making the men catch his fall. "Just walk on it. Move it a little bit," Barry said. Darrell stomps his injured foot lightly and feels the tingling in his heel. "Now walk on it slowly. We'll still help you if you need it," Hannibal said.

Darrell takes a couple small steps as he's still grunting from the wound, but not as much. Everyone claps as the men take him to the sofa of the living room. Phoenix follows behind them. The living room was sage green as there was a rug and a glass table with a wooden circular rim in the center of the floor. The sofa was also sage green. The men carefully set Darrell on the couch. Darrell takes a deep breath, "Didn't think that former members of a corrupt organization had experience in the medical field. Worst than my last surgery, though. Burned like a bat out of hell."

"It was all from personal experience. Don't take it too

lightly. At least we helped you out," one of the men said, smiling. Darrell looked up to notice Phoenix smiling at him, giving him a glimpse of hope. "Alright, where are we sleeping?" Phoenix said.

"Second floor," Darien yelled. He was still in the other room.

"There are three bedrooms up there. All of them have at least five beds. They're old, though, so you might want to be careful with them," Hannibal said.

"Thanks, guys, we appreciate it," Phoenix said. Darien walks into the living room as his footsteps echo from the wooden floor, "We have a curfew though."

"Since when?" Phoenix said.

"Well, we do, we both do, actually, but ours is different. Your situation is special. Try going to bed at around nine o' clock at night. You guys need all the sleep you can get if you want to finish this."

"Alright," Phoenix said. "We can manage that."

Later on that night, Darrell and Phoenix lay in bed asleep

with some of the townspeople, recovering from the events

that took place earlier in the day.

Chapter 4: Departure

March 25, 2021

1046 hours

A couple days have passed. Darrell and Phoenix were just waking up from their sleep. They're walking down the steps as they see the men in the kitchen feeding the people, preparing meals. Darrell was slightly limping, but it's getting better. "You guys hungry?" Darien asked.

"No, we have to get going," Phoenix said.

"How's your foot, Darrell?"

"Still hurts, but I can drive still," Darrell said.

"Good, and speaking of driving, your car's completely

fixed, gas is filled and everything."

"Again, thanks for everything," Phoenix said.

"No problem. You helped us out in the end, so we returned the favor."

They suddenly hear the sound of helicopters approaching the town. "Everyone outside!" Darien yelled. The men stop preparing meals and line up the people towards the entrance. "Phoenix, you two know what to do now. You guys may be our only hope to winning this fight."

"We'll do what it takes to bring these people to justice," Phoenix says with honor.

"Good, now get out of here as soon as possible. Russell might call at any moment. He might hear the helicopters."

As the men order the people out of the shack, they notice two helicopters hovering towards the town. They were at least two miles away. The helicopters had a dark, metallic green finish with a decal of red, white, and blue stripes, with the letters, USA.

Darrell and Phoenix sprint to the garage towards the far side of the town. They budge open the garage doors and see their vehicle. The Lamborghini was flawless as it looked like it just came out of the factory. They climb in the vehicle and work their way out of the garage. As Darrell turns the steering wheel and reverses, they notice the people waving at the helicopters towards the entrance of the town.

As Darrell accelerates to the entrance, Darien waves them goodbye, wishing them luck. "Accelerate further, we need to get away from the helicopters," Phoenix said. Darrell switches into third gear and drives in that gear until he's about a couple miles away from the helicopters. Russell speaks through the communicator as his voice is muffled, "Now, time for your second trial." Phoenix switches to Russell's frequency, "We're just getting started."

Russell's voice sounds clearer now, "For your next trial,

this will take place in the country of England."

"What's the catch this time?" Darrell said.

"The next target will be a woman native in that country. Fortunate for me, the people I'm selecting will be elite members. Rashon was just a warm-up." Russell laughs, irritating Phoenix. "She's been active for only a year, she's quite young for her skills. Her name is Kyla Fisher. Age: 23. Hair color: Blonde. Skin color: Caucasian. Weight: 131 pounds. Let's just say she's very active, she knows her way around the city."

"Why don't you stop beating around the fucking bush?" Phoenix said.

"I'm not here to help you guys out. That's not the purpose of the Trials. I'm just giving you guys information on what's next. Like I said before, either you do them, or else face the consequences. This is the deal, you guys are the targets, you're my guinea pigs."

"Fuck you, Russell." Russell laughs in an evil manner and dismisses.

As Darrell and Phoenix head towards the Wonderboom Airport, they prepare for the flight in the second Trial in London, England.

Chapter 5: Blending In

March 25, 2021

London, England, 1013 hours

Darrell and Phoenix land at the London City Airport in the city of London, England. After they head out of the entrance, they roam around in the streets to get used to the city. Some of the buildings appeared Victorian in architecture as others looked modern. The vehicles used for transportation were similar to the ones back in the United States. "You guys in the city?" Adrian said in a muffled tone. Phoenix switches the frequency in the communicator, "We're just getting our way around."

"Who would be your next target?"

"It's a woman," Darrell said.

"Somebody by the name of Kyla Fisher. She's native here," Phoenix said.

"Alright, I'll look up her background."

Adrian looks up Kyla's background information in the database. "She's pretty young for getting involved into this kind of work. If you see her, her hair is usually combed straight down."

"Well, the youngest that you're eligible of getting in is twenty-one years of age, which is what we found out back when we found discovered the Archives."

"She's only been active for a year. How did she advance so quickly?" Darrell said. Phoenix looks down on her communicator to see Kyla Fisher's picture.

"According to her profile, she's been heavily involved with acrobatics. She's been getting into parkour as she was given extensive training for that kind of field. She also wields

platinum-grade katanas and mostly wears a black stealth suit,

too. Similar to what you have, Phoenix."

"This should be interesting," Phoenix said.

"Know how there's multiple bases that are established?"

"Yes, they could be in the ten thousands range, why is

there so many?" Darrell said.

"Well, like we said before, they've been secretive for

almost thirty years at the time until you guys came along.

With every organization, they're kind of like chapters, but

they don't belong to a specific one. They all just do their own

thing when they're assigned to a mission. Everybody has their

own personality or background that mostly has a reason for

them getting involved with IFHR."

"But what's Kyla like, is she dangerous?"

"Well, she is an elite. She can sweet talk with someone

for a while, but she's known to turn her back in the bitter

end."

"Well, we're not going to put up with that," Phoenix said.
"We need to stay focused."

"Here's one thing that I want you guys to do, though.
Don't go hunting for her just yet."

"Why not? We have to go after her as soon as we can,"
Darrell said.

"We're going to try something different this time. You
guys need to blend in the crowd for this Trial. Try to find a
department store so you can buy a new set of clothes. That
shouldn't really affect your suit, Phoenix. Your suit is light and
thin."

"We just arrived in the city limits. We can't find a
department store anywhere."

"I'll pinpoint the nearest store that's on your tracker." He
goes to the map on the computers and sets a waypoint to the
closest store, which was only a couple blocks away. "Check

on your GPS. You should be approaching a red pin after a couple turns."

"Yep, we see the pin. We should arrive in a couple minutes," Darrell said.

"Specifically for you, Phoenix. I would suggest finding something casual, like a jean jacket and blue denim jeans. As for you, Darrell, you can keep what you have on. She may be hiding out somewhere in the downtown area, somewhere were nightlife is involved."

"What would that be?"

"Stay low, don't slip up. That's the last thing we need on our hands right now. And no drinking, too. So don't try it."

"Didn't plan on it," Phoenix said.

"She'll most likely be hiding out in the West End of London, which is where you're close to. That's where one of the entertainment hot spots are located in."

"We're just about to turn onto another street."

"Alright, Adrian out," he dismisses.

"You have arrived at your destination," the female computer voice said through the navigation system. Darrell parks at a large department store. The store's exterior was painted light blue as there were windows displaying white mannequins dressed casually.

Darrell and Phoenix get out of the Lamborghini and enter the department store. The interior of the store was luxurious as there was checkered flooring and red walls. They quickly walked around as there was a large assortment of clothes to choose from, such as designer's hats, hoodies, dress clothes, and casual wear. "The only thing we need to get for you is a pair of sunglasses," Phoenix said.

"We're in a different country now. We can't use U.S. dollars in this country," Darrell said.

"Then, what can you use?"

"My debit card. You can complete a transaction with no

problem if you have one of those. Foreign exchange is universal, nowadays." They walk towards the section of the dress shirts. They look through the dress shirts as there were different colors and designs, such as two-tone stripes and two-tone squares. "Hmm, not usually the kind of gal that wears this on a daily basis," Phoenix said.

"It's nothing new when it comes to being professional. However, we do work in the same company," Darrell said. Phoenix just looks at him, "Good point." She pushes some of the shirts aside and browses through them. "But our lives our different now. Do me a favor and help me find a good, logical choice to wear in the nightlife. You have to look reasonable in order to blend in with the crowd." Darrell helps her look through the shirts and finds a choice, "How about a black T-shirt with a blue and gray striped dress shirt?" He hands it to her as she checks it out.

"Well, at least it's not all thrown together. Next, we need

some pants," Phoenix said. They walk to the pants from the opposite side of the dress shirts. The section is accompanied by lights from the ceiling as there was a large arrangement of pants to choose from. "Pick any pair that fits you," Darrell said. Phoenix grabs one of the pairs and hangs it over her shoulder. "We don't need shoes," Phoenix said. "Nobody's really going to notice. I'm also going to need a hat, too." They just walk to the hats section by the entrance doors of the store as Phoenix just takes a plain, black hat.

Darrell and Phoenix walk to the counter to get ready for checkout. They see a young looking man with blonde hair, wearing a blue hat and a white and black striped shirt. "Hello, mates," said the man in his British accent. "Where'd you get those clothes?"

"What, from the store?" Darrell said.

"No, the clothes you have on. We don't usually see stuff like that around here."

"Oh," Phoenix said, surprised and nervous, thinking of what to say. "We're part of a film that's coming soon."

"Oh, really? That's cool, what kind is it?"

"Yeah, what is it Darrell?" Phoenix looks at Darrell, waiting for him to give an answer. Darrell looks at her, confused. He suddenly realizes what she's doing. "Oh, it's a spy film," Darrell said, smiling. "Sorry, sir. I wasn't paying attention."

"What's the film called?"

"We can't tell anybody the name yet. It's best if people don't know right now," Phoenix said. "We just started making the film."

"It's all good, I understand," said the clerk. "Did you get everything you need?"

"Yes, sir," Phoenix said. Darrell had a feeling he was missing something. "Oh, I forgot, I'm getting a pair of sunglasses, too," he said as he glanced at a small steel tower on the counter carrying sunglasses by its branches. Darrell quickly takes two pairs of black shades and places them on the counter. "Jeez, Darrell. You're not paying attention. What is up with you?" Phoenix said as she raises her eyebrow, smiling. Phoenix sets her items on the counter as the clerk scans them with a silver, metallic barcode reader. "That will be thirty-six pounds altogether," the clerk said.

"I'll use my debt card," Darrell said.

"We're from the United States," Phoenix said.

"I can tell by your accents," the clerk said. The clerk crouches down to grab a couple plastic bags and places the clothes in them. "Here you go, you're all set."

"Thank you, have a good day, sir," Darrell said.

"You, too."

Darrell and Phoenix walk out of the department store and head towards their vehicle. They start driving away from the department store. "Did you get the clothes?" Adrian said.

"We got 'em," Darrell said.

"Good, you guys should have enough time to head towards the center of the West End. Find a secluded space when you get there to put your new clothes on. If she finds you out and tries to evade, take off your new clothes, pursue her and eliminate her."

"We'll be on it," Phoenix said. "Just as soon as we can find her."

"Beware, she's an assassin, too. That's why she has katanas with her."

"That shouldn't be too hard to do. You can only kill two birds with one stone," Phoenix said.

"Be careful, there's no room for failure," Adrian dismisses.

Darrell and Phoenix exit out of the street of the department store as they head towards the West End of London.

Chapter 6: Vixen

1104 hours

Darrell and Phoenix enter into Leicester Square in the West End of London. The climate was flawless as there were no clouds. The area consisted of several venues like cinemas, theaters and sports bars. Most of the buildings around them were Victorian in architecture. The traffic was moderately dense as commuters filled half of the road from their sight, putting themselves into a traffic jam. "This place is busier than I thought," Phoenix said.

"That's a good thing if your mission is to track down

somebody," Adrian said. "But, it's also a bad thing because the members of IFHR use this as their advantage to keep their work under the grid."

Darrell and Phoenix see their chance and exit out of the traffic jam. As he turns onto another road, he notices a sports bar with a series of newly added LED Lights, showing the sports bar's name on it. The sports bar was Gottfried Nightlife British Sports Bar. "I think we found the place," Phoenix said.

"Good, there's an alleyway that has a parking lot behind the building. Enter through it and change clothes from there," Adrian said. Darrell stops and slowly pulls into the alleyway. He enters the empty parking lot and parks the vehicle. "Good, there's no people here," Phoenix said.

"Turn your ear mics on," Darrell said. They grab their clothes and get out. Phoenix puts on her shirt and hat as she takes off her shoes to put on her jeans. Darrell just puts on his sunglasses. "Alright, before I forget, watch how she talks, too," Adrian said through the mics. "She also has experience with talking people into something. When she does this, don't bluff too much or you'll give yourselves away. If she finds you out, pursue her, no matter what." Adrian dismisses.

Darrell and Phoenix walk out of the parking lot and alleyway and into the street, heading for the sports bar. "Don't fall for anything she has to say," Phoenix said, speaking to Darrell.

As they open the glass doors of the sports bar, they check out the interior. The flooring was made of stained, dark earlywood textures as the walls were burnt sienna. There was a lighted counter that was wide as it was light gray and transparent, showing glass down to the bottom. There were a bunch of different colored bottles and dispensers that displayed several varieties of alcoholic and non-alcoholic beverages. There was a large, open space by the counter that showed people sitting at several circular and rectangular tables. There was a large window that shined the sun's rays down beside the tables. "Why don't we get a drink while we're here?" Phoenix said.

"We can't drink," Darrell said.

"We can get water." They walk to the counter as the female bartender just comes towards the counter. The bartender had blonde hair that extended down to her shoulders as she had white skin and was wearing a purple shirt. "Hello, what can I get for you guys today?" said the bartender.

"Just two bottles of water," Phoenix said. She pulls two bottles of water from under the counter and hands them to Darrell and Phoenix. "Thank you."

Darrell and Phoenix walk towards the side of the counter and sit on the red cushioned bar stools. They notice a woman in a full black leather suit similar to Phoenix's coming through the entrance. She had an expression of anger and determination on her face. She matched the description and portrait of Kyla Fisher. She goes to the counter and orders a bottle of water. "I think we found our target," Phoenix said, quietly.

Kyla notices Darrell and Phoenix looking at her. Kyla had a confused look on her face. She smiles and walks over to them and sits on a stool next to them. They noticed that she didn't have katanas attached to her back. "I saw you guys looking at me over there," Kyla said. "May I help you?"

"No, we just like to look around," Phoenix said.

"Are you guys from here?" Kyla said, joyfully.

"What do you think, lady? Does it sound like I'm from here?" Phoenix said, angrily.

"Well, my name's Kyla. Kyla Fisher."

"Really? That's cool," Phoenix said sarcastically. "Now get lost, you're starting to annoy us already."

Kyla looks at Darrell, "Who's that man sitting beside

you?"

"He's not much of a talker, he really isn't," Phoenix said, getting agitated.

"Well, I'm going to talk to him anyway. He seems lonely."

"You're really pushing it, ma'am."

"Phoenix?" Adrian said, speaking through the ear mic, making Phoenix slightly jump in her seat. Kyla didn't notice. "Phoenix, I know you can hear me. Kyla can't hear me with the microphone, but I can hear her. It sounds like Darrell's in trouble. Make sure she doesn't make a move on him. And don't blow your cover, either!"

Kyla sits next to Darrell and starts to flirt with him, "Hey, you look a little lonely here."

"He's fine, Kyla. Leave him alone," Phoenix said. Kyla ignores her.

"So, sir, what would be your name?" Kyla said, smiling.

She puts her arm around his shoulder.

"I don't give my information to people I don't know. Surprisingly, you sound drunk," Darrell said, annoyed.

Kyla says flirtatiously, "Hmm, that wasn't very nice. Here, give me a hug. It'll make you feel better." She forcefully gives Darrell a hug, making him feel uneasy and nervous. Kyla's action made Phoenix mad, causing her to get up from the bar stool. She walks to Kyla and pushes her off of Darrell, "What the fuck did I just say? You seem like the desperate kind." Kyla gets up from the ground and walks back to Darrell, hugging him tightly. "So, you want to come home at my place tonight?" Kyla said, smiling.

"Get her off of him, Phoenix. Don't let her get into Darrell's head!" Adrian said. Phoenix walks up to Kyla and pounces on her, catching her off guard and letting go of Darrell, falling to the ground. This action caused the people around her to pay attention to the ordeal.

Phoenix stands herself up and takes off her sunglasses and hat, revealing herself to Kyla with an expression of anger. "So, Kyla, you remember me?" Phoenix said, boldly. Kyla was petrified, "No fucking way."

"And I bet you were looking for us, too." Kyla looks around her as the people around them turn their backs and witness them.

Kyla looks at Phoenix and quickly gets herself up by swinging her legs out to stand. She pulls a dagger out of her suit and charges after Phoenix. Phoenix dodges her as Kyla swiftly swings the dagger towards almost all parts of her body. Phoenix attempts to grab her by the arm, but Kyla counter attacks by grabbing her arm and bending it towards her back. Darrell panics and jumps off of the bar stool and runs towards Phoenix's aid.

Kyla takes her dagger and places it just under Phoenix's chin, making Phoenix panic and breathe heavily. Everybody in the bar gasps, surprised and confused. "Nobody better make a fucking move," Kyla warned with anger. "Or else this beautiful looking piece of obsidian will cut through her neck better than what your butcher makes on a busy night." Kyla pulls out a black pistol in her leather suit, placing her other arm on Phoenix's shoulder. "So, what's it going to be, big boy?" Kyla taunted, speaking to Darrell. "Do you want to sell yourself to me, or do you want to save a smuggler's wife that made our plans a lot more interesting than we could have ever imagined?"

"Let her go!" Darrell yelled.

"You have to make a choice, Darrell. Either you give yourself up or die trying? You'll die either way." Darrell's patience is drastically decreasing as his anger suddenly fuels into rage. He says slowly as the emotions flow through him, "I said let her go, you fucking bitch!" He quickly pulls out his white pistol and shoots a scattershot round three feet above

Kyla's head. The shot went through a couple pictures,

shattering through the glass and making them fall to the

ground. The shot also made Kyla jump, releasing some of her

grip on Phoenix. She grew petrified as she widens her eyes in

fear, causing her to breathe heavily. "What the FUCK DID I

JUST SAY?!" Darrell aims down Phoenix's feet as their was an

opening between them. He fires the scattershot as only one

of the three fragments go through the gap, startling the

crowd and making them scream. Some of them ran out of the

bar. This made Kyla completely release her grip on Phoenix.

"Jeez, Darrell, are you trying to kill me?!" Phoenix yelled.

Kyla's fear suddenly turns into focus as she quickly turns

around and bolts out of the doors she came in. "She's getting

away, get after her!" Adrian said to both of them.

"Come on, Darrell. Let's go!" Phoenix said. They bolt for

the doors and enter the street. Darrell throws his sunglasses

down on the ground. They look around and spot Kyla running

towards her vehicle, which is a metallic orange Aston Martin.

They both run after her. "Where do you think you're going,

bitch?!" Phoenix taunted.

As Kyla enters her vehicle, Darrell and Phoenix stop

running by her driver's window. Kyla still looks petrified.

Phoenix punches the window, "Open the door!" Kyla doesn't

listen. Phoenix takes her body and budges on the window

after almost every word she says, "I SAID OPEN THE FUCKING

DOOR!"

Kyla suddenly revs the engine and drives away. "Shit!"

Phoenix yelled.

"Get in your car and get after her! Prepare to do a lot of

running! She specializes in acrobatics!" Adrian said.

Darrell and Phoenix run towards the Lamborghini. While

running, Phoenix takes off her T- shirt and dress shirt and

throws them on the sidewalk. Phoenix grabs her katanas and

sheathes them behind her back. She takes off her shoes and

takes her pants off. She also throws the pants over to the

sidewalk next to the bar. She puts her boots back on as they

both get in the vehicle. "Let's see if she's good with cutlery,"

Phoenix said. Darrell starts the vehicle and begin their pursuit

with Kyla.

Chapter 7: Goose Chase

1120 hours

Darrell and Phoenix accelerate to catch up with Kyla.
They see Kyla turn onto another street. "Quick, make a hard turn!" Phoenix said. Darrell executes a small drift and continues to follow Kyla. She presses hard on the brake and gets out of her vehicle. "Stop the vehicle!" Phoenix yelled. Darrell presses hard on the brake as the tires leave a thick trail of smoke. The vehicles stop by a building that's about thirty stories high as it is metallic gray in texture, similar to an office building.

Darrell and Phoenix get out of the vehicle and pursue Kyla. Kyla quickly pulls open a door in the back of the building and enters inside. "Prepare to run. You're going to have to do some parkour, too," Adrian said. They both enter the building to see a lighted narrow, bland, gray hallway. They see Kyla in the distance, just opening another door. "Come on, Darrell, we can't let her get away," Phoenix said.

Phoenix charges and budges through the door, revealing a room with a green light and windows by the wall, projecting the city of London. They see Kyla running up a stairwell. "Why are you running? I thought you wanted to kill us," Phoenix taunted. Kyla runs onto a wall and vaults over the edge of the stairwell. Phoenix pulls out one of her pistols and fires a couple rounds, but she misses. Darrell and Phoenix run towards the stairwell and execute the same actions as her.

As Darrell and Phoenix enter another floor, they are surrounded by a wide and long hallway that has glass elevators on one side and windows projecting the city on the other side. There were yellow and green lights on the ceiling as the floor was carpeted. They continue to sprint down the hallway as they gain distance with Kyla.

Kyla suddenly heads towards one of the elevators and presses the button beside it to ascend. The glass elevator's curved door slides open as Kyla enters inside it. They catch up to Kyla and stop running. "Where the hell do you think you're going?!" Phoenix said. Kyla presses a button inside the elevator as the door slowly closes. "I'm going one step ahead of you?" Kyla said, boldly.

Phoenix runs up to the elevator, "You motherfucker!" The elevator closes before Phoenix could make a move. She punches the glass door in anger. Kyla looks at them with a petulant expression and a cunning smile. As the elevator starts ascending, she taunts them by waving goodbye. "We're taking the elevator next to her," Phoenix said. They run to the elevator beside Kyla's. Phoenix presses the ascending button.

As Darrell and Phoenix enter inside, they look around its interior. The interior has gray metallic walls as there was a black touchpad. She presses a button with the highest floor, with the number, 88. The button flashed green. The door closes and the elevator starts ascending. The ascension rate is fast as they were already on the fifth floor. "I have a feeling she's taking the same floor as we are," Phoenix said.

"How would you know?" Darrell said.

"They usually do their work secretively."

While ascending, they enter through the floors as they see windows projecting the skyline of London. The skyline was getting more detailed as they climb higher. They look up to see Kyla's elevator. "That's right," Phoenix said. "We're coming for you."

As they pass the fiftieth floor, Adrian calls them, "There will be a stairwell on the eighty-eighth floor. It will be on the rooftop. That's where she'll most likely be going."

"We got our eyes on her," Phoenix said. "And she's got our eyes on us, too. Not very brave of an elite to run away."

As they reach the eighty-eighth floor, the elevator door opens. The floor was dark as the only source of light was the windows from outside. There were office doors and filing cabinets throughout the hallway. "Where the hell is she?" Darrell said. They look around in all directions, but the hallways are too dark to locate Kyla.

Suddenly, they see her crawling down and opening a door, revealing the sunlight. "There she is!" Phoenix yelled. They sprint towards the door and budge it open as they run up a small flight of steps. The steps reveal the rooftop as they exit through. The roof's floor was white as its contrast was enhanced by the sun. They see Kyla still running as she jumps and vaults onto a surface that's about five feet high. The surface is close to the end of roof. Darrell and Phoenix follow her as they do the same actions.

Darrell and Phoenix were too late as she already jumped off of the surface by the time they arrived. They see Kyla jump towards a lower section connected to the building as she coils herself into a somersault. Phoenix panics and breathes heavily as the lowered section appeared to be fifteen feet from her estimate. "You guys have to jump!" Adrian said. "Just do it however you can if want to eliminate her!"

Phoenix slows her breathing down as her and Darrell back up a few steps to get a running start. They jump off. As they are falling towards the lowered roof, they notice Kyla stop running.

Darrell and Phoenix successfully land as Kyla has her back turned. The section they were on was almost completely out in the open as there were no barriers to protect them from falling. There was a door that was located towards the center of the roof that indicates one of the building's several exits. "It's over, Kyla," Darrell said.

"You have nowhere to go," Phoenix said. Kyla folds her arms, "I know, that was the purpose of the running." She turns around and walks toward them. "I picked this building because it would be the perfect spot to cut you guys up. No one would have to know," Kyla said.

"Don't be so stupid, Kyla. Everyone in the organization knows about us. I've heard that trick before, you're no longer top secret."

"We were, until you came along and came for Darrell's rescue. It doesn't work that way."

"I'm not doing it just for him. I'm doing it because I'm now a widow for what you guys did."

"And yet you still haven't learned your lesson yet." Kyla slowly unsheathes her swords and spins them around as she gets into a defensive stance. "Now, let's see if you can save your precious gem from being cut down to several fragments for my pleasure."

Phoenix pulls out her swords as she gives an expression of revenge, "I would like to see you try for yourself."

Phoenix and Kyla charge at each other and viciously swing their swords. They break each other's attacks as their swords make clanging noises. They block each other's attacks as their weapons are grinding against each other. "We take people for granted," Kyla said, taunting Phoenix with an angry expression. "You should've known that by now." Phoenix forcefully pushes Kyla's weapons to the side, breaking her blocking position. She charges after Kyla, but she blocks Phoenix again, entering each other's breaks. "I've already known that, because you guys are a bunch of pathetic excuses that you call humanity," Phoenix said.

"We are humanity," Kyla said. "We just have a different outlook on it." Kyla breaks her blocking position and ferociously swings at Phoenix. Kyla walks towards Phoenix as she blocks her every swing. This causes Phoenix to back up closer to the ledge of the building, pushed against the wall. Phoenix was panicking and hyperventilating. "Aw, what's the matter? Has your will power got the best of you?!" Kyla said. "Do you have any last words before I take your life away along with your partner in crime?"

Darrell slowly walks up to Kyla, hoping that she won't notice. Phoenix sees that her legs aren't protected from her weapons. She kicks Kyla hard in the leg, knocking her off balance. Darrell charges after her and grabs Kyla, standing her up. He then grabs her by her suit and performs a hard punch to her face, giving her a bloody nose. He lets go and punches her in the chest and diaphragm along with a merciless uppercut to her chin. Kyla was feeling dizzy as she walks around, almost falling. She already feels whiplash from dealing with Darrell. "It's true," Darrell said to Kyla. "You are the desperate kind." Kyla gave in to her dizziness and kneels to the ground, dropping her swords.

"You've done well, Darrell. I've got this from here now," Phoenix said.

Phoenix walks up to Kyla and quickly pulls her head up, "You have nowhere to go now." Phoenix takes one of her swords and stabs her in the diaphragm. "You should know what I'm capable of." She pulls the sword out and stabs it back into her diaphragm. Blood starts dripping from Kyla's mouth. "The whole world already knows about you. They'll soon know about us." Phoenix takes her other sword and stabs her deep into the collarbone. "I'm one step ahead of you. You can't fool me no longer. I know what you guys are all about." Phoenix stabs her in her other collarbone. "I would love to kill you right here, but I won't do that." She pulls out her swords from Kyla's body and sets them down on the roof.

Phoenix picks up Kyla and makes her way towards the

roof. "I'll spare you, but you won't be living any time soon."

Phoenix said. Kyla is coughing from the blood in her mouth.

"Because this marks the end of the second Trial!"

Kyla's eyes widen in petrification and fear as Phoenix

throws her over the roof. While falling, Kyla sees the world

around her blur before her eyes. As she comes in contact

with the ground, most of her bones break as her spine

fractures from impacting the cement sidewalk, creating a

loud cracking sound. The people on the street start panicking

as they witness the body thrown from the roof. Blood starts

spilling out from Kyla's body, causing people to run away.

Phoenix looks down and breathes heavily with anger and

anguish, giving no remorse from her actions. "We took her

down," Phoenix said through her mic. "I threw her off of the

roof."

"Holy shit, Phoenix," Darrell said, surprised from her

actions.

"Good, now go to the nearest exit and get out of London as soon as you can," Adrian said.

Darrell and Phoenix sprint towards the door near the center of the roof and budge through it. They run down a couple flights of stairs and enter a hallway full of elevators and windows. They enter an elevator and descend down to the first floor.

They open the door they originally came in and run towards their vehicle. They get inside as Darrell starts the engine. He accelerates and makes their way out of the street. As they pass by the building, they see the people gather around Kyla's body as some of them are taking pictures from their phones. "Now, for your third Trial," Russell said. Phoenix switches to Russell's frequency, "It wasn't too hard, Russell. Why don't you invest in a challenge besides just choosing a random member?"

"Oh, you won't have to worry about that in the next

Trial, Phoenix! This one will be a definite challenge for you as this will be a test of your mental stability!"

"And how would that be a test?" Phoenix said.

"In the third Trial, it will take place in a remote location in Brazil, specifically a rich forest area. There will be a complex with several buildings there, kind of like a large town."

"How will that be a test of our mental stability?" Phoenix said.

"Because the complex has the same characteristics of one of the historical funny farms, but more brutal and modern." Russell laughs wickedly.

"Funny farm?" Phoenix said, confused.

"Insane asylum," Darrell whispers.

"You're going to be looking for a man inside the complex that's in one of the many cells of the people that are in there. His name is Edward Fleming. Age: 25. Hair color: Black. Eye color: Brown. Weight: 210 pounds. He was active for two years until he was found out by authorities."

"Oh, that's surprising," Phoenix said, sarcastically.

"In IFHR, once you get found out by authorities, we sneak in their prisons and take them in for isolation, which is basically our version of prison, but with a more violent twist," Russell laughs again. "Let's see if you can stand yourself on this one, Phoenix."

"What are you plotting, Russell?" Phoenix was losing her patience.

"You'll see in due time," Russell dismisses.

They head out of the West End of London and enter the airport to take flight, awaiting what's in store for them in the lush forests of Brazil.

Chapter 8: The Mountains

March 27, 2021

Mantiqueira Mountains, Brazil, 1206 hours

Darrell and Phoenix are driving on a mountain range in the forests of Brazil. There were damp hills surrounding them as they were going on a straight road. "Where are you at right now?" Adrian said. Phoenix switches the communicator to his frequency, "We're in Brazil, particularly a mountain range." Darrell stops and turns onto a dirt road.

"Be careful on the roads, they will be slightly damp from where you're at."

Darrell drives towards two more hills as they obstructed

his sight ahead of him. As he drove between the hills, they saw several gray buildings in the distance surrounded by mountaintops. The buildings appeared no higher than seven stories and were connected into an intricate complex, similar to a small city. The complex appeared to be ten football fields in area size. "Wow," Darrell said.

"What is this place?" Phoenix said.

"From my coordinates, that would be Base No. 00047, which is one of their many establishments they call the IFHR Medical Facility. They made it look like a town," Adrian said.

"I thought they didn't care about their kind," Phoenix said.

"They don't. The place is a fucking joke. Their 'medical facilities' are used as insane asylums. Most of them have agents that were caught in the act, but some just get out of control. Too unstable to tell between what's reality and what's not. Fleming fits in the mental part of the facility."

"What did he do?" Darrell said.

"Fleming was convicted of a multitude of crimes. Some were unthinkable. He was convicted with aggravated murder, and attempted murder." Darrell was halfway towards the base as he started to see smaller buildings and parked vehicles scattered around inside it. "In his record, he was known to strangle some of his victims by force, literally choking his victims to death with just his hands. He has a tight grip on people."

"Well, yeah, if he can choke people with just his hands," Phoenix said.

"He's really strong, too. He was also known to mercilessly beat up his victims in the most sensitive areas on the body, such as their temple, neck, and their skull. He broke bones of some victims by bending their elbows back until they snapped and twisted their necks."

"Holy shit, that's fucked up," Phoenix said.

"But he's not the only one being held captive in there. There are hundreds of other inmates that have severe mental stability conditions that make them so twisted, it drastically drains their sanity, but Fleming is one of the worse in there. I would be cautious going in if I were you. This isn't a regular settlement." Adrian dismisses.

Darrell stops by the large, gated, steel doors of the base's entrance. "I'll take it from here," Phoenix said. She gets out of the Lamborghini and runs to the touch pad by the side of the steel doors. She holds the buttons, E and OVERRIDE near the touch pad and waits as the circuit noise gets distorted and the communicator's blue glow expands. "C'mon, don't shock me again!" As the pad's screen reads as ACCESS GRANTED, she immediately releases the buttons and steps away from the doors as they slowly open.

As Darrell drives through the entrance, they see the complex's layout in most of its entirety. There were roads that are exactly the same as used on public city traffic. The layout appeared to be that of a town that's next to a major city. "Wow, this is what you don't see every day," Phoenix said, looking around seeing the buildings while Darrell was driving around. She spots a large, wide building that's mostly white in color with shorter sections connected around it. "Park into there, a lot of cars are there. That could help us blend in with the rest of them," Phoenix said.

Darrell turns on another road and heads towards the white building. He slowly pulls into the parking lot of the building as vehicles were mostly covering it. They parked between a white sedan and a red city car. They both get out of the Lamborghini and walk towards the entrance, which was only about a couple blocks away. "I didn't think they would have city cars, too. Why would they have them, that's very unusual," Darrell said.

"This looks like a town, Darrell. Maybe this is a place for

testing," Phoenix said.

They walk up to the entrance as Phoenix prepares to override the door's touch pad. She presses and holds E and OVERRIDE and stands back. The door grants access as they both slowly enter inside.

Darrell and Phoenix walk into a dimly lit hallway that had cerulean blue walls, a dim shade of blue. There were two flights of stairs which lead up and down. The hallway was quiet as there were no sources of background noise. They see a steel table with cabinets and lockers embedded into the wall above the table. "Let's check over there," Darrell said softly. They run up to the table and lockers and search through them.

"If they're always trying to keep things secret, they always have a place to put things. They don't usually grant patients access to just roam around. That's not what it was like in the old days when the so-called doctors tortured them for a living." Phoenix said softly. They look through most of the lockers and cabinets, but they were empty. "Damn it, nothing!" Phoenix exclaimed quietly.

They have one more locker to open. Phoenix opens it and finds a modern key that's ahead of its time. It doesn't look like a traditional key used in households. It was metallic silver and was the size of a quarter of the palm of someone's hand. There is a small digital code that was embedded in it. "C113?" Phoenix said, confused. The screen quickly swiped to another text, showing Fleming's name. "I think we found what we were looking for."

"Congratulations, you're opening the door quickly than I thought," Russell said. Phoenix switches to his frequency, "I'm just getting started, Russell. This is way too easy."

"Well, then. This should be a challenge for you." Phoenix gets frustrated as Russell is talking. "Once you enter that room, just remember how far you came just by putting every one of us on your list. We always have tricks up our sleeves, we're always one step ahead of you."

"*Tst*, really?" Phoenix said sarcastically. Her and Darrell start walking up the steps to enter through the B level. "Then you better change your sleeves by the time I see your face. I'll coat them with blood."

"Wow, I can tell you're losing your mind already. This should be your home. Are you scared for what has to come?"

Phoenix smiles boldly, but brazenly, "If I was scared, then why don't I feel any sympathy for every person I took out?" They walk up to the C level and see a clean, white door with a touch pad.

"You keep thinking like that. You don't know what's behind that fucking door. We have plenty of surprises for you guys," Russell said.

"I thought you weren't trying to help us out. Don't even try to help us. We already know what you're capable of."

"I would certainly hope so. After all, you're still the

targets. Or should I say, test subjects for this type of

situation?" Russell dismisses. Phoenix presses s and OVERRIDE,

unlocking the door.

Chapter 9: Madhouse

1223 hours

As Phoenix pushes open the door, they see a brightly lit, wide room with a hallway stretch. There are hundreds of cells that had steel bars and touch pads for added security. They looked on the sides of the cells to see they were from numbers C399 - C300.

They both looked upon a room with a window in the distance. They only saw the silhouettes of figures of two people standing and a person sitting helplessly in the chair. It showed agents with white suit jackets with white blood stained aprons carrying different tools. The agents couldn't

see through the window. The window was designed a certain

way, so that way the patient couldn't see the outside of their

room. There was a man inside the room with the agents that

was sitting down. He barely showed movement and had

bloodstains on him. He had nothing but underwear on and

was coughing out blood profusely. The agents showed no

remorse. "Take him down, he can't suffer anymore," one of

the agents said. The man eyes reddened as his chest

asphyxiated and died, leaning over one side of the restrained

chair. They were surprised to see what they witnessed.

"What the hell is going on?" Phoenix said, panicking.

Darrell and Phoenix walk towards where the cells are

and see the inmates. They all wear the traditional IFHR attire.

Black suit jacket, dress pants, shoes, and a white dress shirt.

The cells were mostly dark as they all have a small light

embedded on the side of the ceiling. The cells have a table

below a mirror on the side as there was a small bed on the other side.

Behind them was a man eating his lunch like a wild boar off of a metallic tray. Halfway through eating his bologna sandwich, he heard Darrell's and Phoenix's footsteps. He stops eating and jerks his head up and quietly growls, looking menacingly just below the mirror.

"Sir, are you okay?" Phoenix said to the inmate. The inmate they were near was sitting on a steel chair, facing the opposite of the bars.

The inmate behind them heard them talk and jerks his head up more and widens his eyes. He then jerks his head and spot Darrell and Phoenix. His face turns into rage and snarls loudly at them. This startles Darrell and Phoenix. "Holy shit!" Phoenix said, causing her to jump and look back and see the other inmate. He violently flips his tray over, almost breaking the mirror. He charges at the bars and grabs a hold of them with all of his force. The bars were made to be resistant to the inmates to prevent damage and allowing them to escape.

Darrell and Phoenix look back at the inmate sitting down. He slowly backs up and groans like a zombie and looks at them with wide eyes. Phoenix starts to get terrified. The inmate slowly twists his head to one side and gets up from his chair. He then jerks his head straight and charges at the bars. He yells at the top of his lungs and forcefully grabs the bars.

Suddenly, they hear other inmates yelling and screaming, even making onomatopoeic sounds. "I think they know we're here," Darrell said, terrified and paranoid.

"No shit!" Phoenix said.

They run past the cells as they see some of the inmates snarl and growl, charging at the bars. One of the inmates startles Darrell and Phoenix. The inmate was grabbing the bars with full force and starting pulling on them violently. He looks at them with rage and mania flowing through his body. "I WANT YOUR HEAD! WE ALL WANT YOUR HEAD! I WANT YOUR BLOOD ALL OVER ME!" the inmate yelled. He hisses and snarls loudly, increasing the levels of terror in Phoenix's eyes. Her and Darrell start hyperventilating and sprint away from the inmate.

They look to see another inmate sitting on a chair looking in the mirror. He starts getting enraged, "Where are you, Phoenix?! I want to see your face again!" He quickly gets up from his chair and punches a hole in the mirror, cracking it instantly. "WHERE ARE YOU?!" he yells at the top of his lungs. He slowly turns as he's breathing heavily. He sees Phoenix and charges at the bars, "THERE YOU ARE! NOW GET OVER HERE, SO I CAN SNAP YOUR NECK!"

Darrell and Phoenix sprint away from the inmate's sight. They heard a loud cry from another inmate that can be heard from the entire room, making them stop again. They see an

inmate sitting down with a lunch tray, crying profusely. He

was holding the orange from his tray and looks down on it.

"It'll be okay, it'll all be over soon!" he said to the orange,

petting it as if it was an animal.

The inmate slowly looks at the bars of his cell and spots

Darrell and Phoenix. He yells and smiles immensely while still

crying profusely as he sees Phoenix. Emotions were going

through his mind as he was experiencing joy, rage, and

sadness simultaneously. As his emotions grow more

overwhelming, he drastically increases the grip on the orange

and squeezes the juice out of it. The juice quickly came out of

it as it splattered across the floor and walls. The inmate's

body was shaking as he was now holding the orange that's

now half of its original size. "THE ORANGE IS DEAD!" he yells

out at Phoenix.

Phoenix starts to shake as the terror increases. The

inmate then throws his tray on the floor, almost bending the metal and charges at the bars, making Phoenix jump. Darrell and Phoenix continue shaking as the acoustics of the yells and screams echo throughout the room.

Suddenly, a loud alarm sounds throughout the room, which alerts the agents by the window. Darrell and Phoenix look up and gasp as the agents run and exit out of the room. Darrell spots a door at the side of the room and points it out. "Let's go that way! That must be a way out!" he yelled. They sprint to the door to see it has a touch pad.

She overrides it and budges through the door only to see more inmates mischievously behaving out of control. The cell numbers were from C299 - C200. They sprint past the cells as the inmates continue screaming and pulling the cells' bars. "Ahead of us must be Fleming," Phoenix said. They stop running as she overrides the door.

They budge through to see the layout of the cells to be

different than the other rooms. The walls were dark blue and

were accompanied by lights hanging from the ceiling. The

inmates' behavioral activity from C199 - C100 was more

severe than the previous sections. Most of the inmates

grabbed the bars and snarled loudly. Some of them

screeched as it almost mimicked a hawk's. "Holy shit!" Darrell

said. Some of them attempted to kick and punch the bars out

with full force, but only hurt themselves. "C113 should be

close," Phoenix said. The inmates resumed their screaming.

"SHUT THE FUCK UP!" she yelled, reacting to the screaming.

Her yelling didn't effect the magnitude of the inmates.

They sprint to the other end of the room until they stop

by Cell C113. Phoenix inserts the key into the side of the cell

as its text flashes quickly and beeps. She waits as the bars go

down into the ground.

Chapter 10: Conviction

Inside the cell was different and about three times the size than the ones from Cell C399 - C300. The room was longer as it was lighted in the center and had dark blue walls. There was a bed that's right by the bars of the cell. Darrell and Phoenix notice a bulky man standing in front of a mirror as he notices them walking towards him. He had his hands folded behind his back. There was a closet door that's beside the mirror. The man looks menacingly as they draw in closer.

"Fleming," Phoenix said cautiously. "Are you Fleming?" No answer. Just a dead look on his face as they stop walking to him.

"Wow," Fleming said, in a quiet and calm voice. "Would you look at that?"

"Look at what? Are you proud to be in here?" Phoenix said.

"I *was* proud, but not anymore. I used to walk as a free man. That is until they took me in."

"You know you're guilty. It's time to face it," Phoenix said.

"Every day I'm in here, it increases my insanity to a point where I can't control it. I mean, I can, I just don't want to."

"How did you benefit from killing those people? Did it make you feel good?"

"Only to a certain point. Would have been better off if I was in a regular jail."

"Why did you kill these people?"

"I heard that you were the targets," Edward laughs. "I'm surprised you guys even came this far." He stops talking suddenly and jerks his head, widening his eyes. He starts talking in a delusional tone as he appears to speak with voices in his head. He puts his hand by his ear, "What? What's that you say?"

Phoenix gets petrified, "Darrell, step back." They both step back as Fleming continues to talk to himself.

"You want ME to kill them?!" Fleming makes a cackling laugh like a hyena and walks to the closet door. He talks in a screeching tone, "I would be happy to oblige to your command!" He opens his closet door and yanks a steel baseball bat with spikes on them that are sharp as thorns. The bat was heavy as it was around seventeen pounds. However, the bat was composed of titanium and carbon, signifying its lightweight, yet powerful, damaging effects. "Because when it comes to being free, I'll do anything to get that back!"

He jerks his head to look at Darrell and Phoenix. They both get scared as they start to hyperventilate. Fleming starts yelling as he's walking towards them with the bat and swings it. "Oh, fuck! Darrell, let's get out of here!" Phoenix panicked. They turn around and make their way towards the end of the cell. Fleming charges towards them and attempts to strike, but manages to break one of the legs supporting his bed. "Don't worry, I JUST WANT TO PLAY!" Fleming yells.

Darrell and Phoenix run to the exit door near his cell. She quickly overrides it and budges through the door. Fleming grunts as he swings the bat towards Darrell, but barely misses him by a couple inches. "C'MON, DARRELL!" Phoenix yelled. Darrell runs through the door and enters the hallway that's similar to the back entrance.

"Quit running, it's not FAIR! NOT FAIR!" Fleming yelled. He threw the bat while they were running down the steps in the hallway of the B level. The bat made a clanging noise as its bottom stuck to the bottom of the floor. "Damn, this son of a bitch is crazy!" Darrell yelled. Fleming sprints down the steps and yanks the bat out of the floor as Darrell and Phoenix run down towards the A level.

Fleming catches up to them as they get out of the steps. Phoenix overrides the door and budges through as Fleming was only a couple steps away, swinging at the side of the door and braking the touch pad.

Darrell and Phoenix quickly get into their vehicle as Fleming gets into the red Fiat city car next to them. He reverses and make his way out of the parking lot and towards the road. "Shit, he's going to kill somebody!" Darrell yelled.

"Get after him, you have to kill him!" Adrian said through the communicator, startling Darrell and Phoenix.

Darrell reverses and heads towards the end of the parking lot to catch up with Edward, which he is only about fifty feet away. Edward turns right and heads for the base's

exit. Darrell turns in the same direction and speeds towards

Edward's rear bumper. He switches lanes and accelerates

until he's by Edward's tire. He then viciously rams him,

causing Edward to enter a series of unforgiving barrel rolls.

Pieces of metal break off of the city car as he heads towards a

wide pole that's strong as steel.

While Edward's in a barrel roll, the spins were so fast

that it caused him to fly through his windshield before the car

impacted the steel pole, bending it like the shape of a fortune

cookie. Part of his face scraped across the asphalt by the time

he touched ground.

Chapter 11: Word of Mouth

Darrell thrusts the brakes and halts the car beside Edward's damaged and bruised body. Him and Phoenix get out of the Lamborghini and rush to him, crouching down beside him. Fleming was still alive, but just barely. His face was severely lacerated from the impact as he had two black eyes and bloody nose. His arms were bruised as there were some cuts that made blood slowly gush out. He could barely move his body. He's coughing out of his mouth, whereas small amounts of blood splattered out, hitting the ends of his lips. "Now tell me, what are they planning?" Phoenix said.

Edward speaks, but just barely, "We......... don't...........

give............ out............ information."

"Really? Of course you can, a few people belonging in

your circle were brave enough to do it. You could be another

one of those people if you're willing to cooperate."

Edward make a hollow laugh, "I've...... had...... my......

share...... with....... cooperating..... for..... far..... too...... long."

Phoenix pulls out one of her daggers and clenches it

towards his neck, "Well, you're going to cooperate whether

you want to or not!"

"I would..... swallow your pride....... right now.... if you

want to know...... what's next for you."

Phoenix slowly moves the dagger away from his neck,

"Then spit it out, Fleming. Don't test my patience."

"If you knew what I went through from the start, you

would not live with yourself for the next moment after."

Phoenix gets angry and puts the dagger back towards his

neck, "Just tell us what to FUCKING EXPECT!"

"This is your only chance if you want to make it out for the next step. Russell has been telling us about you a lot." He coughs as blood comes out of his mouth. Phoenix sighs and commands Darrell, "Darrell, get up to him, make sure he survives long enough to give an answer."

Darrell stomps on the ground and gets up, "Damn it!"

"Just do it, Darrell! I don't feel comfortable about this either!" Darrell walks up to him and crouches down, pressing down on his chest to slow down the blood loss. "Now tell me, Fleming. What are you planning?"

"I'll start off with a riddle to put a staple on your mind. This will help you on your way. Towards the valley of the east, you will find a route in the land of the rising sun. But they will ride at night, where the skies are their blackest light. They will ride like the lightning in the sky, dodging lights like a thief working in the night. But it will be a race against time, unless you beat your rival in due time. Once you slip up,

they'll know who you are. But be very aware. Because once

you make an alliance, prepare to expect the retribution of

IFHR." Fleming passes away as he gags from his blood and his

eyes redden.

"Wow," Darrell said. "That's a lot to take in."

"Oh, I know it is," Russell said as they were still on his

frequency. "Now time to prepare for your fourth trial."

"We're not going anywhere until you tell us where to

go," Phoenix said.

"Then I guess you'll be shit out of luck just sitting around.

I used Fleming as an accomplice to spread the word of

mouth. Hope you can understand riddles." Russell laughs and

dismisses.

"Shit, he dismissed!" Phoenix said. She gets up as they

both walk to the Lamborghini. "Come on, Darrell. Let's get

out of here and try to figure this riddle out before they pick us off on the spot."

An alarm suddenly sounds off throughout the base, alerting Phoenix. "That means now!" Phoenix said. Darrell quickly gets up and sprints to the car and gets inside. They propel towards the base's entrance and drive away before they could call out the agents. "Shit, that was close!" Darrell said.

Phoenix starts to get a headache as visions flash in her mind again. She starts to see the building that she pictured back at Washington, D.C. "Phoenix, what's wrong?!" Darrell said.

"There's something that jumped in my mind again."

"What is on your mind? Do you see something?"

Phoenix stops as she is surprised, "Actually, yes. I do see something."

"What do you see?"

"I pictured this when I drove us out of D.C.. I saw a

building that was in the dessert emitting a red light on its top

at night."

"What do you think it could be?"

"I honestly don't know. I had no idea I had this ability.

This just started happening. This may be a message of some

sort."

"So, are you saying you're partially psychic?"

"I would not know. I never practiced in fortune telling.

I've lost my ability to think straight, I only focused on one

goal."

Darrell enters through the plains of the mountain range

where it appears to be in the middle of nowhere. "Let's try to

decipher this riddle before we get into the jet," Darrell said.

"The valley of the east would be in the eastern

hemisphere. The land of the rising sun is a popular phrase

referring to the country of Japan," Phoenix said.

"But they will ride at night, where the skies are their

blackest night. Which means it will take place at night, and vehicles would be involved. It would be an oxymoron if we think horses will be involved."

"They will ride like the lightning in the sky, dodging lights like a thief working in the night. There's going to be some high speed driving involved. The lights means it will take place in a city."

"There's only one city I know that has a lot of lights in Japan."

"That would be the capital of the country."

"But it will be a race against time, unless you beat your rival in due time. It may be a race because it involves going against the clock with other people."

"Once you slip up, they'll know who you are. But be very aware. Because once you make an alliance, prepare to expect the retribution of IFHR."

Phoenix think about the last segment of the riddle. She

suddenly gasps, "We already did that."

"How? Adrian didn't betray us."

"That's the point of a riddle. You have to figure it out! We made an alliance with Russell, but we slipped up!" She grunts in anger. "Do you know what this means, Darrell? It means they know we're working with Adrian now!"

Darrell breathes heavily in shock, "Son of a bitch."

"We're heading to Tokyo, Japan. We still have to figure out who's the target. We have to notify Adrian as soon as possible."

They exit out of the mountain range and head to the nearest airport with their jet, preparing to go to Tokyo.

Chapter 12: The Streets

Tokyo, Japan, 2054 hours

Darrell and Phoenix are still flying in the obsidian skies as the jet is just above the clouds. "It looks like you're approaching a nearby airport," Adrian said.

They exit the clouds and see a lighted runway from below that emitted white and sky blue lights. "We see a runway," Phoenix said.

Darrell slowly pushes the yolk down to carefully descend. As they approach the runway with an altitude of about a thousand feet, he releases the undercarriage and flies through the runway. The wheels of the undercarriage skid on the newly paved asphalt.

They stop moving on the runway as they exit out of the jet. After Darrell opens the rear latch, they jump down to ground level. They sprint to the Lamborghini and exit out of the airport.

They head into the downtown area of Tokyo as the streets are lit up from the buildings and streetlamps. The buildings have sponsors and company names as they were mostly in Japanese dialects. They look upon a large group of customized vehicles with varying colors and vinyls. The vehicles ranged from coupes, muscle cars, and supercars. "Looks like your intentions were right when picking up from Fleming's riddle," Adrian said.

"Looks like they're organizing a street race. All of them don't look like they came from the factory," Phoenix said.

"Well, get in there as quick as possible. They may start

the race at any moment."

Darrell turns and pulls up next to an orange Mazda with blue tribal decals and blue rims. Darrell was in shock, "How many cars are there?"

"There's thirty-six vehicles altogether," Adrian said. "I'll look through the database to find the target's name and vehicle." He scans through the computer in the auto shop and finds a match. "I found a match. He's native in the country."

"Who is it?" Phoenix said.

"His name is Takeshi Matsuo. Age: 21. Hair color: Black. Eye color: Blue. Weight: 158 pounds. He's only been a member of IFHR for about six months."

"Wow, that's our youngest and most recent target to date when it comes to their time of initiation," Phoenix said.

"He's been active in street racing long before he was recruited by IFHR. He started racing when he was seventeen years old, so he has some experience behind the wheel."

"Is there more to his background check?"

"He's been known for rebelling against authority even before he was recruited. He was caught speeding several times throughout his career and is known to shoot down his rivals during a race, sometimes killing them."

"What vehicle does he drive?"

"He drives a dark purple Nissan GT-R with gray-white stripe decals on both sides. He also has a carbon spoiler."

"What class are they?"

"They're all elites-" Adrian suddenly gasps. "Wait a second, something's not right here."

"What's wrong?" Darrell said, alerting him and Phoenix.

"I forgot to mention that my brother's participating in that race!"

"Your brother?!" Phoenix said, surprised. "I didn't know

you had a brother! Why didn't you tell us?!"

"He used to work for the organization, but he had enough and joined the same situation that I'm in. Or as the organization coins those people as 'smugglers'."

"What vehicle does he drive?"

"He's on my map, he should be next to you. He drives a 2009 orange Mazda with blue tribal decals and a carbon spoiler. His name is Alex Wortham."

"Oh, shit!" Phoenix said, startled by the vehicles' engines revving, signaling the preparation for the race. "The race is starting!"

"Alright, please watch out for my brother! I need to see him again soon! He doesn't know that I'm still alive. Here's a couple quick things. This is a sprint race. That means from point A to B. I'll track you and my brother while you're in the race. You're yellow and he's red on my map."

"Alright." Phoenix dismisses.

A blonde haired woman holding a white flag that's

wearing a white T-shirt, shorts, and shoes walks in front of

the drivers as they still rev their engines.

"Remember from London, Darrell. You have to blend in.

Rev your engine," Phoenix said.

Darrell puts the Lamborghini in neutral and revs it as he

hears the loud, whistling V12 engine. The woman with the

flag slowly raises it until she extended her arms out to their

highest point.

As the woman quickly lets the flag down, all of the

racers, including Darrell, spin their tires and jolt past the

woman, leaving thick trails of smoke by the witnesses around

them.

Chapter 13: Rivals

Darrell gets his weapons ready as they pass one of the drivers. The drivers weave in alternating directions and pass each other as they drift to the left. Takeshi was close to first place as Adrian's brother intentionally falls back. Darrell looks in the rear view mirror, "I don't think he's even trying to race."

"Let's not worry about him right now. He probably has his own intentions against them," Phoenix said.

Some of the racers ready their weapons and fire

machine guns at each other. The metal of the vehicles was heavily armored, similar to Darrell's Lamborghini. This startles Phoenix, making her prepare her weapons. "Start shooting!" Phoenix said. Darrell activates the machine guns with the magnetism and armor piercing rounds. One of the vehicles fire at Darrell's front bumper, which was a metallic yellow Honda coupe. Darrell fires the machine guns at the coupe. The Honda explodes in flames in the air as the bullets ate through the rear bumper.

Darrell weaves through a couple of the racers and attempts to accelerate towards the target, but Takeshi's vehicle bolts away without giving him a chance. One of the racers attempts to ram them to the side, but Darrell barely budges.

Darrell moves ahead and shoots two of the vehicles from behind, making them explode in a fiery inferno and fly in the air. He gets in between some more of the vehicles and prepares the magnetic pulse, setting it at 23% at its power

levels. All of the opposing vehicles were in the south pole. He

activates the magnetism in the south pole as the pulse

violently pushes them apart, knocking eight vehicles out of

the race.

Suddenly, Alex Wortham is shooting at a couple of the

racers in the distance. He picks off two vehicles as he pops

out their tires, making them swerve and spin on their rims

and hit a building. Darrell and Phoenix were shocked. "Now

we can worry about him," Darrell said.

Darrell accelerates and catches up to the opponents.

There are twenty-five left in the race. They enter into a

tunnel as their vehicles' engines echo throughout it. One of

the racers puts their window down. He pulls out a shotgun

and aims at the Lamborghini. "Shit!" Phoenix yelled. "He's got

a shotgun!" Darrell abruptly turns away from the shotgun's

aim. The driver fired his weapon, but accidentally blasts the tire off of another racer, making him swerve and impact the tunnel walls.

Darrell turns again and accelerates towards the racer with the shotgun. The racer panics and turns to swerve out of the way. Darrell shoots one of the tires, making the racer go into the air. He raises the angle of the machine guns by pulling back on two yellow switches on the steering wheel and fires at the vehicle's gas tank. The vehicle explodes as the sound resonates from the narrow space of the tunnel. Darrell accelerates just in time before the totaled vehicle could impact him.

Darrell and the other racers exit the tunnel and reenter the city as the buildings' lights and lamps illuminated the streets. "Looks like Alex is on our side, but we have to take Takeshi down if we don't want our asses to become twisted metal!" Phoenix said.

Darrell accelerates with the rest of the drivers as they

are approaching a small bridge. Alex accelerates past a couple of the drivers as Darrell follows. They spook them as the drivers accelerate, causing them to shoot their machine guns from behind. "See if this vehicle has shotguns," Phoenix said.

Darrell's Lamborghini is starting to take damage to the hood, but is not significant as it only creates dents. A couple of the drivers' bullets managed to impact the windshield, creating small cracks on the side. "Shit!" Phoenix panicked. "DARRELL, HURRY!"

Darrell panics and quickly looks at the buttons while traveling at about a hundred and fifty miles per hour. He sees a button lit in red that's shows an icon of a pistol with three lines exiting the gun. "This might be it," Darrell said.

"Activate the armor-piercing, let's take care of these motherfuckers," Phoenix said.

Darrell presses the buttons and focuses on three vehicles

on the targeting screen. Once the screen locked on a target with a yellow reticle, he fired two loud rounds of titanium-grade shotgun shells with sharpened tips and blasts through the driver's rear bumper. "Shoot him again," Phoenix said. "Try their tires."

Darrell moves the shotgun towards the back tires and blasts a large hole through them, partially melting through and cutting through the rim. The vehicle creates sparks as it jumps on its damaged rim. Due to the high rate of speed, the vehicle gives in by jumping in the air from the built-up friction of its rim. Darrell aims at the gas tank and directly fires through it, exploding as the fire consumes the vehicle.

Darrell accelerates to another vehicle and moves the shotgun to its side. He fires a couple rounds at the front passenger seat, piercing through the door and through the driver inside it. Alex also uses the shotguns in his weapon and destroys the vehicle in front of him. Darrell accelerates further until he is beside Alex.

They both accelerate at full throttle and switch to their machine guns. "Looks like there's something different here," Darrell said, looking at the buttons by the weapons. He specifically looks at the ammunition types. There's a button with a flame accompanied by three curved lines. He presses it along with the magnetism and armor-piercing options. The button represented the heat ammunition, signifying more heat and it creates more damage to objects.

Darrell locks on to one of the five vehicles on his target screen. He fires rapidly at one of the vehicles and cuts right through the metal of the rear bumper. The vehicle flies in the air, creating a raging fireball. Him and Alex shoot at two vehicles and pick them off, making them spin out of control and impacting the barriers of the bridge. They both accelerate to the other two vehicles. Darrell and Phoenix were sweating as the situation grows more tense. As Darrell and Alex approach the sides of the drivers, they ram them and knock them out of place. They shoot them afterwards, penetrating through their windows and puncturing their tires and rims. The drivers spin out of control and impact the barriers.

There are fourteen vehicles left. Darrell accelerates and switches to the shotgun with armor-piercing rounds and he shoots one of the driver's tires, causing the driver to swerve and hit the other driver. Darrell shoots again at one of the driver's other tires, making it go in the air. He accelerates under the totaled vehicle just before it could impact the Lamborghini's roof.

They exit the bridge and enter back into the city limits. They see a group of roads that split and curve in different directions. Darrell goes up an entrance ramp that goes to the right as Alex goes in the opposite of him. Darrell sees Takeshi going on a different road from Alex. "Shit, we're losing him!"

Phoenix said. "Looks like we're splitting up for right now. He has his share, we have ours."

"We have six vehicles to take out!" Darrell said. "Hang on, we're about to touch grass! It looks like a small park!"

Darrell speeds into a park with a few sidewalks and a few tall trees. Him and the six vehicles were weaving around the sidewalks and trees as they fly through at speeds of around a hundred miles per hour. "Damn it, we can't take them down around here!" Phoenix said, frustrated from the terrain they were currently on.

Suddenly, they catch a break as they come out of the trees. There was a ledge that had a barbed wire fence to prevent people from climbing over. The racers abruptly turn towards the direction of the fence and break through it, making clanging noises. They exit the park and jump down to enter back on the road. Sweat is pouring down Darrell's forehead as his heart is racing from the situation. "Hang on!"

Darrell said. He abruptly turns towards the fence and jumps down onto the road. He was approaching a barrier on the side of the road, so he turned the steering wheel hard enough to drift away from it. The drift was long as the tires screeched loudly and emitted a large cloud of smoke.

Darrell straightens the Lamborghini onto a lane and accelerates to catch up with the racers. As he switches to fourth gear, he slows down to drive beside the racers. The rate of the vehicles' speed is still pacing at a rapid rate.

They enter a small tunnel as Darrell and Phoenix aggressively look at the other racers. They keep a steady pace as they were in a drag race. "Don't make a move just yet, they're probably wanting you to something. Wait until we're almost out of the tunnel," Phoenix said. "Ready your weapons now. I don't care what you use, just do it."

They are fastly approaching the end of the tunnel. "Accelerate!" Phoenix yelled.

Darrell slams the throttle as the vehicle jolts past the racers. He activates the rear machine guns with the modifications still online and fires at one of the vehicles on the target screen. After the racer's vehicle explodes in flames, he works his way around a couple other racers. The bullets are ripping though the fine metal of the racers' vehicles, igniting them into flames. Darrell deactivates the machine guns and switches to the rear shotguns. He locks on to one of the three remaining vehicles. He fires at the vehicle with the heated, armor piercing rounds and explodes while flying in the air with scraps of twisted metal. He aims at the two other vehicles and destroys them, making them spin out of control and impacting the barriers, rendering them useless.

"Alex is still chasing down five vehicles, we still have to find Takeshi," Darrell said.

They suddenly see five racers emerge from the side along with Alex pursuing them. "Shit!" Phoenix said, surprised while no reaction time was given from the appearance of the racers. Alex and the racers keep driving on the same road he was driving in and starts shooting at the racers, taking them out and disappearing from Darrell and Phoenix's sight. "Our focus is on Takeshi now."

Darrell keeps driving as he looks around the city block. He looks in the rear view mirror to see what he thinks is a lighted flare in the distance. The light was getting bigger as it was drawing in closer to Darrell. "Shit, it's a missile!" Darrell yelled. He looks down below the missile to see Takeshi's vehicle fastly approaching. Takeshi activates the nitrous and drastically increases speed to gain distance with Darrell in a matter of seconds. Phoenix panics and looks around. "There's a tunnel right over there, take it!" she yelled.

Takeshi was now caught up with Darrell as he was about a second behind him. He fires another missile after Darrell enters the tunnel, destroying the lights that were within the blast radius of the missile.

Takeshi drifts into the tunnel and continues to pursue Darrell. He fires another missile at the side, barely missing the Lamborghini. Darrell swerves to the opposite of the blast radius, dodging the explosion.

They exit the tunnel and reenter the view of the night skies. Darrell sees another tunnel to the side, but there was no lighting, just pitch black darkness. He makes a hard turn into the tunnel and turn on his headlights. Takeshi was still right behind them as he shines his headlights behind Darrell.

"What's he doing?" Phoenix said. Takeshi switches to another ballistic weapon type. He fires a charged projectile as it hisses and flies through midair. Darrell panics as the projectile was coming closer, but it impacted the ceiling. The projectile exploded on impact and had a larger blast radius, destroying the brick material into fragments. This also caused the tunnel to shake from the shock wave.

Suddenly, the tunnel's interior starts to crumble down from the entrance and the center. "Shit, he used a mortar!" Darrell yelled.

"Fire one back! If he's an elite, then you must have it, too!" Phoenix said.

Darrell accelerates and looks down to feverishly look for a ballistic weapon. He pressed the button that had a smoke cloud with a target reticle, activating the mortar for the rear as it pointed at Takeshi. "Put him in his place," Phoenix said boldly.

Darrell moves the barrel upward and aims it at the ceiling. He fires the mortar and blasts the bricks off as the debris rains down on Takeshi, totaling his Nissan. The ceiling turns to rubble as it starts to bury Takeshi, crushing him from the weight of it inside his vehicle.

The ceiling keeps collapsing as it follows Darrell. "Go faster, we have to get out of this tunnel!" Phoenix yelled. He accelerates and opens the flap in the center console

containing the button for the nitrous system. He presses it as

the vehicle's speed increases drastically, losing distance with

the crumbling tunnel. Blue flames come out of the exhausts.

Darrell and Phoenix's bodies are pushed against the seats

from the force of the speed as the Lamborghini travels at a

blistering one hundred and seventy miles per hour.

They see Alex fly past the tunnel as he had no racers to

pursue. "There's Alex!" Phoenix said. Darrell drives out of the

tunnel just in time before the interior was completely buried

in its own material. "Stop the car!" Phoenix yelled. He thrusts

the brake as the tires screech loudly, pushing around towards

the dashboard from the sudden deceleration.

The Lamborghini comes to a complete stop as they look

around in an attempt to spot Alex. They see his vehicle, but

he's far in the distance, only to turn onto another block in the

city.

"Shit, we lost him!" Phoenix yelled.

"We have to get our car fixed before we head out," Darrell said.

"Hmm, looks like you're taking this game a little too far," Russell said through the communicator.

"We're just getting started," Phoenix said.

"Oh, really? It looks like you need a little bit of more practice since your last training session." Russell laughs devilishly.

"We don't need training, we can take care of ourselves!"

"I've caught you communicating with Adrian back at Brazil. That's a big infraction in the Trials, you broke one of the rules."

Darrell and Phoenix gasp in surprise. "His voice got caught in between the frequencies. His voice was distorted through my communication system. Do you think I would be that damn stupid after working with IFHR for five years?"

Russell continued.

"Yeah, so what if he's helping us? At least he has the damn courtesy to help! He's not mentally numb and heartless like you are!" Phoenix said.

"But being heartless is a requirement in the organization. He didn't have that requirement. Now, we're going to have to step things up a knotch since you two decided to behave like rebellious, disobedient children!"

"What could you do that's so bad? Are you going to keep sending vehicles and your pathetic henchmen after us? This shit is getting too easy if that's the case."

"I'm not going to tell you anything about important information anymore now. I'll keep telling you the targets' names and the locations, but I will be more limited about their backgrounds."

"YOU WEREN'T GOOD ENOUGH ANYW-" Phoenix was interrupted as Darrell yelled at her. "Phoenix, calm down!"

Darrell yelled.

Russell laughed in an evil manner, "You keep up that attitude, miss. Or else you two will suffer even more. Oh, yeah, that's right, we want you to suffer!" Russell dismisses.

"Shit, now what are we going to do?!" Phoenix yelled.

"I don't know, but let me tell you something," Darrell said. "You need to learn how to be quiet at certain points because it will only make matters worse!"

"Well, Darrell, I can't FUCKING help it!" He knows we're working with Adrian now and it is most likely going to get worse now!"

"Well, no shit!"

Phoenix looks disgusted, "You know what? Why don't you try losing someone you love dearly? Why don't you walk in my shoes?"

"You guys alright?" Adrian said through the communicator.

"Not really, we just got done having a heated argument,"
Darrell said.

"What's going on?"

"Russel knows about us now," Phoenix said.

"Damn it! I knew this would happen!" Adrian yelled.
They could hear him punch the computer desk back at the
auto shop. "How's the car doing?"

"It needs work, a lot of dents and some bullet holes are
around the vehicle. The windshield's partially damaged,"
Darrell said.

"Alright, I'm going to find a good auto services place that
could take care of your vehicle within a couple days. It's going
to be far from where you're at to avoid arousing suspicion."

Adrian scans the map for auto services locations within a
two hundred mile range. "Shit, this is unbelievable!" he
yelled, thinking about when Russell discovered their
whereabouts. "Alright, I found a location within a hundred

and twenty-nine miles from here. It'll be away from the city

limits. The people in that place specifically work on your type

of vehicle. I guess this isn't the only country that has

smugglers with different races and ethnicities. It'll be in the

rural areas in the middle of nowhere."

"Alright, we'll try to find it," Darrell said.

"Good, because we have to stay under the radar more

often now. I'll be here to help, but the coordinates should

connect to the vehicle's GPS." Adrian dismisses.

Darrell downloads the route map on the GPS after

Adrian's selected destination appears on the screen. They

cruise through the city to eventually find their way to the

auto services shop.

Chapter 14: Family Ties

Darrell and Phoenix head into a secluded area where there are small hills and bridges that were scattered across the landscape. "That's where my brother should be hiding out," Adrian said.

Darrell keeps driving until they see a large building that was allegedly the size of a warehouse. It was lit up on all corners of the building. "That should be the place," Phoenix said.

As they approach the warehouse, they park in front of a

garage door. The garage door opens automatically as there was nobody around it. Darrell pulls into the warehouse and parks in there. The warehouse's interior was partially lit in scattered spots as there were work stations that each served a different purpose.

"Close the door!" a man yelled. The door closed quickly behind them. Darrell and Phoenix couldn't locate the man. They walked around to see a few men in black welding outfits walking to various stations. They were all native to Japan. "Hey, sir?" Darrell said. He was talking to a man that had black short hair with a stocky build. He wore a black T-shirt with blue jeans and black shoes. He was standing in front of a desk that was lighted above it. There were various tools laid out that looked sleek as they didn't appear to what people would see at a hardware store. There were also several buttons and computers that appeared to be advanced than its present time. "We have a car that needs fixed."

Darrell turns around and saw Alex's vehicle raised on a platform that's ready for repair and bodywork. The man turns around and faces Darrell and Phoenix. The man talked in a deep voice, "How may I help you?"

Darrell hesitated as him and Phoenix were nervous, "We just got out of a race. A couple of them almost shot through the window."

The man just looks at them for few moments, "Let's take a look at what you're trying to tell me." They walk to the garage door to check out their Lamborghini. The man walks around to see the vehicle's overall damage. "Hmm, looks like your vehicle needs a lot of work. The tires are alright, need to fix the windshield, especially the bodywork. The whole body's pretty much shot with dents and holes."

"Do you know how to fix this, and if so, how long do you think it will take?" Phoenix said.

"Actually, I do. I share the same blood as Adrian."

Darrell and Phoenix were shocked by his statement. Phoenix said, "Are you-"

"Yes, I am who you think I am. I'm Alex Wortham. I'm worked on elite vehicles for quite some time. There's nothing we can't fix."

"How long have you been in the organization before you decided to become a smuggler?"

"Just as long as Adrian has been out, for almost a year as of today. I'm just as tangled in the situation as he is right now."

"How did you manage to get out alive?" Darrell said.

"Adrian and I were separated because we were family. They don't allow bonds to be made in IFHR, which pissed me off in the long run. I went through three years of hell while working in there."

"What was your side of the story?" Phoenix said.

"These men in here, the five of us, we may originate

from other countries, but we've managed to communicate at a level." Alex makes a gesture, telling Darrell and Phoenix to come closer. Alex says quietly, "They're starting to speak our native language, but I didn't have to teach them. They pretty much learned on their own." Darrell and Phoenix back away as he was done talking quietly. "But here's my side to the story. Around a week before they headed off into New York City in 2020, my men and I have been negotiating an escape plan to get out of there."

Alex goes into one of his flashbacks. He continues, "We were in a large room where agents were surrounding each corner. It was a room that was similar to this, only nicer, cleaner, and bigger. Large enough to fit at least three hundred vehicles." The room was bright white as there were platforms that carried vehicles for working on. "As the alarm sounded, the agents startled, including us. One of them said, 'Come on, the targets are out again!' The five of us just stood there. 'You better fucking listen to us, don't fucking start rebelling. You know what will happen if you do,' the agent warned us. A couple of them stayed and walked up to us. They pulled out their pistols and aimed it at us, thinking their so damn tough to puncture our fucking skulls. But what they didn't realize is that in our business attire, we had a few tricks up our sleeves."

"What'd you do?" Phoenix said.

"With no reaction time, we pulled out our weapons. A couple of us had submachine guns and fed them with lead, killed them right on the spot. They didn't see it coming at all. They died before they even touched ground. So I yelled at my men, 'Come on, let's go. We're not far from an exit! Grab their weapons and find some more! We each need vehicles and tools, too! We're booking out of here!' Weapons can be found anywhere within the organization. There was a small room next to the garage we were in and opened it. Hundreds of weapons were on display in that long hallway. We broke

the glass and grabbed the weapons only to see a few agents

budge open the door in the distance. The agents were

running towards us. 'Let 'em have it!' I yelled." They fired at

the agents as the bullets pierced cleanly through their bodies,

killing them instantly. "We bolted out of the weapons room

and hopped in any vehicle that wasn't occupied. My vehicle

was the orange Mazda, one of the only sports cars in the

garage that didn't fit in the supercar category, but I could tell

it was definitely an elite type when I looked inside."

Alex drove around the platforms and towards the large

garage door. He got out of the Mazda and overrode the

security pad with his communicator. "As the garage door was

opening, more agents came out from the entrance of the

garage. All of the men except for me were in the vehicles.

They started shooting their machine guns, which made me

bolt back into my vehicle. Missed me by mere inches. We all

activated our vehicles' weapons and shot at them as we floored it out of the garage."

"Did you see Adrian?" Darrell said.

Alex was starting to feel sad, but didn't cry, "No, we just drove away, didn't think about anything else. I never saw him again since." He exits his flashback, "We customized our vehicles' bodies, so that way we could stay under and hopefully start anew. But they figured us out too quickly. They've been looking for us here for a while. We've just been fighting and running ever since. And that's how we ended up to where we are now. I don't think we can survive like this much longer if things don't change quickly."

"They're still after us, too. Russell went rogue, did you hear about that?" Phoenix said.

"Yeah, that crooked bastard. I knew he wasn't right from the start! He always had a thirst for inflated power. That's all he wanted was to feel that sense grow to a consuming level."

"Yeah, he's a madman," Darrell said.

"What's he doing with you guys?"

"We're still the most wanted in the organization, they've still been tracking us down ever since Darrell was picked for cancellation. They're after me, too, because I helped him escape," Phoenix said. She whispers, "He's making us do the Trials."

"What's that?" Alex whispers.

"We're given ten of them in which we have to kill a target in order to regain our freedom, but I know that's not what he's going to do."

"How far?"

"We're on trial four."

Alex sighs, "Alright, we'll get your vehicle fixed in close to pristine condition within a few days. We should have enough metal left specifically designed for a couple elite vehicles. We're running low on bulletproof glass as we only have a couple sets left."

Alex turns around and sees the men welding parts as showers of sparks come out of the burners. He takes both of his hands into his mouth and whistles, grabbing the men's attention. "Hey, we just got an elite vehicle in the shop. We need to fix this one within a few days. It's an emergency situation!" he yells.

The men run to the tool desk that's located opposite from the other one and head towards the damaged Lamborghini. The men yell at them, making Darrell and Phoenix move out of the way, startling them. "Just ignore it, it's an emergency situation, right?" Alex said.

"Do you have any place to sleep?" Phoenix said.

"Yes, it's located on the other side of this shop. It's still in the warehouse, though. I'll show you around."

They walk away from the men inspecting the Lamborghini and walk past the platforms. They stop at a door as Alex opens it with the hand scanner. The room revealed metallic walls and beds with blankets and pillows. "It may be uncomfortable, but you'll get used to it after a while," Alex said. "I would get as much sleep if I were you. We have extra clothes for you if you need it."

"Thanks, and it was nice to meet you," Phoenix said.

"We'll talk later, we don't have time to do the meet and greet tonight."

Darrell and Phoenix walk into the room as Alex closes the door. They withdraw their weapons and place them on shelves next to them. They then get ready to sleep for the night and close their eyes.

Chapter 15: Brand-spanking New

April 2, 2021

0917 hours

Darrell and Phoenix wake up after four days of hiding with Alex. Phoenix gets up from her bed and reequips her weapons. She walks to the door, but realizes she can't open it with the hand scanner. Alex opens the door as Darrell just awakens and sits up from his bed. "Are you guys ready to hit the road?" Alex said.

"Yes, just when we get all of our weapons ready," Phoenix said. "Is the car fixed?"

"I think you guys'll have to see for yourselves."

Darrell equips his weapons from the shelf as him and Phoenix walk out of the sleeping room. "I would look away from the light if I were you," Alex warned them. The men were welding parts together as the burners emitted a bright blue light. Darrell and Phoenix continued to follow Alex to their Lamborghini.

As they stopped in front of the Lamborghini, Darrell and Phoenix were surprised from the appearance of the vehicle. "Looks just good as brand-spanking new, doesn't it?" Alex said, giving a proud smile.

"You guys did a good job, thank you," Darrell said.

"We did our best. We didn't have to mess with the interior. It wasn't affected. We also changed the oil to give you a performance boost."

"This vehicle has enough performance, don't you think?" Darrell said jokingly.

"Your car's oil was going bad. Plus you need all the speed

you can get for the situation you guys are in. I'll open the garage door for you."

He runs to the tool desk that's closest to the garage door and holds down a red button. The door opens slowly as Darrell and Phoenix get in the Lamborghini.

Darrell rolls down the window as Alex walks up to their vehicle. "Thanks for the help," Darrell said.

Alex puts his arms on the window. "No, problem, but thank my brother mostly. He's the one that's mostly helping you through this. You haven't got to know me yet."

"Why are you being hard on yourself? You don't seem like a bad person."

"I'm not, I have a self-deprecating sense of humor. Sometimes it's good medicine to have a little humor when things go bump in the night." Alex smiles. He took his arms off of the window. "Well, I guess it's time for you to head out. The more you wait, the less time you have to do what you need to do.”

“But, what about you?” Phoenix said.

“We’ll meet each other again in due time. Give greetings to Adrian for me.”

“We’ll make sure to touch base with him. We always do,” Darrell said.

Darrell and Phoenix waved goodbye to Alex as he did the same. “It was nice meeting you!” Phoenix yelled.

“My pleasure,” Alex said.

Darrell drives out of the garage and makes his way into the dense forests of Motosu-michi as the skies were clear with no clouds present. “Alright, time for the fifth trial, the halfway stretch of my test,” Russell said through the communicator.

“Why don’t you try something different for once than trying to taunt us with your false sense of power?” Phoenix said.

"Oh, I promise you, it will be very different this time, I guarantee it!" Russell laughs. "Your next target will be in the city of Dubai in the United Arab Emirates. His name is Ravindra Varman, native to the country. Age: 31. Hair color: Black. Skin color: Pallor-Caucasian. Weight: 193 pounds. He's been active in IFHR for three years. This is very similar to the previous trial, but let's just say things will be more edgy in this one."

"And what do you mean by that?" Phoenix said, angry.

"What did I say before? I'm not going to tell you specifics anymore, since you decided to do things your way."

"You were never good at telling specifics anyway."

"You will see what's coming for you when you arrive. The city's is so nice to be decimated." Russell laughs and dismisses.

After a couple of hours of driving, Darrell and Phoenix arrive at the airport. They place the vehicle in the jet and take off to enter the rich and advanced establishment of Dubai.

Chapter 16: Paradise

April 2, 2021

Dubai, United Arab Emirates, 2147 hours

Darrell and Phoenix arrive at an airport nearest in the city area of Dubai. After they exit out of the airport and into a highway, they see the bright, vibrant, skyline, making its landmarks stand out. One of them was the Burj Khalifa, which is the world's tallest skyscraper to date, a height of around three thousand feet. As they entered into the city limits, what mostly captured their vision were the several skyscrapers and the transportation choices. This was the city of the future.

The overall city composition was clean as the technology

levels were about ten years ahead of present day. The transportation was the most advanced out of all of the other countries as they were mostly all high performance vehicles.

"What's the news?" Adrian said through the communicator.

"We just entered Dubai. Looks like paradise here, at least for now," Phoenix said.

"Yeah, the city's technology's ahead of its time."

"Our target's name is Ravindra Varman. We still don't know his whereabouts yet. Motherfucker's pushing it this time."

"Hold on, I'll try to locate him on the map." Adrian looked up Ravindra's profile to locate him. He wasn't anywhere to be found. "Shit, I can't locate him!"

Suddenly, three supercars emerge from a city block and drift in front of them, blowing smoke in front of Darrell's windshield. They then drive away in the distance. "What the fuck, assholes?!" Phoenix yelled.

The supercars suddenly fire a few machine gun bullets from their rears at the Lamborghini, startling Darrell and Phoenix. The bullets made them become more alert. "Looks like we have company," Phoenix said.

Darrell floors it and immediately switches to second gear as he does an intense burnout. He immediately accelerates and weaves around the traffic to pursue the three supercars. He readies the machine guns and fires at one of them. "Two can play at that game!" Darrell said while switching to another gear. He continues firing and blows out one of their tires, making the supercar run on the sparks. He switches to the shotgun and uses the heated ammunition. He fires a couple rounds through the windshield and kills the driver as they saw parts of the seats tear apart and blood splattering on the windshield. The car swerved and T-bones into one of the commuters, destroying both vehicles.

Darrell switches back to the machine guns and activates

the magnetism and armor-piercing rounds. Both of the vehicles fire their rear weapons at Darrell as he locks onto one of the supercars. He fires at it and destroys the vehicle, making it pop its tires and fly in the air. He accelerates and delivers the same fate to the third vehicle.

Two more supercars suddenly drift onto the road in Darrell's rear view mirror and pursue him. "Shit, we have more!" Darrell yelled.

While accelerating, there was a row of Dubai police vehicles ahead of them. The police vehicles were also comprised mostly of supercars. "Just zip past them, they're no use!" Phoenix yelled. He turns the Lamborghini onto a lane and speeds in between the police as the supercars follow him.

After they pass the police, they all sounded their sirens as there were five of them. They accelerate and start to pursue the supercars and Darrell. "Oh, great, what the hell are the cops going to do?!" Phoenix yelled. The supercars

fired their machine guns at the rear bumper of the

Lamborghini, Darrell activates the rear shotguns and fire at

one of the supercars, obliterating a portion of its front

bumper. He fires again and pops the front tires, causing it to

fly in the air and barely missing the police. He turns the

shotgun towards the other supercar and delivers the same

fate as it misses impacting the police by only a few feet.

"Takes care of that," Phoenix said. The police are still

traveling at blistering speeds. Phoenix glances in the rear

view mirror and looks at the police vehicles. She tenses up,

"Accelerate, Darrell! They're right on our tail!" Darrell goes

full throttle as he weaves through traffic. "Why aren't they

stopping?!"

Suddenly, without warning, one of the police vehicles

fires a couple machine gun rounds at the Lamborghini. Darrell

and Phoenix were startled as the bullets came in contact.

"Shit!" Phoenix panicked. "Get your weapons ready!" They're fucking decoys, damn it!"

The police decoys resume the hot pursuit as they attempt to apprehend Darrell and Phoenix.

Chapter 17: Decoy

2209 hours

The decoys line up side by side as one of them fire at the Lamborghini. The same decoy that fired accelerated and was going for the rear. Phoenix looks back and panics, "Darrell, do something!" Darrell switches to the rear shotguns and activates the heated ammunition. He aims at the center of the decoy's front bumper, showing the Koenigsegg emblem. He fires and blasts a hole through the metal and into the interior, instantly killing the agent inside. He then blows out the agent's tires, making him skid on the rims.

The four remaining decoys separate and weave around traffic to catch up with Darrell. One of them drives beside him. Two of the decoys fire their machine guns at the Lamborghini. Darrell switches to the machine guns with the armor-piercing and magnetism options.

While Darrell was firing, the decoy beside him nudges him, shaking the interior and startling Phoenix. This caught Darrell off guard. While angry and provoked, she rolls down her window and readies her assault rifle, aiming at a tire. She fires multiple rounds, shredding the tire while pieces of rubber and steel come off. She then shoots through the decoy's window and penetrates it as a couple bullets travel through the agent's head, spilling a few brain fragments on the passenger seat. "Let's blow this one out of the pack," Phoenix said brazenly. She fires through the door again as it chips through the decoy's interior. The bullets eventually work its way towards the engine as its a mid-engine sports car. The bullets penetrate through the modified engine and ignites the vehicle into flames, releasing a small shock wave.

The decoy driving towards the totaled vehicle quickly weaves away from it and continues to pursue Darrell. One of the decoys accelerates and attempts to immobilize him by knocking him in the side, but Darrell decelerates just in time. The decoy was now in front of him. "Finish them," Phoenix said. Darrell fires the machine guns at the decoy in front of him. He switches to the shotguns and blasts a couple rounds through the interior, destroying the vehicle and making it fly in the air.

There are now only two decoys left as they were in front of Darrell. They both accelerate and activate their nitrous systems, emitting gold-yellow flames from their exhaust tips. "Shit!" Phoenix yelled. "Darrell, step on it! Go full throttle!"

Darrell accelerates and now pursues the decoys.

"Doesn't make sense for the police to become the mouse,"

Darrell said.

"Maybe they're planning something. Make them go up in smoke." After weaving through traffic, Darrell fires the machine guns in a long distance. Only a few rounds hit one of the decoys. Darrell tries to lock on one of them, but the screen couldn't pick up the target. "Shit, can't get to them!" Darrell yelled.

"Go faster, use the nitrous system!"

"Phoenix, how the FUCK are we supposed to get through these people while going two hundred and-"

"Just do it! There's a clear zone up ahead!"

Darrell exits the traffic. He flips open the flap on the center console and presses the red button to activate the nitrous system. The vehicle suddenly experiences a sudden jolt of acceleration and speed, making them pull back on their seats. He catches up with the decoy that he tried to take out. He fires again as he chips away at the rear bumper and tires.

The tires blow up and create sparks. He fires through the rear

window and kills the agent inside it.

Phoenix spots the decoy by the side in the distance, but

is too far away. From her estimate, he appeared to be about

a couple hundred yards away. "Darrell, step on it, we can't let

him get away!" Phoenix yelled. Darrell turns away from the

totaled decoy and works his way around traffic.

Darrell catches up and enters in the same lane as the

decoy. He tailgates him, making him gain distance faster

towards the decoy. "Blast him off the road," Phoenix said. He

fires the machine guns at one of the rear tires. He then

switches to the shotguns and aims at the rear window. He

fires multiple rounds at different areas of the vehicle,

destroying the rear bumper, tires, and the window. The

decoy gave way as it flew in the air. Darrell moved the

weapon upwards and fired at the chassis and gas tank. The

vehicle ignited in flames and created a small shock wave in

the air. Darrell accelerates under the decoy just before it wass able to come in contact with the Lamborghini. The vehicle touches ground and impacts a commuter. "Shit, that was close!" Darrell said.

"Where's the target?" Adrian said through the communicator.

Phoenix was reminded, "Shit, we still have to find Ravindra!"

Suddenly, a fleet of vehicles drift in their way by the distance, making Darrell panic and slam on the brakes. He comes to a complete stop as more vehicles come in from the side. They were making the formation of a circle. They were blocking traffic in all directions as a few honked their horns. The vehicles had armor plates attached around their bodies as they matched the color of their car paint. There were fifty vehicles surrounding him. Darrell was in the center of the circle. "What the fuck is going on?" Darrell said.

"Don't get too comfortable, Darrell. I knew they were planning something. This is way different than the incident in Tokyo," Phoenix said. They notice a gap in the circle as it was the distance of two car lengths. They see a chrome white metallic high performance car pull up slowly to the circle, filling the gap. The vehicle was a Porsche coupe that had multiple armor plates on its body and chrome rims.

The Porsche pulls out of the circle and pulls up until it is nose to nose with the Lamborghini. The Lamborghini was surrounded with dents, holes, and scrapes, but still operated like new. The Porsche briefly flashes its headlights. "Shit," Phoenix said.

"What?" Darrell said.

"Flash your lights like they did, that means we have to get out of the car." Darrell sighs and flashes his lights.

Chapter 18: Secrets

2221 hours

A man in IFHR attire opens the car door and stands on the road. Darrell and Phoenix get out of the car and walk up to the man. The profile Russell gave matched the same description as Ravindra. "Wow, it's a shame that police have to be involved in this," Ravindra said.

"Ha, please, they were decoys. You think I would fall for that one?" Phoenix said.

"You're in for a reckoning." He looks around and waves his arm out. "Look around you, you're surrounded in every direction."

"And I should be scared, why? I've killed your kind one too many times before. I'm so used to this," Phoenix smiles brazenly.

"Alright," Ravindra also smiles brazenly. "Here's a question I want to ask."

Phoenix pulls out one of her pistols and aims it at Ravindra's forehead, "Do you really think I want to hear what you have to fucking say? You're starting to piss me off already!"

"Everyone, ready your weapons!" All of the vehicles surrounding them had machine guns come out of their front bumpers, aiming at Darrell and Phoenix. Darrell had sweat pouring down his face as Phoenix was shocked, but stood her ground. "How rude of you to interrupt me. If you do it again, we'll kill you on the spot right now."

"Even if you kill us now, I'll still remember you all as

pathetic fucking cowards."

"You can call us out as many names as you want, you still don't know what we're about. After all, we do have a homicidal lust for power." Ravindra clenches his fists. "And it feels FUCKING GREAT!!!" He breathes heavily.

Suddenly, Ravindra pulls out a remote control device that shines in silver with blue metallic buttons. "So, I have this device for the next step in this trial."

"What the hell is that?" Darrell said.

Ravindra speaks menacingly, "For years, there was a construction zone that was established below this city in 1997 without any knowledge. There were no witnesses. They couldn't find any traces." There were five buttons on the remote control. He cunningly smiles, "And when I press one of these buttons, it will activate a portion of the masterpiece under this fine settlement. But when I press the button on the bottom, I will activate it all at once, and it will destroy a large amount of this fine and delicate city." He looks around and sees the tall buildings lighting up the street as his anger and arrogance is blinding him. "Such a pure and beautiful investment. *Oh*, how I'm going to miss this city in its entirety." He sniffs the air and breathes heavily, but slowly. "Releasing that feeling makes it so much worth it in the end," Ravindra said.

"You'll never get away with this!" Phoenix yelled. Her and Darrell charge at him, but one of the vehicles in the circle fire a couple rounds from their machine guns, barely missing them both. They were startled as they stopped running. They were face to face with Ravindra now. He pulls out a pistol and aims it at Phoenix. "Good," Ravindra said. "You're listening for once." He puts his thumb on the bottom of the device. "We're self-admittedly mad people. We all should be in the psych ward, but that's not enough for them to fill all of us, isn't it?"

"You wouldn't dare!" Phoenix yelled.

"Watch me." Ravindra smiles nefariously and presses the bottom button. No effect. "What?" Darrell said. "Nothing happened."

"Looks like your batteries are dead," Phoenix said as she was about to pull the trigger on Ravindra.

Suddenly, the ground starts shaking like an earthquake, slightly knocking Ravindra, Darrell and Phoenix off balance. The shake caused some of the vehicles to sound their alarms. The road was being broken apart within a twenty-mile radius. Ravindra shakes his head and folds his arms, "You seriously lack patience." Curved and cyan lighted transparent walls were rising up from the damage road as it destroys the buildings and vehicles surrounding it. "What the hell is going on?!" Darrell yelled.

"I don't know!" Phoenix yelled. They were in shock as they were overwhelmed from the sudden events. The walls surround the circle of agents' vehicles as the walls continue to rise. They feel the road push upward below them. The construction rises upward to about five hundred feet in the air. The construction revealed itself to be a dome. There was a platform below the asphalt as it was accompanied by a steel twenty-foot stand from below the city. The area from the dome is now a sinkhole. The people below the ground were screaming and crying in terror as they saw the vehicles get damaged and the buildings surrounding it collapse.

The stand holding the asphalt slams down back into ground so fast, the vehicles were left in the air. The vehicles, Darrell, Phoenix, and Ravindra begin freefalling as Darrell and Phoenix scream in terror. The platform was quickly rising back up as they land on it after a ten foot drop. They were crouched down as they were breathing heavily. The construction formed into a spherical shape. "Wow, you guys need to get out more," Ravindra taunted. "Your hell is just beginning. You're the first to test this out for us. Welcome to the Dome. Let the trials resume, you're only halfway there."

Ravindra walks back to his vehicle as Darrell and Phoenix sprint to the Lamborghini. They get in the vehicle. "What do you think this could be?" Darrell said.

"Don't know, definitely not what I pictured at D.C.," Phoenix said.

There was a timer in red digital lighting above them, starting at ten seconds. "This may be an amplified version of destruction derby," Phoenix said.

As the timer goes down to five seconds, all of the vehicles rev their engines. "Five....," Phoenix said. Darrell was holding a steady note in his vehicle to get a good start. "Four.... three.... two.... one."

The numbers turned green as all of the vehicles circled around the Dome in order to take down and ambush Darrell and Phoenix. The fifth trial has begun.

Chapter 19: The Dome

Darrell slammed on the throttle. "Get used to the structure first," Adrian said. "Make small circles and gradually accelerate." Darrell turns and ascends as half of the fleet was in front of him. Some of the agents were shooting at his rear bumper, making him accelerate faster. He fires the shotgun and already knocks down three of the vehicles, making them fall and roll down to the platform of the Dome.

Some of the vehicles move upward towards the equator of the sphere. "Move upward, I'm going to try to take some out by the sides. You get the front and rear," Phoenix said.

She tensed her body up from the changing momentum of the vehicle. She pulls out her assault rifle and rolls down her window. "Roll your window down, too." Darrell rolls down the window on the side of the steering wheel while breathing heavily and having a tight grip on it.

The Lamborghini is slightly dropping down as he wasn't going fast enough. "Shit, we're dropping!" Darrell yelled.

"Go faster! The higher you are, the more speed it requires!" Phoenix yelled. Darrell keeps the throttle going as he climbs up to two-hundred and twenty miles per hour. Phoenix leans against the seat to prevent being sucked out of the vehicle and cocks her weapon. She moves back and fires at a couple vehicles above her. She blew out their tires and shot through their windows. They decelerate and fall down, instantly rendering them useless and totaling their vehicles. "Hold still, Darrell, this will only take a moment." A couple vehicles are turning towards Darrell as she aims at them. Just before they could impact him, she fired at the two vehicles in a split-second, knocking them out of the ordeal. "Take care of the vehicles up front, go off with a bigger bang this time!"

Darrell switches to the mortars and locks onto ten vehicles. He fires one and blasts the agents into oblivion as car parts and twisted metal are scattered everywhere. The radius created a shock wave near him. "Turn!" Phoenix yelled. He turned just in time before he could impact the totaled vehicles ahead of him. A small group of vehicles behind them fire their machine guns. Darrell switches to the rear shotguns with the heated ammunition. He fires multiple rounds, picking off a total of seven vehicles, making the count lower to twenty-eight.

Suddenly, most of the vehicles except for Darrell's and Ravindra's begin to scatter in varying directions. Some decided to change course and begin driving in a full 360°

circle, reaching to the top of the sphere and horizontally around.

The vehicles immediately started shooting at each other as they were picking themselves off in all directions. The platform started to get filled with a pile of totaled vehicles and dead agents. "Holy shit!" Darrell said. "It's every person for themselves now!" Darrell keeps driving straight around the equator of the Dome and pursues Ravindra. While accelerating, Phoenix panics and sees a few vehicles pursuing and shooting machine guns at each other from above. "LOOK OUT!" Phoenix yelled. The vehicles drive downward as one of them explodes in front of them as they missed Darrell by mere inches.

Darrell and Phoenix survived the sudden death by the skin of their teeth. There were only four vehicles left including Darrell and Ravindra. The two vehicles behind Darrell accelerate and shoot at his rear bumper. He activates the rear shotgun with the heated ammunition and fires at

them, eliminating them out of the group. They explode and

roll down the platform with the rest of the vehicles.

There was only Darrell and Ravindra now. "There's only

him now," Phoenix said. They see Ravindra accelerating at an

alarming rate. "What the hell is he doing?" Phoenix's eyes

followed with Ravindra's Porsche as he was making a circle

around the equator, making his way towards Darrell. "Shit, he

must have activated his nitrous system! Use yours!"

Darrell flips the flap for the nitrous system and activates

it. The Lamborghini is experiencing a sudden jolt of

acceleration and speed, making him and Phoenix pull back on

the seats. He could hear the loud whistle of the Porsche's

engine fastly approaching behind him. "How fast are we

fucking going?!" Phoenix yelled, gripping her arms onto the

seats.

"TWO-EIGHTY!" Darrell yelled. That was the fastest

they've pushed the vehicle to date. However, that wasn't its

top speed. Elite vehicles are capable of doing so much more.

Darrell rolls his window up as Phoenix rolls most of hers up.

Ravindra is behind them, shooting at the Lamborghini's rear.

Phoenix sees him smiling nefariously as he appeared to be

laughing. She gets aggravated, "You just keep on laughing,

bud, because there's nothing funny about living a life of

foolish pride!"

Phoenix cocks her assault rifle as Ravindra accelerates

until he's beside Darrell. "Roll your window down again,"

Phoenix said. Darrell rolls his window down halfway as she

aims at Ravindra's vehicle. "You're finished, Ravindra,"

Phoenix said boldly. She tenses up as she tries to keep control

of the weapon while the Lamborghini's operating at high

speed.

Phoenix takes a heavy, deep breath and fires at the

passenger window in Ravindra's vehicle. Darrell tenses up

and breathes heavily as Phoenix continues firing. The bullets eventually penetrate through and strike Ravindra in the jugular vein as he gags and unintentionally makes a full turn down to the platform. He hits the totaled vehicles with unforgiving force and explodes on impact, squishing his body inside and flattening the vehicle like a pancake. "Okay, you're going to have to slow down, but turn *slowly* while doing so!" Adrian said.

"You heard him, Darrell, do it!" Phoenix yelled.

Darrell slowly decelerates and turns towards the platform, eventually coming down to a cruising speed. He then puts the vehicle in a complete stop. He slowly pulls into an empty spot on the platform that's not blocked by the totaled vehicles. They had smoke emanating out of them.

Darrell and Phoenix were breathing heavily as their hearts were racing. The adrenaline got the best of them as they both felt dizzy. "I think I'm going to fucking puke,"

Darrell said.

"Me, too," Phoenix said. They rolled their windows down and stuck their heads out. They forcefully purge themselves as they vomit onto the platform. After vomiting a couple times, they calmly breathe and get back inside the car. The rear bumper was severely damaged as there were multiple dents and bullet holes around it.

The walls of the Dome slowly come down as there was only the platform with the vehicles suspended in the air. The stand holding the platform slowly pulls down until it reaches the city's ground level. Due to the sinkhole in the middle of the road, there appeared to be no way to cross the road. "Great, now how the hell are we supposed to get across?" Phoenix said, frustrated.

Suddenly, a lighted surface similar to the platform emerges from the sinkhole and connects to the platform they're on. The expanded platform was big enough for them to make it across the road.

Darrell slowly drives off of the platform and onto the road. They see people screaming and running away from the sinkhole as they cried from the devastation. "You give up yet?" Russell speaks through the communicator.

"Nope, we're just getting started," Phoenix said, smiling brazenly. "Oh, and considered our purging a souvenir for that trial. But it's not a congratulations for you, it's for us. We're still standing. Your agent's creation worked, but you didn't think we would backfire, would you?" Phoenix said.

"Oh, don't you get too comfortable, now. Just you wait, the fun is just beginning for you guys. You haven't experienced the climax of this game yet!" Russell laughs nefariously. "Now, time for the sixth trial."

"Lay it on us, don't waste our FUCKING time!" Phoenix said, growing impatient.

"The target's name is Konstantin Stankevich. He's in

Saint Petersburg, Russia. Native to the country. He's been active in IFHR for three years. Age: 28. Hair color: Black. Skin color: Tanned-Caucasian. Weight: 186 pounds. That is all I will give to you."

"Oh, we'll figure it out, I promise you that," Phoenix said, still smiling brazenly.

Russell snaps, "You know? You keep breaking the rules and you're pushing my buttons. Keep it up and you'll suffer the consequences!"

"And if we don't listen?" Phoenix said sarcastically.

"Don't you dare do it!" Russell threatened. "I'm telling you, if you keep disobeying, you don't fully know what I'm capable of!"

"Oh, yeah? Watch us, I bet you are somewhere."

"You know what? I dare you to get assistance from Adrian again. We'll see how long we can further push this envelope."

"I accept your challenge, Russell. We're one step ahead of you."

"We'll see in due time, Phoenix. We will see!" Russell laughs and dismisses.

Adrian speaks with a distorted voice, "Where's the next trial?"

"Saint Petersburg, Russia. The target is Konstantin Stankevich," Darrell said.

"Alright, I'll download his profile and give you details by the time you arrive there. How well is the car?"

"Managing, but it's seen better days," Phoenix said.

"What's the damage?"

"Rear bumper underwent several bullet holes and around the body," Darrell said.

"You're going to have to pull through on this one. I don't think this trial will involve much of vehicular combat. Your elite vehicle should be fine for a few more combat situations, but after that, I think it's done."

"Alright, we'll do the best we can," Darrell said. Adrian

dismisses.

Darrell and Phoenix head out of Dubai as they leave the

devastation caused from the Dome. They go to the airport

and take off as they prepare to go to Saint Petersburg, Russia.

Chapter 20: Roaming

April 4, 2021

Saint Petersburg, Russia, 1941 hours

After Darrell and Phoenix land at a nearby airport, they cruise around the city with the same damage from Dubai. The city overall looked vintage from the buildings. The vintage lamps lit up the streets as there were also wet roads. People were looking on and staring at the damaged Lamborghini. "Just ignore them," Phoenix said. "They're going to know soon, anyways."

"You in Saint Petersburg?" Adrian said. Phoenix switched to his frequency, "Yes, we are. We just arrived."

"I found Konstantin's background." Phoenix looks down at her communicator and looks at Konstantin's facial portrait. He had a clean cut of hair as he had a black goatee surrounding his lips. "He's one of the best known assassins in IFHR. Recently in the city, people started randomly disappearing on the streets. Authorities say that he leaves the corpses in alleyways and murders in secluded areas. The description of the deaths were usually slit throats and deep cuts through their chests."

"Where do you think he could be?" Darrell said.

"Can't find him, just keep looking, the buildings almost look the same as each other there, so it's hard to tell where to find an assassin. Try going for the city's landmarks. Remember, this will most likely not involve vehicular combat, so use yourselves as weapons. Do you guys still have enough ammo?"

"We should. I have three full magazines of the assault

rifles left. I barely used my pistols. I still have all of my daggers," Phoenix said.

"I'm still set for my pistols, only used a few bullets," Darrell said.

"Alright, good, because you might need to use your tactical strategies in this one. I think I found his coordinates," Adrian said. A red dot appears on the map back at the auto shop in Los Angeles. "For the landmarks, try the State Hermitage Museum, it's a big open place. I believe that's where Konstantin and his men are hiding."

"How can you tell?" Phoenix said.

"The vehicles used have IFHR tracking devices below them, remember?" Adrian dismisses.

Darrell and Phoenix keep roaming around the city until they work their way around the State Hermitage Museum.

Chapter 21: Unfinished Business

2003 hours

Darrell and Phoenix arrive at the entrance of the State Hermitage Museum. "Pull in slowly," Phoenix said. Darrell drives into the area outside of the museum. The perimeters of the museum was lit up all around. The open area was about the size of half of a football field. "Shit, there are vehicles already there. Those look like vehicles that IFHR would use. Let's make our way into the museum, there's another open area in the center."

Darrell pulls up to the entrance doors of the museum.

They get out of the vehicle and ready their weapons. "Stay quiet, we're not here to sight-see the exhibits," Phoenix said firmly.

They enter inside the museum and see the flawless and magnificent interior. There where pillars that supported the ceiling that contained possibly hundreds of historic and religious paintings. The pillars and floors shined around Darrell and Phoenix as they were waxed. "Looks like the coast is clear in this room. Let's try to make it towards the center. It will be a long walk from here," Phoenix said while having a tight grip on her pistol.

"Damn, this place is huge," Darrell said.

After three minutes of walking to the end of the room, they enter another one, which has a couple flights of steps that curved on both sides and sculpted ornaments scattered around. "There's nothing here, either," Phoenix said. Her and Darrell look around while readying their pistols in case of a sudden attack. Phoenix points to one of the doors. "Let's take it to my left. Let's try to stay on the first floor of this place. It may take a while for us to get through the center.

After going through several hallways and rooms, they eventually find a room that leads towards the center from outside. "This may be it," Phoenix said. "Get your weapons ready."

They both open the large doors and step into the center. They walk around the large center to see if anyone was there. The center was surrounded by the vintage architecture of the museum as it created a square around the area. Phoenix turns on her ear microphone and sets it to Adrian's frequency, "Adrian, there's nobody here."

"They're somewhere around the museum, keep looking," Adrian said.

Darrell activates his ear microphone, "We're in the center of the museum."

Suddenly, they hear doors being kicked open from the side, startling Darrell and Phoenix. "Agents, I found them!" a man said in his Russian accent.

"Where are they at?!" a strong male with a Russian accent said. They were all Russian IFHR agents.

"They're in the center!"

"Darrell, ready your weapons now!" Phoenix said quietly. She cocks her pistol and aims it at the doors the agents are in. The five agents start bolting out of the doors and walk to the center with arrogance and determination. "Ah, there you are," said Konstantin in his strong voice. He sounded arrogant. He had two swords sheathed behind his back. He was standing in the middle of the men. "Thought I'd never see your face again."

"I'm not finished with you guys just yet," Phoenix said.

"You know what? You're right, we do have our own share of unfinished business." Konstantin and his men walk up to Darrell and Phoenix, but maintain a distance from them. "That was a fair fight during the civil war in 2020. Only passed by the skin of your teeth. I bet your country's still suffering from the traumatic side to it." Konstantin laughs.

"Go ahead, keep laughing, you son of a bitch. I'm surprised that your pride hasn't got the best of you yet," Phoenix said.

"But pride is our calling, it's in our bloodline. We are all brothers and sisters of bloodlust against each other and people from the outside."

"If you were brothers and sisters, then why do you end up killing each other?" Darrell said.

"That's how we succeed when it comes to settling business in IFHR. Barrett was nothing compared to this. I hope that name rings a bell in your head, Phoenix." Konstantin laughs with no remorse.

"I know damn well who that is!" Phoenix said.

Konstantin shakes his his head and smiles, "Hmm, I see.

All of those emotions through all of that time has blinded you

in the long run. Remember New York City?"

"Yeah, that bastard killed my husband in cold blood.

Motherfucker deserved to get a bullet through his head!"

"The authorities have been looking for you ever since."

"That's a lie," Darrell said. "If the authorities were

looking for us, then why weren't we interrogated a year after

that?"

"They canceled the case," Konstantin said. He was

getting frustrated. "Want to know why? Because THEY

FOUND OUT ABOUT US! They realized some of the agents

you killed during the chase were FUCKING IFHR AGENTS!"

"Yeah, you're getting exposure now! Your organization's

no longer a secret!" Darrell said.

"You know? IFHR was a top-secret government that was

established by the current United States president, Lavensa?"

"Yeah, there were rumors, and we expect that they're true," Phoenix said.

Konstantin talks in a psychotic tone, "Oh, they're *REAL* true. I'll give you a hint for the next trial. It will be in the nation's capital, that is all I will give."

"You better tell us everything or I'll shoot you right on the spot!" Phoenix said as her and Darrell aim their pistols at Konstantin and his men.

"NOT SO FAST, LEYTON!" Konstantin yelled. "We're going to do things differently here. Drop your firearms right here, right now." Konstantin's men, Darrell, and Phoenix drop their weapons on the ground. They all ready their daggers and knives. Phoenix still has her swords on her back. "Because if you want to get out alive and complete this trial, you better cut your way through this one."

Suddenly, two more men sneak up behind Darrell and Phoenix and grab a hold of them by their neck while holding daggers, knocking them off guard. "Split up!" Konstantin

yelled. While they were both taken hostage, Konstantin and

his men run towards the doors they come from.

Chapter 22: Stealth

Darrell and Phoenix are struggling as the two agents

have a tight grip on them. Phoenix suddenly kicks one of

them in the knee, making him let go. Phoenix quickly turns

around and slashes him in the face with one of her daggers,

cutting through his cheeks and nose, killing him. She then

grunts and punches him in the face, knocking him to the

ground. She charges at the other agent and pulls one of her

knives out. She stabs him in the hip and in the temple, killing

him as he lets go of Darrell. Darrell breathes heavily as he

experienced his brush of death. "Come on, let's go after

Konstantin!" Phoenix yelled. They both sprint towards the doors Konstantin and his men went into and begin the pursuit of the sixth trial.

As Darrell and Phoenix charge through the doors, they enter a room that's dim in light as there were curved flights of stairs and exquisite furniture. "There's light on your communicator if you can't see," Adrian said.

"The light's acceptable in this room, we're scouring out to find them," Phoenix whispered. "Stay close and low, Darrell, they could be anywhere." They go through the room and scan it, but there are no agents around. "Nothing here." They go to another door as Phoenix peeks through the keyhole.

There was an agent inside a hallway filled with paintings in the distance. He was talking through his communicator, "What the hell do you want us to do, Stankevich?! They could still be alive. Who knows how many of us they fucking killed?!" the agent yelled.

"Keep a watchful eye out for them," Konstantin said through his communicator. "Stand your ground, we can't let them head to Washington, D.C. The uprising will continue if they survive. Cut them up if you have to. You better not take the coward's way out!"

Phoenix gets angry as she is surprised, "Wait, what uprising?!"

"What happened?" Darrell whispered.

"Apparently there's an uprising in the United States, and it's at the damn capital, too! We have to kill these men quickly."

Phoenix tightly grabs the doorknob and turns it. "Stand back," she warned. She quietly opens the door as Darrell gets behind her. They enter the hallway and look for hiding spots. The agent was far away from Darrell and Phoenix. They cling across the walls as they were hiding beside a podium. The ceiling was providing dim natural light from outside as it

made it easier to see.

Phoenix realized she let go of the door, which made it

creak and slam, alerting the agent. "Shit!" she mouths out.

"Stankevich! They may be inside the building! The door

closed by itself!" said the agent, petrified.

"What are you waiting for?! Don't stand there, take

them out!

The agent fast walks to the podium as he pridefully pulls

out a silver switchblade made of platinum metal. "Hope your

ready for the uprising!" the agent taunted.

As the agent reaches the podium, Darrell and Phoenix

quickly get out of cover and pull their knives out, ambushing

the agent. The agent tries to fight back, but Phoenix cuts

deep into his collarbone before he was given a chance. The

agent yelled in excruciating pain. He was about to call

Konstantin, but Darrell charged at him and punched him in

the face, knocking him to his knees and dropping his communicator. He takes the agent's hand and breaks a couple of his fingers. Phoenix takes her knife and uppercuts him through the center of his neck and chin. Blood was quickly gushing down as he was gagging. She yanks out the knife and gives him an expression of rage.

They both run to the opposite end of the hallway and cling beside the door. Phoenix looks at Darrell and points the numbers, "One, two, three." She quietly opens the door as they enter another hallway with arched ceilings and beveled walls. They slowly walk up the stairs and peek at the end of the hallway. The agent was in the distance. He heard their footsteps as they walked up the stairs. They cling up beside the walls as the agent turns around. He walks towards their direction and pulls out a knife.

Phoenix quickly gets out of cover and throws a couple daggers with her quick reflexes. The daggers chop air as they cut a deep hole into the agent's thighs. He yells from the sting of the cut as it echoes throughout the hallway. Phoenix and Darrell charge at the agent and start cutting him with their daggers. The agent yells louder, begging for mercy.

"Help me!" the agent cried.

"Come on, fight back, you can't let them get away!" Konstantin yelled.

The agent makes one more yell before Phoenix cuts him deep in the center of his throat. The cut was deep enough for it to go through the back of his neck. "Come in, agent!" Konstantin said. "AGENT!" Phoenix yanks out the dagger as Konstantin heard the agent gagging over the communicator. "SHIT! Agents, they're in the building, we are being ambushed! Scan the museum and be prepared when you see them! Stop at nothing to take them down!"

"Shit! Come on, Darrell!" Phoenix said. They both start running towards the end of hallway. As they approach the end, they budge through a door and enter another hallway. They sprint through the hallway as the light from outside shine on the floor and walls.

Suddenly, the two remaining agents budge through the door and block their way. Konstantin wasn't with them. They pull out their knives and daggers. "It's all in a hard day's work when you accomplish something," one of the agents said.

"Oh, I'm not finished with mine yet. My work isn't quite done until I eliminate the source of the problem," Phoenix shakes her head.

"Maybe we can help you finish it, but in this case, we can do it by our standards," the other agent said.

Darrell and Phoenix prepare their knives and daggers as them and the agents charge at each other. They start swinging their knives as they block each other. Phoenix was about to drive a dagger into one of the agents' chest, but the agent blocked her attack. He pushed her away and temporarily stunned her.

Darrell is fighting the other agent as he swings his knife close to the agent's forehead. They block each other, but Darrell saw his chance. He slams his daggers down on the ground and drives his fist into the agent's chest, striking him by the heart. The agent made an "Oomph!" and bent over, covering his chest with his hands and applying pressure. Darrell grabs one of his arms and pulls it. He takes his arm arm and twists it backwards, braking it and snapping it like a twig while accompanied by a cracking sound. The agent yelled in agony from the twist, making him kneel down. Darrell knees him hard in the chin, making him go back wards. He quickly grabs a hold of the agent and snaps his neck, killing him.

Phoenix gets up as the remaining agent charges at him. Darrell sees the agent grabbing Phoenix and pushing her against the ledge. She panics as she sees the distant ground from outside. The agent looks at her with taunting intentions and slowly brings the knife to her. The agent laughs nefariously, "Now, you're going to do things our way, Mrs. Leyton! The only way this will work is if you comply with us for *just* a moment!"

Darrell sprints towards the agent and pulls him off of Phoenix. He then grabs a hold of the agent and violently throws him to the wall that's opposite of Phoenix. The agent attempts to strike Darrell, but he blocks the agent with his forearm. Darrell punches him in the throat, making him drop his blades. Darrell quickly picks up one of his daggers and grabs a hold of him, holding him in a hostage position. The agent panics as Darrell holds the dagger to his Adam's apple. Darrell gets tense as he says in the agent's ear, "Don't you move, you bastard!" The agent tries to break free from his grip, but it was too tight. Darrell takes his fist and punches him in the hip, "I said." He punches him, "DON'T!" He punches him again, "FUCKING!" He punches him once more, "MOVE!" The agent grunts and hyperventilates.

"That's enough, Darrell, I'll take it from here, but keep him in your grip. Make sure he doesn't move," Phoenix said.

Phoenix walks up to the agent and puts the edge of one her daggers to his neck. "Wow, would you look at that?" she said. "You say that you work in numbers, but you guys are so scatterbrained, you don't even know how to react when you give in by the time I'm around. With every one of you that I kill, my message grows stronger. And I will stop at nothing to make people know who you really are." Darrell makes his grip tighter around the agent's neck. "Slit him in the neck, Darrell. Put him out of his misery."

Darrell quickly slits the agent's throat as blood rains down his business attire. Phoenix takes her dagger with both hands and executes him by stabbing into the center of his skull. Blood splatters towards her and Darrell's hands. The agent's eyes roll back into his head. Darrell lets go of the agent as Phoenix pulls out the dagger from his skull. Phoenix breathes heavily as she looks down on the agent's body as his blood spreads around it. "Let's go find Konstantin," Phoenix said.

Darrell and Phoenix run to the door and budge through it. They go through the hallways and rooms in order to find where Konstantin is hiding.

Chapter 23: Bloodline

After running through several rooms and hallways,

Darrell and Phoenix enter a room that was white in color and

had chandeliers on the sides. They see Konstantin standing in

the center of the waxed floor, looking at Darrell and Phoenix.

"It's over for you, Konstantin," Darrell said.

"Oh, it's not over yet," Konstantin said.

"We've killed off your henchmen, you might as well give

it up," Phoenix said.

Konstantin laughed, "You think I would show any

remorse? We don't have remorse. We don't care who dies or who lives."

"I'm from the opposite side of what you believe."

"I would love to kill you two smugglers, but you two were never in the organization to begin with. You're trying to make it look good for the public to see, so that way they could be fine again."

"Isn't that what society's supposed to be? Free? Peaceful? Somebody has to make a change one way or another. They can either take the message or just go on with their lives."

"Unlike you, we follow in a different code of ethics, we take and benefit from others. We take each other for granted. We kill for the thrill, it's in our bloodline to possess that power. We've done it for so long, it's obvious you've had your fair share."

"I kill for a multitude of reasons, and with every agent I

kill, I'm one step closer from shutting down the main source."

Konstantin pulls out his swords, "Well, in that case, why don't we fight to the death? Blood for blood, the choice is yours."

Phoenix unsheathes her swords and prepares the fight with Konstantin. She throws a sword to Darrell, "Don't worry about how to use it. Just block and swing. It's that simple."

Darrell, Phoenix, and Konstantin charge at each other and begin the sword fight. They all swing at each other and block attacks. Konstantin catches them in a break as their swords grind against each other. "Maybe you should follow a different pastime instead of focusing on killing us!" Konstantin yelled, echoing throughout the room.

"Why would I do that? I'm just doing it to protect the people!" Phoenix yelled. She breaks out of Konstantin's hold and continues to swing. Darrell was about to swing at Konstantin, but he caught Darrell before he had a chance. He performed a counter attack and sliced through Darrell's pants, but the cut wasn't deep. Konstantin laughs with no remorse. Darrell was still able to fight.

Phoenix keeps swinging at Konstantin and attempted to strike his hip, but he blocked her. He saw that Phoenix's chestal region was unprotected, so he charges and rammed her, pushing her to the ground and knocking her off balance. She coughs from the impact as she lays on the ground. Darrell yells and charges at Konstantin while he has his back turned, but Konstantin blocks his attack. He grabs Darrell and pushes him hard, knocking him to the ground and temporarily stunning him.

Konstantin turns his attention back to Phoenix. He walks up to her and says with pride, "I never understood humans. I've never had that ability and never will." He raises his sword and brings it down in an attempt to execute Phoenix.

Phoenix suddenly strikes Konstantin in the chest by

stabbing through his diaphragm, making him gag and widening his eyes. She gets up as he drops his sword. She walks up to Konstantin as he kneels to the ground, "You know what? I never understood them either." She pulls the sword out and tightly grabs his neck. "Because when it comes down to killing somebody for no logical reason, it sparks a question that can't be answered." She cuts through his diaphragm again, making blood come out of his mouth, "And whatever you're planning at the United States, I expected it to happen! I wasn't surprised! Los Angeles is now a city of ruins!" She pulls out the sword and cuts into his diaphragm again. "I said I would spread message, but this one will be worded differently just for you!" Konstantin keeps gagging as more blood comes out of his mouth.

Phoenix gets close to Konstantin's face, "If you ever try anything, I mean ANYTHING, you and the rest of your organization and your omnicidal leader, Arkwright will fall until there's nothing left!" She pulls out the sword and slashes him in the neck, making blood splatter onto the floor. Konstantin's eyes roll to the back of his head as he falls face first to the floor. The blood starts spreading around his body as the circle grows.

Phoenix looks down on Konstantin's body and breathes heavily as she shakes from his blood on her hands. She sees Darrell rolling around trying to get up. She walks up to him and lets her arm out to help him up. "Are you alright?" Phoenix said while grabbing the sword from his hand. "I'll help you up." She pulls Darrell up and checks his pant leg. "Did he cut deep?"

"I don't think so." Darrell grunts from the cut in his leg. "Son of a bitch, it stings!"

"Let me check it." Phoenix pulls up his leg to see that it only cut through the thin layer of his skin. "Doesn't look like he cut deep, but we're going to have to find a bathroom if there is one in this place. We have to get there fast if we want to get to D.C. in time."

"I have the blueprints for the museum, they should be in the Winter Palace, which you are in. They should be located by the Main Staircase of the building. It isn't far from where you're at," Adrian said.

"Alright, we'll find it, because Darrell needs to get cleaned of his wound before it gets infected. It's not a serious wound, Konstantin didn't cut deep," Phoenix said.

"Make it quick, because over here, it says on the news that there's an uprising at the capital. Get over there as soon as you can. I knew something like this would happen."

"Alright, we'll probably clock out of Russia in a half an hour, if not, then later. That is if we can find a bathroom."

"Alright, but don't make it too late. I'm downloading the blueprints to your communicator. You'll get them in a minute." Adrian dismisses.

Phoenix puts her arm over Darrell's shoulders, "Come on, let's get you cleaned up and get out of here." They work their way out of the room and try to find the Main Staircase. The museum's blueprints showed up on her communicator. She looks down at it, "Alright, good, that saves us plenty of time."

After ten minutes of going from room to room, Darrell and Phoenix find the Main Staircase and locate the bathrooms. They go to the bathroom doors and budge through them, revealing a luxurious interior. The walls and floor were made of marble and other fine materials that shined throughout the room. She goes to the sink and wets a couple paper towels. "Lift you leg up. Just pat them on your leg and the bleeding won't be as bad," Phoenix said. The bleeding started to dissipate as Darrell patted the towels on his leg. "Alright, let's get out of here, our car should still be outside."

They walk out of the bathroom and into the entrance room of the museum as Phoenix waits for Darrell. He was slightly limping, but was strong enough to walk on his own.

"I'll wait for you," Phoenix said.

After Darrell caught up with Phoenix, they budge through the doors and head for their vehicle. They get inside the vehicle as Darrell starts it. "Are you still able to drive?" Phoenix said while buckling her seat belt.

"Yeah, it's just a cut," Darrell said. He backs out of the museum's area and heads into the streets of Saint Petersburg. "You just want to keep breaking the rules, huh?" Russell said through the communicator. Phoenix switches to his frequency, "Why don't you put us up for the challenge? This is getting *way* to easy!"

"I do have a challenge for you, indeed. Stankevich has given you the word of mouth about the seventh trial, but since you keep breaking the rules, I'm not going to say the targets' names."

"I swear, if you try anything, Russell, I'm warning you right now! We will stop at nothing to take you down!"

"You would kill me anyways. However, I will tell you the gender of the target, it is a female that's fighting against the uprising at the United States' national capital. Better get there quick before I ruin the surprise!" Russell laughs and dismisses.

"WHAT SURPRISE?!" Phoenix yelled. No response. "Shit! Darrell, let's get to D.C. now!" Darrell accelerates through the streets and makes his way to the airport.

After they arrive at the airport, they quickly take off in the jet and venture to the homeland, where an uprising and a revolution is beginning.

Chapter 24: Wasteland

April 6, 2021

Washington D.C., United States, 1245 hours

Darrell and Phoenix prepare to land at an airport nearest to the White House. "Looks just the same as it was before, a wasteland," Phoenix said. The climate in D.C. was cloudy, but it didn't rain. Both lawns of the White House had smoke around them as there were small pits of fire. The buildings and homes around the capital were decimated as they were invaded and had smoke coming out of them.

Darrell opens the back hatch of the jet as Phoenix gets out and pulls the Lamborghini out. He closes the hatch as

Phoenix switches seats for Darrell to drive. "Where are you at now?" Adrian said while they were pulling out of the airport and entering the highway. There were totaled vehicles that were scattered around the road.

"We're in D.C.," Phoenix said.

"How bad does it look?"

"The gardens of the White House are badly affected." Phoenix glances at the South Lawn of the White House and notices a large amount of people covering the lawn while carrying signs and torches. "Stankevich and his men were right."

"What's going on?"

"There's an uprising at the capital."

Adrian sighs in fear, "Shit, the news was right. I knew that this day would come."

"Russell didn't give us the name of the target this time. He's really dumbing down on us. She's a female."

"I should be able to find her whereabouts by categorizing in the database. Give me just a moment."

Adrian sets the map to Washington, D.C. and scans the database. He goes through their current whereabouts and clicks on Washington, D.C. He clicks female and finds a match. "I found two possible matches. One's at the White House."

"What is her name?"

"I'll transfer the data to your communicator." A picture of a female shows up on the communicator. "Alice Walker. Age: 29. Hair color: Blonde. Skin color: White. Weight. 170 pounds. She's been in the organization for four years. She's one of the most notorious members of the organization. She's heavily involved in committing populicide in multiple countries. Be careful on this one."

"They better not try anything when we show up," Phoenix said. Adrian dismisses. "Let's try to find my parents first. They live here."

"Why are they here? Why would they stay in a place that's decimated by an organization attacking the capital?" Darrell said.

"My parents used to work for the government. It was a family secret. They acted completely different when I married Warren. They may still be at their house if IFHR didn't drive them out already. Let's go see if they're still home."

"We have to find them fast before the uprising inflates in scale."

"Ready your weapons by the time we get there, just in case they show up as uninvited guests. I'll tell you the address and guide you there."

Darrell drives around the vehicles on the road and make their way to Phoenix's family house. Papers and other debris were floating in the air from the wind. Phoenix can only hope if her parents are alive again.

Chapter 25: History Lesson

1312 hours

Darrell and Phoenix eventually enter the suburbs of Washington, D.C. and cruise through the curved roads of one of the several neighborhoods located within the capital. Specifically, they're in a small neighborhood, which is about fifteen minutes from the White House. The neighborhood was unaffected as vehicles were still parked in people's driveways. "Looks like they didn't come here yet, but they might be working their way here," Phoenix said. "My parents' house should be a few houses on the left here." She points to a white two-story house. "Just park by the side of the road."

Darrell parks by Phoenix's parents' house. "Ready your weapons in case IFHR shows up," Phoenix said. They get out of the vehicle and walk on the driveway while preparing their weapons. As they walk up the steps to their front porch, Phoenix knocks on the door. "Hello?" she said. She didn't hear any footsteps. "Anybody there?" She knocks again, but there was still silence. She knocks harder, "Mom?! Dad?!" No response.

She focuses on the doorknob and realizes it's unlocked. "Why would they leave it unlocked during an uprising?" she wondered. She slowly opens the door as her and Darrell enter the house. They entered the living room, which looked vintage in texture. There was a floor and walls that were stained in rich golden oak. There was a round glass table with a soft, white tablecloth in the center of the living room. There was a black leather couch beside a window as the sky glared dim light in the center of the floor. There were small particles of dust throughout the house. Darrell whispered, "Smells like this house hasn't been used for a while."

"Keep an eye out. Why don't we head into the kitchen?" Phoenix whispered. While they walk towards the kitchen, the floor creaked, alerting her parents. "Eleanor, they've entered our house!" her father yelled, his name was Gregory Hadaway. There was a staircase on one side of the kitchen. They hear footsteps as Darrell and Phoenix see her parents. Her parents run down the steps as her father carries a shotgun and her mother carries an assault rifle. Gregory and Eleanor both wore business suits, similar to the attire of IFHR.

As Phoenix's parents come off of the steps, they point their weapons at Darrell and Phoenix. Gregory appeared aged as he had a gray beard. He still had his black hair. Phoenix noticed he was blind in one eye, shocking Phoenix. Eleanor still had her blonde hair as she kept her sunglasses. "What the hell are you doing in my house?" Gregory said desperately in his mature sounding voice, pointing the shotgun at Phoenix. Phoenix raises her arms and drops her weapons. She panics, "Dad, it's me, your daughter, Phoenix!"

Gregory and Eleanor were surprised to hear her voice. Gregory's fear turns into relief as he lowers his weapon, "Phoenix?"

"Is that really you?" Eleanor said in her mature voice, shedding a tear.

"Yes," Phoenix said. "It's me. Phoenix Leyton."

Gregory and Eleanor drop their weapons and run to her, both giving her a hug. "I thought we would never see you again!" Gregory cried.

"They killed my husband a few years ago. I've been fighting them ever since," Phoenix said, crying.

"Who's this guy that's with you? What's he doing here?" Gregory said as he sounded protective. Him and Eleanor let go of Phoenix and look at Darrell in a serious manner. "Who are you?" Gregory said. "What are you doing here?"

Darrell raises his arms, "I'm not here to hurt you."

"How do I know that? You wear the same attire as

them."

Phoenix gets in the conversation and walks up to Darrell

and Gregory, "Because he was the next target, and I helped

him escape. His name's Darrell Friegman, and he sure can

drive out of a situation."

Gregory lets out his arm and shakes his hand, "Nice to

meet you, sir."

"With pleasure, Mr. Hadaway," Darrell said.

"How long ago was this?"

"It's a long story. And how do you know about the

organization, Dad? You and Mom seem to know a lot,"

Phoenix said.

Gregory hesitates, "Because your mother and I used to

work with Lavensa before he became President."

Phoenix got angry, "Why didn't you tell me this before?!"

"It was a secret. It was corrupt from the start."

"Then let's start off with when you guys got involved in the government."

Gregory takes a deep breath and starts from when him and Eleanor got involved with IFHR, "When your mother and I got out of school, we were originally living here that was once known as a beautiful establishment of our country. Washington, D.C. was so beautiful when your mother and I were attending school together. We both shared the same interests, which involved politics. We both became involved in the government in 1990, we were twenty-two years old at the time."

"What was the position for Lavensa?" Phoenix said.

"He used to work as a conspiracy theorist, one that actually thinks and digs in to figure out if it's really true or not."

"Did he become rogue, too?"

"As a matter of fact, he did," Eleanor said. "That's when it all happened. He started to become narcissistic, I guess you could say. He kept mentioning that he wanted to create an organization that could help change the world. he named it the IFHR, the International Foundation of Human Resources. That's when he started to change."

"What happened with Lavensa? How did this all begin?"

"We found out that he began torturing people for interrogation reasons. He started recruiting people, random people and created a group to start out with. One of his first torture methods were bounding them to a chair and hitting them with heavy objects if they didn't spill the information. Him and the people he recruited went after random criminals, similar to what a vigilante would do."

"They were killed in secret," Gregory said.

"How did it get to where it is now?" Phoenix said.

"After a few years of passing, the number of people grew by the thousands. They started to get their own attire, the same attire you're wearing, Darrell. Just as simple as if you're going out to a formal event. Then, the men he recruited decided to do their own part, they started to get violent. However, Lavensa decided not to intervene," Gregory said.

"Why?" Phoenix said.

"Because he realized that it was getting out of hand, but he couldn't stop it. He quickly became outnumbered. All of the men abandoned him."

"What about Arkwright?" Darrell said.

"Arkwright was one of his first men he recruited. Ever since Lavensa was left behind, Arkwright was one of the people that decided to take over. He was a prideful bastard, that's for sure. One of their first establishments was in 1993. The establishments got more advanced in technology over the years, that's how they look so far ahead of our time in their interiors."

"What happened to Lavensa after that?" Phoenix said.

"Donovan Lavensa started his presidency in 2018. He didn't smile on his first day. The first lady didn't even know what to expect of him. She didn't know about IFHR back then. She probably knows now since it's circulating in the media. I saw you guys on there a couple of times on the news. They showed your portraits."

"Are we in the Most Wanted?" Phoenix said.

"No, the people in the country decided to revolt against authorities because there's claims that many people outside and inside of the government have researched the organization's background. They all found traces that lead towards Lavensa himself. This might be the year he'll get the axe. If he wants any redemption, he needs to tell the truth about his involvement with IFHR."

"Wow, that's a lot to say," Phoenix said, surprised.

"That's how it happened. He still says that he wants to change the world, but is he doing that?" Gregory finishes explaining the ordeal. "Let's get you guys out of this mess. It's not safe here anymore." Gregory grabs Phoenix's arm, but she steps back.

"No, that can't be done," Phoenix said, scared.

"Why?! You suffered long enough, Phoenix!"

Phoenix hesitated and breathes heavily, "We're still being watched by Arkwright. We can't do this. Darrell and I have to take him down before he kills more people!"

Gregory goes up to Phoenix and places his hands on her shoulders. Phoenix was terrified as she looked down. "Phoenix, look at me!" Gregory said. Phoenix looked into her father's eyes. "What did he do to you guys?"

"We're in something called the Game of Trials. We have to kill a set number of targets in other countries in order to become free. Darrell and I have to stop him!"

"Then why don't we fight our way through together?" Gregory gives Phoenix a hug. "It'll be alright. You and Darrell have to finish this before it's too late."

All of them get startled as they hear the loud engines of vehicles coming onto their street. "Everybody, ready your weapons!" Gregory yelled. They pick up their weapons and run towards the windows in the living room. They slightly peek out to see a few Arma tanks and black heavily armored Chevrolet SUVs with silver battering rams approaching their house. "Shit, close the blinds! They're approaching our house!" Everybody closed a window blind and peeked through the windows as agents get out of their vehicles. "This neighborhood's clean! Check this white house! There may be people in there! We need to deliver the targets to Alice!" one of the agents yelled.

All of the agents from the SUVs walk up to their house

while carrying several firearms, such as modified assault

rifles, pistols, and shotguns. They walk up the porch steps as

they all make loud footsteps with their dress shoes. "Find a

spot to hide and give them hell. If they want to ambush us,

we'll ambush them!" Gregory said.

Darrell and Phoenix crouch down and hide behind the

couch as Phoenix's parents go into the kitchen. Phoenix's

family and Darrell wait as the agents prepare to fight them.

Chapter 26: Ambush

1331 hours

The agents kick open the door as they move their weapons around with flashlights attached to their barrels. "Agents, search the room!" one of the agents said. A few agents enter the house and begin searching. Darrell and Phoenix stand up and aim at the agents. "HEY!" Phoenix yelled, getting their attention. "Looking for us?!" They both start firing at their chests and heads, instantly killing the agents as the bullets make permanent marks in the walls, creating more dust.

"That takes care of that bunch!" Darrell said.

Phoenix's parents were covering beside the walls at the edge of the kitchen as they were crouched down with their weapons raised. Gregory's voice echoed, "Oh, don't you get too comfortable, boy! There's definitely more coming, and Mom and I have plenty of firepower to deliver them! You guys get in here and go upstairs! Your mother and I are going to try to flank them, but make this fast! We'll be on the sides of the kitchen. I want you guys to flank them upstairs, too. They could find their way up there as well."

Darrell and Phoenix get away from the couch and sprint towards the stairs in the kitchen. "Hurry before they shoot you on the spot!" A few of the agents fire a couple rounds at the kitchen as they whistled, barely missing Darrell and Phoenix by mere inches.

They breathe heavily as they enter the brown stained hallway filled with rooms. "You watch out in my bedroom and I'll guard my parent's room. Close the blinds when you get in there. They'll most likely try to get in the bathroom. There's a big window in there," Phoenix said.

Darrell and Phoenix split up and go to their assigned rooms. They kick open the doors and enter inside. Her parent's bedroom was luxurious as there was a queen size bed in the center with soft, velvet red blankets with ivory colored pillows. She ran to the window, which was halfway towards the ceiling and the size of a small television frame. She closed the blinds and peeked through to see vehicles with the IFHR insignia drive onto her street. She also saw agents running onto the grass with a steel chrome ladder and raising it just below the window of the bathroom.

The room Darrell's in was plain as there was only a one-person bed with a small television on top of a dresser. He runs to the window and closes the blind. He peeks out cautiously to watch the agents climb up the ladder. "When we get in, watch your six!" the agent on the top yelled. "I'll

shoot the window!"

"Shit!" Phoenix yelled. "Darrell, you know what to do

now! When they enter through the bathroom, we're flanking

them! Keep an ear out for broken glass!" Darrell and Phoenix

reload their weapons until they have a full magazine.

The agent on top of the ladder pulls out his assault rifle

and fires at the window, shattering it immediately. Phoenix

and Darrell run out of their rooms and cock their weapons.

They go into the hallway and enter the bathroom.

The agents were startled as Darrell and Phoenix aimed at

them. Phoenix yelled as adrenaline was flowing inside of her

as she and Darrell mercilessly fire at the agents with full

force, giving them no time to react. The agents flew back

against the wall as they were barraged with bullets. The walls

that were once a clear and clean white was now a different

color as they were splattered and stained by their blood. One of the agents tries to squeeze through the window. Darrell and Phoenix walk up to the agent as she's focused on revenge and determination. "How dare you break into my house as an uninvited guest?!" Phoenix said. She goes up to the agent and pulls out one of her daggers. She cleanly slices three of his fingers off as the agent yells in pain. She fires at the agent in the arms, making him lose his grip. He then yells again and falls to his death, cracking his spine and skull. "Come on, Darrell!" Phoenix yelled. Darrell could see the rage in her eyes. "Let's go the window and give them ALL OF THE FUCKING HELL THEY DESERVE!"

Darrell and Phoenix lean out of the window and aim at the agents. "You take one side, I'll take the ladder and the other side!" Phoenix yelled. They both yell with energy and fire repeatedly at the agents running towards the ladder. The amount of dead bodies were increasing they executed multiple headshots and chest shots. She sees a few more agents trying to climb up to the bathroom window. She fires one round at the agent on the top of the ladder, knocking him off. "Darrell, we're taking this ladder down! No counts, we're just doing it!"

Phoenix grabs one side of the ladder as Darrell has the other. It was a heavy ladder as it was made of layered titanium. They push with brute force as the ladder slowly tips over. She yells and fires at the agents holding onto the ladder from down to up. As the ladder falls to the ground, it crushes the agents' bodies, braking their bones. "Don't FUCK with the Hadaways!" she yells at the top of her lungs.

Darrell and Phoenix jumped as they heard shotgun blasts in the kitchen. "Shit, they're in the living room! Come on, Phoenix!" Darrell yelled. They sprinted out of the hallway and downstairs.

Phoenix's parents were shooting their semi-automatic shotguns in the living room as the agents storm in. The bullets shot holes through their chests and blew some of their heads off. "Should've swallowed your pride before it ate you from the inside!" Gregory yelled.

"No wonder you guys have been secret, you're a bunch of fucking cowards!" Eleanor yelled.

"You better count your FUCKING blessings next time, you omnicidal bastards!" They keep firing as bodies pile up in the living room. One of them escapes the shower of bullets and makes their way into the kitchen. Gregory gets up and turns the agent around. The agent was emotionally numb as he saw the rage in Gregory's eyes. "Stay away from my family!" Gregory puts the shotgun to the agent's forehead and blows his head off, spreading brain matter all the way to the kitchen counter. Their house now looked like a slaughterhouse.

Darrell and Phoenix enter the kitchen and into the living room, ignoring the blood and bodies surrounding them. They see more agents storming into the living room. They run to the door and shoot the agents approaching it. "Welcome to D.C.! Special greetings from the Hadaways!" Phoenix yells.

Suddenly, they see two agents with full body suits made of heavy silver armor. Their chest plates had the IFHR insignia on their left side. The masks had a front glass cover as metal covered the back, similar to what Darien Summers pictured in his flashback. The armored agents run into the door and enter the living room. Darrell and Phoenix try to intervene by shooting at them, but they had no effect. The armored agents turned their attention to them and pushed them violently against the walls, temporarily stunning them.

The agents run to the kitchen and pull out their assault rifles, which were chrome in color. "Don't you dare hurt them!" Phoenix yelled. They see her parents and hit them with brute force in their chests with the butt of their assault rifles.

"What are you going to do?" one of the agents said in

their distorted tone from their armored suits. Gregory

groaned in pain as Eleanor cried for mercy. "Shut up!" one of

the agents yelled. They took the butts of their assault rifles

and bashed them in the foreheads, bruising them and

knocking them out cold.

"Mom! Dad! No!" Phoenix yelled in shock. They picked

up her parents and hoisted them over their shoulders. The

agents walked up to Darrell and Phoenix and grabbed them

by their shoulder, squeezing them. One of them speaks to

Phoenix, "You better find us if you want to see your family

again." The agents violently push Darrell and Phoenix against

the walls again, temporarily stunning them. They fell down

and collapsed as the agents walk out with her parents.

Darrell tries to get up, but the push slightly bruised him

in the hip. "Don't move yet, wait until their vehicles exit the

street," Phoenix said as they were both hyperventilating.

"Agents!" one of the armored agents yelled. "Put them

in one of the SUVs! Make sure they don't wake up!"

Two of the agents get out of one of the SUVs and takes Phoenix's parents, placing them in the passenger seats. The armored agents go inside one of the tanks as they all start their vehicles, slowly making their way towards the end of the street. "We're going to follow them," Phoenix said. "Come on, get up, let's go."

Darrell and Phoenix get up and start walking away from her parent's house. They get in the Lamborghini as Darrell starts the vehicle. He turns around and follows the path of the agents. While turning, he saw the vehicles in the distance. There was a large amount of SUVs behind the two Arma tanks. "Keep a distance from them," Phoenix said. "They're most likely going to the White House." They turn on the highways and see the totaled vehicles scattered around. They weave around the twisted metal to get around.

After ten minutes of driving, the fleet turns left and

enters the center of the South Lawn Fountain where the people are still waving their torches and signs. "Go fast now, we're going to get the people's attention," Phoenix said. Darrell accelerated and turned into the area of the lawn. He drives through the grass as the people yell in shock and fear. Some people moved out of the way as they almost got ran over by the Lamborghini. The vehicle was in the middle of the crowd.

As Darrell and Phoenix got out of the vehicle, they saw a large stage with three nooses placed in front of the White House supported by a steel bar that's twenty feet in the air. Phoenix saw the two agents in one of the SUVs grabbing her parents and taking them to the stage. They were still unconscious at the time. "What?! No, you can't do that! You will NOT do that!" Phoenix yelled. She starts running to the stage, but the armored agents guarded the bottom of it. They block their path by grabbing a hold of her, picking her up.

"Let go of me!" She starts punching the helmet of their suits,

but no effect. The agents throw her and pushed her back.

One of them raises their assault rifles, "Don't you move!"

The agents on stage put Phoenix's parents by the nooses

and carefully slip their necks in and tie their hands behind

their backs. Shortly after, a blonde haired woman with the

same leather suit as Phoenix walks into the center of the

stage. She has an ear microphone for everyone to hear her.

"Alice Walker," Phoenix said in anger.

Alice stands in the middle of the stage as she begins to

speak, getting the crowd's attention.

Chapter 27: Execution

1347 hours

Alice starts speaking with inflated pride, "Everyone's attention is needed. If you don't pay attention, we'll shoot you right on the spot." The armored agents aim at the crowd. "We want justice!" the crowd said. Some people in the crowd started saying vulgar words at Alice. "We are the IFHR, the International Foundation for Human Resources. As you can see, for two years, we've been chasing down a target that goes by the name of Darrell Friegman, but he was assisted by Phoenix Leyton. They're right in the middle of the crowd beside that tathered Lamborghini." She points to their

Lamborghini, making the crowd draw their attention to Darrell and Phoenix. One person said, "We've heard about you. You were on the news."

"Is it true that it's all a conspiracy?" another person asked Phoenix.

Phoenix hesitated, "Not anymore. It's out there now."

Phoenix's parents wake up as they groan from their bruises. They notice that they were kneeling down with nooses around their necks. "What the hell is going on here?" Gregory said. He feels the fibers of the rope, making his neck feel slightly tight. "Mom! Dad!" Phoenix cried.

Alice turns her attention to Phoenix's parents, "Oh." She goes to one of the agents beside her as they hand her a baton. "Her parents woke up. Just in time for the next step in the termination process."

"I'm warning you right now, you fucking bitch! If you ever try anything, I will hunt down in a heartbeat!" Phoenix yelled.

The crowd cheered from Phoenix's statement. Alice was getting aggravated, "Oh, the crowd wants to go against us now? I specifically said to pay attention. At least you're doing that part." She walks up to Phoenix's parents and readies the baton. "Hi, my name's Alice. Alice Walker. And this will be the day that will also be your last." She swings the baton and hits Gregory in the shoulder blade. Gregory yells and cries in pain. She then turns her attention to Eleanor. "And as for you, Eleanor, you'll suffer the same fate!" She swings her baton at Eleanor's shoulder, bruising her even more. She cries from the pain as it grows.

"Please don't do this!" Phoenix begged.

"Now that I have your attention, Phoenix, we're going to give your parents one last chance before it's time for them to go," Alice said. She turned her attention back to Phoenix's parents. "So, do you two have any last words for your daughter? We'll start off with you, Mr. Hadaway."

Gregory grunts and coughs from the pain, "Phoenix....., I hope....... that you find a way...... to take these bastards down."

"Alright, and how about you, Eleanor? Got something to say?"

Eleanor said, "Phoenix, it'll be alright...... Your father and I..... love you... to death...... Take these bastards down. Do it..... for the world!"

"Enough with the charades. Don't waste my time! Now let's go on with the termination process!"

Phoenix sprints after the stage, "You motherfuckers, don't you da-"

The armored agents grab a hold of Darrell and Phoenix, preventing them from moving. More armored agents go up to the stage and grab the ropes by their feet. They pick the ends up and pull back with unforgiving force on the nooses, lifting Phoenix's eyes up and suspending them in the air.

Phoenix gasped as they pulled the nooses tighter around

their necks. Phoenix's parents were gagging as their faces

started turning red. Alice smiled with no remorse as she lifted

her arms out and looked up in the sky.

Phoenix's parents gave in to the grip and passed away.

Phoenix started wailing as she saw her parents die in front of

her eyes. "Wow, finally got your attention, Phoenix," Alice

said.

Phoenix's sadness turns into rage, "I'm going to kill you

all!

"It's over now, Phoenix. You got caught this time!"

The armored agents holding Darrell and Phoenix threw

them down on the ground and punched them, knocking them

out cold. "You boys sure do a good job every time!" Alice

said, congratulating the agents. She points at the crowd.

"Now, to all of you people who have all of your torches and

signs, you know who we're all about. Your protest means nothing now!" She turns the microphone off and yells to the agents on stage, "Some of you take her parents off of the nooses. Some of you get Darrell and Phoenix and put them in an SUV. One of you get their vehicle. Make sure they don't escape again."

The agents follow all of Alice's orders and take Darrell and Phoenix away from the stage. They we're taking them to an establishment that was close to the White House, but a different one from where they escaped from. The one they're traveling to is far more disturbing than any other bases they went to.

Chapter 28: Visions

Phoenix was in a dreaming state, a state where it appeared to be nowhere. She was fully clothed as she had the same suit from while she was awake. She's laying on a desert landscape as the sun and clear blue skies made the desert sands more vibrant. She stands up and studies the environment around her. "Where am I?" she said, worried and scared. She walks around as she can only see barren wasteland. "There's no way out."

"Phoenix," Warren's voice was sounded as it was loud

and echoed in the distance.

"Warren? Is that really you?" Phoenix sounded delusional.

"Yes. Are you wondering why you keep visioning that building?"

"Yes, I want to know the answers of how to stop this."

"Keep going straight, you'll find the answer."

"Alright, I know I can trust you." She walks straight as she can see a tall building in the distance.

"Go ahead, keep going, it'll look familiar to you."

Phoenix keeps walking towards the building in the distance until she's a couple hundred feet away from it. She looks up to see a black building as there was a needle on top, indicating its highest point. The building's architecture had arches on its sides. There was also a large, square fence that surrounded the perimeter of the building. "There's nobody here," Phoenix said.

"This is a dream, you're fine. This building is the key to stopping him. A route towards your salvation." The dream's landscape starts to become dark as the environment loses its color. Phoenix panics, "But wait, what about you?"

"Don't worry about me, you will see me again. You and Darrell have to stop him before it's too late."

"Warren, no!"

The dream fades away into black, signifying the end of it.

Chapter 29: Restraint

1523 hours

Phoenix wakes up from her dream and sees that she is restrained on a gurney made of cement. The room she was in was small and confined and also made of cement. The room was dark as there was only one light shining down on her, dangling from the center of the ceiling. She notices a security camera in a corner of the room. Everywhere she goes, there will be cameras recording her every move since the technology has increased in drastic levels. The bands were tight enough to where she is stuck. She was only wearing a bra and a pair of pants. She panics as she struggles to break free from the restraints. She hyperventilates and grunts while she tries to push her body through the bands.

Phoenix pushes her arms down hard and slowly works her way out of the restraint's hold. The cement brushes against her skin as it scrapes, She can feel the cement scratching her skin as they become red, but didn't bleed. She tried moving to the side, but the restraint still has a hold on her. She takes both of her arms and starts pulling on the restraint pressing down on her upper chest.

Phoenix pushes with all of her might in an attempt to break the restraint. "It's getting weaker," Phoenix said. The restraint started to become weaker as the hold became looser. She pulls one more time and snaps the restraint, making a loud cracking noise that sounded like the lash of a leather whip.

There were two restraints left, one on her femurs and one on her ankles. She moves her legs until her feet are down facing the ground. She sits up and sees her legs. She leans forward and lifts up the restraint by her feet with all of her might. She was grunting as she felt the tight grip on her hands. She slides her feet out of the restraint and focuses on her legs now. She lifts the last restraint and slowly pulls out.

She was starting to lose grip, which made her let go. The restraint snapped back on her thighs, creating a burning sensation. She grunts as she grins from the pain. She pulls up the restraint again and slides her legs out completely. She's now free and sits on one side, breathing heavily after exerting herself.

Phoenix's anger builds as she recollects Alice executing her parents. "I'm coming for you, Alice. All of you. I will stop at nothing to spill your blood on the ground."

She hops off of the gurney and sprints to the door next to her. She pulls and twists on the doorknob, but it's locked. She looks around the room for a solution. She finds a metallic baseball bat and a large flashlight. She walks to the bat and

flashlight to pick them up. "This should do the trick," Phoenix

said. She runs to the door and swings at the doorknob, slowly

knocking it off.

After Phoenix opens the door, a dark pathway made of

cement shows up in front of her. "Shit, what is this place?"

she said. She shines the flashlight and runs through the

pathway. As the pathway curves, she realizes she's currently

underground, trying to escape.

Chapter 30: D.C.

1534 hours

Phoenix runs around the pathway until she finds another path leading to the right. She goes into that path and runs through it. While running through, she sees a cement table showing all of her weapons and her communicator. "Alright, there's all of my weapons, but where's my suit?"

She notices a crate that's also made of cement beside the table. Everything in the pathways are made of cement. She goes to the crate and opens it. It reveals her black leather suit. She quickly grabs it and takes off her pants. She pulls herself into the suit and reequips her weapons. She sheathes

her swords behind her back and places her firearms and

throwing weapons in her pockets. She clenches her fists and

says, "Just like old times."

She runs through the pathway and makes a left. There

was a small staircase along with a door. "I have to find

Darrell, too."

Phoenix budges open the door and reveals a dim and

clean corridor. She knew she was inside one of the bases of

IFHR.

Chapter 31: Revenge

1541 hours

Phoenix walks out of the darkness and into the light as she clings by a wall. She peeks her head out to see a few agents walking away from her sight. "She should be dead within a few days. As long as she's still in that restraint, she's not getting out," one of the agents said as his voice echoed and faded away. She runs up to the door closest to her in the hallway and overrides its security pad.

She pushes open the door and startles the agent inside. There were computers and filing cabinets across the walls while a window projected their reflections. The agents panics

and runs for the door next to the mirror. "Help! She has

escaped!" the agent yelled. Phoenix grabs a hold of him and

throws him against the filing cabinets. She is consumed by

revenge and rage as she pulls out of her daggers. She cuts a

deep hole into his collarbone, making him scream and cry in

pain.

She gets up in the agent's face, "Shh, it'll be alright." She

punches him in the face as he thuds to the ground. She

pounces on him and pins him down. "Because even when I'm

done with you, it will NEVER erase what you did to my

family!" She takes her thumbs and squeezes his eyes, gouging

them. She then slices his neck execution style as blood

splattered onto her suit.

Phoenix pulls the dagger out and runs to the door next

to the mirror. She pushes open the door and sees a room

that's vast in area. She was on a small steep bridge as there was a drop that was three hundred feet above her. On the ground, the floors and walls were white. There were forklifts, supercars with varying colors, and military vehicles all with the IFHR insignia on them. It was like a large warehouse.

Two agents open a door ahead of her as she walked to them, ignoring the dangers of falling off the platform. The agents were alert and shocked as they saw Phoenix alive. While Phoenix charges at them, the agents aim their pistols at her. She pulls out one of her knives and strikes them in the chest. She twists the knife and increases the sting of the cut as she looks at him by the fire in her eyes. The agent gags from the blood spilling out of his mouth and kneels down.

The other agent tries to stun her by performing a melee attack with his pistol, but Phoenix counter attacked. She punched him in the face and stabs him in the mouth. His eyes roll back in his head and kneels on the platform. She violently pushes him and knocks him off of the platform, falling to his death. She heard his bones crack as his internal organs were bruised and damaged. She goes back to the agent she stabbed in the chest and cuts into his heart. More blood showers out of his chest as it spills on the platform. She kicks him down as he falls to his death, suffering the same fate as the other agent.

Phoenix runs to the door and budges through, revealing a hallway that's lit by beige lights. She sees more agents scattered around the hallway as they aim their weapons at her. She pulls out her assault rifle and shoots all of them in their heads. She felt numb after they all thudded to the ground. Their blood spreads around as it forms circles around their bodies, creating a large puddle of blood.

Phoenix walks over the agents as puddles of blood splash from her footsteps. All she saw was red in her eyes as she looked down on their deceased bodies. She overrides the door ahead of her and sees a room filled with agents. It was organized like a lobby room. There were desks and filing cabinets as there was a checkered floor. All of the agents were startled and aimed at her.

Phoenix raises her weapon and fires at their heads as some of them have brain matter exit out of their skulls. She runs to the double doors ahead of her and sees the outside world. The skies were still cloudy and dark. She was surprised by the two agents guarding between the doors. They were about to attack, but Phoenix blocked them just in time. She uppercuts them both with her daggers in the chin at the same time. The daggers went through the roofs of their mouths as the sharp metal can be seen inside. They were gagging as blood came out of their neck and mouth. She pulls the daggers out and kicks them to the ground.

Ahead of Phoenix was a fence that surrounded the perimeter of the base. She looked back to see the base's establishment number, 00012. "No wonder it was so big,"

Phoenix said. She looked to see black armored SUVs and Arma tanks bearing the IFHR insignia. She didn't see the orange Lamborghini parked anywhere. "Shit, I guess I'll use one of the SUVs." While running to one of the SUVs and getting inside, she realized something in her head. She gasped, "I have to find Darrell and Alice. I better find them fast!"

Phoenix starts the vehicle and reverses, facing the fence's front gates. She puts it in drive and plows through the gates, damaging the lock in the middle of them. There was a refinery in the distance as the building emitted black smoke into the sky. She noticed it was another base as there was a building that showed the establishment number, 00013. She accelerates into the long straight road to find Alice and Darrell.

Chapter 32: Numbing of the Pain

Phoenix accelerates on the road as she looks over the SUV's weapon systems. The vehicle has the same capabilities as an elite vehicle. "Her head will be mine," she said to herself. The fence still kept going in the distance as she kept accelerating. The fence revealed that it was a large area owned by Base No. 00012. She notices a few agents in a couple SUVs about to pull away from the gates and turn onto the asphalt. They were driving on dirt roads by the gates.

Phoenix activates the shotguns along with the heated

ammunition type. She fires one round at one of the agents' SUVs, making small dents on their sides. She accelerates past them as they turn and pursue her. "That's right, you follow me. I'll strip you off the road," she said as she saw the agents in her rear-view mirror. "Let's see if you like to be blown away." She activates the mortars by the rear bumper and aims at them with the target screen.

Phoenix fires one mortar, but the agents dodge just before it could make its impact. The mortar exploded as it made a small crater on the road. The agents behind her started firing machine guns at her rear bumper. The agents start accelerating, gaining distance with Phoenix. She isn't intimidated, "That's right, you keep shooting."

Phoenix switches back to the mortars. "Because you should know your limits when it comes to planning bittersweet revenge when you kill off the ones that are dear to you." She locks on and fires the mortar at one of the agents. The mortar creates a shock wave and impacts the agent's vehicle, destroying it as it explodes and parts go everywhere. The mortar created a chain reaction as it affected the other agent. The other agent swerved and rolled over multiple times into the dirt as large pieces of metal come off of it. She looked in the rear-view mirror as she felt numb from the explosions, "Go to hell, you bastards." The agents' vehicles are burning as they are engulfed in flames. "I'm coming for you, Alice, and I WILL kill you!" She accelerates and follows the path of what she's hoping is an IFHR base in the distance.

Chapter 33: Bloodlust

1624 hours

Phoenix notices a large building in the distance as the clouds above it were gray and thundering. "That must be the other base," she said. She leaned her head forward to see the base's establishment number, 00017. "Where would the first base be?" She looked to the side to see that there was a large group of sports cars and supercars. She doesn't see the Lamborghini. "Where the hell is the Lamborghini we have?" Surrounding Base No. 00017 was a fence along with Arma tanks and black SUVs.

She reaches the front gates of Base No. 00017 and slowly pulls in, slowly driving around for an entrance. While turning on a corner, she notices the tathered Lamborghini that Darrell drove. She turns around the base to park by the entrance, which has silver steel double doors. The entire base was made of steel.

She walks up to the doors and overrides the security pad. "Better count your blessings now, Alice," she said. "Because I'm coming for you!" The doors slowly slide open, revealing a large room with raised floors and platforms scattered around. The floor was lit by dashed yellow lines as the walls were lit by white dashes. The colors of the walls were the mix of dark green and navy blue.

There were agents scattered around on the floor and platforms as they all draw their attention to Phoenix and ready their weapons. Phoenix draws her black dual pistols and aims them at the agents. She gives a bold facial expression. "Give it your best shot, boys!" Phoenix yelled. "Because there's plenty more of where these bullets came from!"

Phoenix bolted to the side and sprinted to one of the raised floors. "Get her!" one of the agents yelled. The agents on the ground fire their assault rifles at Phoenix as the ground becomes a pulse-pounding kill zone. Phoenix narrowly escapes as she sprints up the raised floor. She sets foot on the platform and readies her assault rifle. She shoots and already kills a couple agents. She puts her firearm away and pulls out one of her swords. One of the agents pulls out one of his daggers and attempts to strike Phoenix, but she blocks him. She slides under and slashes him in the ankle, making him tip over. She get up and grunts as she slashes a deep and clean cut through his hip, killing him. She runs up to another agent and slices him in the face and chest, killing him as well.

Phoenix sprints to the other side of the platform and pulls out her dual pistols. She clings onto the wall and performs a wall run. She aims at the agents running on the raised floor and shoots in an alternating pattern, delivering headshots one by one.

Phoenix jumps off of the wall and returns to ground level, charging at the remaining agents. The agents surround her, forming a circle. There were ten of them. Phoenix wasn't intimidated from their arrogant looks. They all each pull out a blade. Some were swords as others were daggers or knifes. She gets ready and looks at them with determination while in a defensive stance.

Two of the agents charge at her and prepare to swing at her. Phoenix blocks them just in time before they could strike. She kicks one in the knee, knocking him off balance and cuts him in the collarbone. She blindly swings at the other agent in the front of his chest as blood pours down on his suit.

Six of the agents charge at Phoenix and swing at her with their daggers and knifes. She quickly draws her daggers and strikes a couple through their necks. She dodges from a close encounter by one of them and stabs through the back of his skull. She yanks it out as blood squirts out from the agent's head and charges at two of the agents. The agents swing at her, but she blocks. She takes both of her arms and stabs them through their chins at the same time, killing them instantly. She pulls the daggers out as they fell to the ground. She charges at the agent with the last agent with the daggers. She jumps and uppercuts him in the neck, exiting through the back of them. She yanks out the dagger and puts them back in her suit.

The two remaining agents charge at Phoenix with swords and swing at her. Phoenix blocks their attacks and strikes them in their hips, making them kneel to the ground. She charges her sword and slashes them through their skulls, cutting off half of their heads. She looks down at the dead agents with rage and sprints under the platform.

There was a large security door ahead of Phoenix that was eighty feet tall. "I know you're somewhere, Alice. Best prepare yourself," Phoenix said to herself. She takes her communicator and overrides the security pad.

As the door opens, it revealed a large room that's lighted from white thin lines in its corners. As Phoenix looked straight ahead, she saw Alice Walker with her arms folded. Phoenix looked past her and was shocked as she saw Darrell chained up inside a cage by his arms and legs. He was wearing nothing but a pair of underwear and a taped mouth. There was a red digital timer above the cage. "So, how do you like change?" Alice said brazenly while looking at her fingernails.

"Nothing makes anything better. Killing you won't

change the fact that you killed my family," Phoenix said, aggravated.

"It's what we do in the organization, Phoenix. That's how it's always been." Alice walks around the room and smiles arrogantly. "Hey, I'm in the same boat as you are." Phoenix only expresses hate and disgust as Alice talks. "When I was your age, I was estranged by my parents. I started rebelling when I was fifteen. Got into trouble, trouble was the only thing I knew. I was never guided properly by my parents. They were never there for me."

"And why the hell should I care?"

"So, I started to do things my way. I ran away from home and practiced homicidal activity to make a living. I was so grateful to have IFHR recruit me. It gave me another chance to see the world again."

"So, your way of spreading the message is through killing innocent lives all because you were such a spoiled little bitch when you were a kid?"

"I never liked my parents' rules. They're long gone, now. They fell ill when I was sixteen. Never got a chance to say goodbye."

"That's your own damn fault. You should've took a look in the mirror before you fell into that sickness that we call temptation!"

"Let's not get too sidetracked here. Let's focus on Darrell for a minute. You see him in that cage back there?" Phoenix looks at the cage and gets enraged. "Under him is a large pool with old, shorted out wires trying to trade electrical current." There were small crooked waves of static popping out of the pool and making crackling noises. Alice slowly pulls out both swords from behind her back. "There's a twenty minute timer on him. With every second that drops down, the cage lowers and gets closer to the pool. Once the timer hits zero, the water will enter the cage and electrocute him, frying him until he's nothing but an overcooked corpse of what was SUPPOSED to be an easy target!" Phoenix gets more enraged.

Alice walks to the side of the room and presses a red button on the wall, activating the timer above the cage as it's going down. The cage lowers as the hydraulics make a noise above Darrell, causing him to whimper and panic."You see, Phoenix. The organization is very complex in its methodical structure of execution. And I have a feeling that you understand at least part of it. You've killed off a countless number of us in the organization, we negotiated that you could be one of us. You should try it, maybe we can work together," Alice said.

Phoenix pulls out her other sword and holds both of them, "Barrett may have took Warren by refusal, but when it comes to you and me." Phoenix gets in a defensive stance. "I'd rather choose death before dishonor!"

"Well, in that case, we can fight to the death just the way you like it!"

Phoenix and Alice charge at each other and engage in a duel.

Chapter 34: Death Before Dishonor

1641 hours

Phoenix and Alice swing at each other as they grind with brute force. They step back and parry at each other and swing again. Phoenix goes for Alice's hip, but Alice blocks her. Alice kicks her in the diaphragm and knocks Phoenix back, but she doesn't fall. Alice charges at her and swings at her. Phoenix blocks her attack and swings at Alice. They keep swinging at each other until they grind against each other's swords. "So, should I slow down for you or are you ready to give up?" Alice taunted. Phoenix breaks Alice's parry and walks up to her. "I don't give up on family. Family never dies!" Phoenix yelled.

Phoenix swings multiple times at Alice with brute force as this caused Alice to back into a wall. Just before she could touch the wall, Alice jumps and swings one of her swords, but Phoenix ducks just in time before Alice could strike. Alice takes her fist and punches her hard in the cheek, making Pheonix fall to the ground. Alice charges and raises both of her swords up in the air. Phoenix rolls to the side before Alice could execute her.

There were eight minutes left on the timer. Darrell was panicking as he was getting closer to the pool. Phoenix quickly gets up and sprints behind Alice's back. She takes her arm and puts Alice in a forceful headlock. Phoenix says in her ear, "So, you want to try to try something new?" Alice is struggling as she's gagging from her grip. "You'll be slipping just like the rest of them. Time for you to pay your debt after what you've done!"

Alice kicks her in the knees as Phoenix's knee was free. She stuns Phoenix and throws her to the ground in a short distance. Phoenix drops her swords as one of them skids far to the side. Alice walks up to her as she shows an expression of hubris. "So, you really think you could get this far?" Alice said. She stops walking and prepares her swords. "I got you in the crosshairs. You have no more family to run to now. Warren's dead, your parents are dead, you have NOBODY now!" She kicks Phoenix hard in the hip a couple times while she's still laying on the floor. "And now we can finally end this once and for all!" Phoenix coughs as she can feel the bruise in her hip. "I'll give you a chance right now, I'll let you, only you, survive. You can either surrender and let Darrell die, or you can join me and I'll give you a chance at life again."

Phoenix looks at Darrell as he still panics, begging her in his muffled voice. "We would all love to have another chance," Phoenix said. Darrell muffles a loud "NO!"

Phoenix quickly takes her sword and stabs Alice in the diaphragm. It exits through her back. She gags as blood comes out of her mouth. Phoenix gets up as she yanks out the sword. "But I don't believe in committing homicide to prove a point! Especially when you killed my family!" Phoenix yelled. She pushes Alice to the ground and pins her down. She pulls out two of her daggers, "And here's your one-way ticket to hell!" She takes the daggers and stabs them deep into both of her eyes. Blood gushes out of her eye sockets as Phoenix can hear the daggers enter through her brain. Phoenix yanks them out of her eyes and gets up. She looks down at Alice's body and feels release, but is still angered by her parents' death and the overall situation.

Chapter 35: Escape

Five minutes were left on the timer. Phoenix rushed to the cage as she saw it getting lower, making Darrell panic even more. He was moving his body around as he makes a muffled cry for help. "Don't worry, Darrell. Just calm down, the power switch is right here!" Phoenix said. She runs to the lever that has the word POWER above it. She pulls it down with brute force as the lever is heavy. She grunts as she continues to pull it down. The lever makes a loud circuit noise as the timer disables and the water stops crackling from the power source.

Darrell takes a deep breath and closes his eyes. Phoenix realized there was nothing to unlock the cage beside the power switch. "Shit, where's the keys?" She draws her attention at Alice's body and runs to it. "Maybe she has it. I'll be back, Darrell." Darrell makes another muffled cry as he panics again.

Phoenix crouches down and searches Phoenix's body for the cage's keys. "Come on, where the fuck are they?!" She felt something in Alice's pocket. She reaches in her pocket and pulls out a set of keys. "Fucking bitch." She runs back to Darrell and unlocks the gate. She pulls open the door and grabs Darrell. She pulls him out by his upper body first. Her body shakes as she carries his weight. She almost tips over as she drops Darrell to the ground. "Damn, you're fucking heavy!" She goes to Darrell's aid and pulls out one of her daggers. She cuts the bands around his hands and legs behind his back and turns him around. She quickly pulls off the tape on his mouth like a hair wax strip. Darrell yells from

the tape as his mouth was red. "Are you alright?" Phoenix

said.

"I'll be fine, that woman stripped me down. It's getting

worse," Darrell said.

"I know, you don't have to tell me that twice. She killed

my parents." She looks at Alice's body in the distance.

"What's next for us, Phoenix?" Darrell said.

Phoenix hesitated, "We'll find out soon enough, but first,

we have to find your clothes. They can't be far away from this

room. Do you need help getting up?"

Darrell takes his arms and pushes away from the ground

to stand himself up. "Wasn't in a coma. Only lasted for a

couple hours," Darrell said. Phoenix overrides the door

beside the power switch and enter a dark hallway. She turns

the flashlight on with the communicator and shines it

throughout the hallway. She whispers, "Doesn't seem like

there's any agents around here. Don't hear any footsteps.

Where do you think you last had your clothes?"

"They're in the room next to the way you came from to

fight her. It's behind us."

Darrell and Phoenix turn around and walk to the door

beside the room that's open. Phoenix prepares to override

the door, "Stand back, Darrell. Hold it in for too long and the

electrical overload will throw you back. That's what

happened to me when I broke into your room in the base

back at D.C."

Phoenix overrides the door and enters the room. The

room's lights automatically turned on after they detected

their movement. There were groups of neatly creased suit

arrangements that had the traditional colors of the IFHR

attire. Darrell's clothes were on the floor as they were thrown

around the room. His weapons were also scattered around

the floor. She looks up at the security cameras planted in the corners and yells, "That's right, keep documenting

everything. IFHR's going to be famous. You're no longer a

secretive conspiracy sting anymore now. You're in the media,

just like how everyone was saying before!"

"Phoenix, don't yell! They could still be around the

building somewhere. Let's get out from the way you came in.

Is the Lamborghini still there?"

"It's parked by the side of the building. Still looks the

same as before."

Darrell scrambles as he puts on the clothes of his suit

and re-equips his weapons. "You ready?" Darrell said.

"That's a stupid question, Darrell. You know the answer

to that."

"Then, let's go! Let's get out of here! The uprising may

get worse!"

They sprint through the room Phoenix killed Alice in. "It's

not getting worse, Darrell. It's getting better, they're routing for us!" They exit the torture room and enter the room with the agents' dead bodies. They exit out of the base and sprint to the car.

Darrell and Phoenix enter the vehicle and work their way out of the base's perimeter. As they enter the road, they pinpoint the coordinates to their jet. "Surprise!" Russell said with arrogance through the communicator. Phoenix switches to Russell's frequency and yells in rage, "I will fucking kill you! I warned you not to try anything, but you crossed the line!"

"And I should be scared of you? You break the rules, you get the punishment. There are consequences when a rebellious child falls into disobedience."

"How funny of you to say! You won't be laughing when I have you in my death grip!"

"Time for the eighth Trial. This one will take place in Rome, Italy. This target will be a male as he worked in the organization for three years. That's all the information.

You've pushed my buttons for far too long this time!"

"Well, I don't have sympathy for omnicidal maniacs like you!"

Russell dismissed. "What's the news, anything?" Adrian said as his voice was distorted.

Phoenix switched to Adrian's frequency. "Alice killed my parents. They really pushed the fucking envelope this time," Phoenix said, enraged.

"Where's your next trial?"

"It's in Rome, Italy." Adrian suddenly gasped, "Are you serious?"

"What?! What's going on in Italy?!"

"I've been tracking my brother. He's on his way there right now! Come to Los Angeles as fast as possible! By the time you land, I'm organizing to come with you guys! I can't let them get to my fucking brother!"

"Can you find the target?!"

"Yes, he's on his way there, too." Two red dots are blinking on the sky blue map at the auto shop as they are located at the eastern region of Europe. "By the rate they're going, however, we only have a few days to get over there."

"What's his name?"

"Nero Armetta. Age: 30. Hair color: Black. Skin color: Pallor-Caucasian. Weight: 179 pounds. He's a madman. He's not a guy to mess around with. He's known to kill people in ways that are disturbing in nature. He's already killed over three hundred people since his initiation in IFHR. Get over to Los Angeles before Nero gets to Rome first."

"You heard him, Darrell. Step on it. We have to get to his brother."

Darrell accelerates as they eventually head back into D.C. to get to their jet. They take off and prepare to meet up with Adrian in the ruins of Los Angeles.

Chapter 36: Briefing

April 7, 2021

Los Angeles, California, United States, 1232 hours

Darrell and Phoenix roam around the ruins of Los Angeles as the skies were as clear as the ocean, showing the devastated buildings and totaled vehicles on the roads. Some of the vehicles were scattered in multiple places as some were heavily distorted and twisted in shape from the start of the Civil War of 2020. People on the streets were kneeling down and crying as the sights around them kept reminding them of IFHR's destruction of the city. Phoenix shakes her head negatively as she sees a woman crying on the sidewalk and says to herself, "You're not alone, I'm in the same boat as you are."

After a few minutes of roaming, they see the abandoned auto shop. They notice Adrian making hand gestures to get their attention. "There's Adrian, pull up to there," Phoenix said. Darrell slows down and turns in front of the garage door. He straightens the wheelbase as Adrian sprints away from the garage door. "What's he doing?" Phoenix said.

"There's probably a door by the side of the building," Darrell said.

There was a small pin hole by the side of the building that was by a square tile that resembled the texture of the auto shop. Adrian walks up to the wall and pulls out a small hex key and enters it into the hole by the square. He turns the key as the square flips open and reveals a security pad. He manually puts in the combination without overriding. Part of the side of the wall slowly opens. He walks through the kitchen as the wall closes behind him. The wall that closed was right next to one of the kitchen counters. He goes to the garage and presses on the hand scanner to open the garage door.

Darrell and Phoenix were surprised that the door was opening. "How in the hell did he get in with no outside doors?" Darrell said.

"Like you said, there may be something around the building," Phoenix said. Darrell pulls into the garage as they see Adrian giving hand signals to slowly pull forward. "Come on, just a little more!" Adrian yelled. Darrell fully pulls the Lamborghini into the garage as he parks it.

Adrian runs to the Lamborghini and looks at the overall damage. He was shocked as he gasped from the several bullet holes, dents, scrapes, and chipped paint areas surrounding the vehicle. He signals Darrell and Phoenix to get out. They get out of the car and walk to Adrian. "Holy shit, guys! The damage to the car!" Adrian yelled, panicking.

"We couldn't find any special repair shops on the way," Darrell said.

Adrian suddenly calms down and breathes heavily, "Hey, better safe than sorry. Elite-class vehicles can put up a good fight, huh?"

"I don't think it'll last longer after all of the combat it went through. Although, we've been getting away from vehicular combat in the last couple trials," Phoenix said.

"You're right, but by the looks of it, most of your Lamborghini's armor is still intact. However, it seems that it can only survive a couple more emergency combat situations judging by its condition."

"Put Alice right in her place after she killed my parents," Phoenix said, enraged.

"I'm really sorry to hear about that, Phoenix."

"What are we going to do now?" Darrell said.

Adrian looks down and sighs, thinking of a solution. He

looks at Phoenix, seeing the pain and hatred in her eyes.

Something pops in his head, "Alex, my brother!"

"What's wrong?!" Phoenix said, concerned.

"Rome, Italy, remember?! He's heading there right now

along with Nero! We have to get weapons ready and load the

vehicles onto your jet!"

"Then, what are we waiting for?!" Phoenix yelled. Her

and Darrell start sprinting to the Lamborghini.

"NO, we can't leave just yet!" Adrian yelled, stopping

them from getting in their car.

"Then, what the hell do you want us to do, Adrian?! Do

you want your brother to be killed?!"

"I don't want my brother dead, but we have to plan first!

Follow me to the computer room!" Adrian storms to the

kitchen door as Darrell and Phoenix follow him. They enter

through the kitchen. "And how did you manage to get inside?

There wasn't a door before," Phoenix said. They stop walking as Adrian points to the wall beside the counter. "That was actually a door. The organization always kept hiding their secrets, you should've known this by now," Adrian said.

They run up to the computer room as Adrian rushes to bring up the map and database. "Let's see where my brother's at," Adrian panicked. He clicks on the map to zoom in between Russia and the continent of Europe. He finds two red blinking dots slowly moving as they were separate. "I found one blip in Belarus right now. They're in Minsk." He clicks on the dot and checks the profile. "That's my brother." He clicks on the other dot. "The other one's in Kiev, Ukraine." He clicks on the dot to view the agent's profile. He was shocked as he gasped. "Shit!" He yelled.

"What?!" Darrell yelled. Adrian pointed at Nero's dot, "There's Nero. He's heading the same way as Alex, and it's not very far from Rome."

"How much time do we have?" Phoenix said.

"Well, from the rate of speed they're going right now, we have just about a day to book out of Los Angeles."

"Well, then we better get moving. If it involves family, then what are you waiting for?"

They head out of the computer room and stand by the wall Adrian broke that was beside Russell's bedroom, which held the weapons and armory. He puts in the combination for the safe door and opens it with brute force. They go down the steps and revisit the weapon displays containing a large assortment of firearms. They walk to the pistols and assault rifles. "Are there any weapons you guys need to change? Now's the opportunity. I don't think you'll need armor for this one."

Darrell and Phoenix go to the pistols as Darrell picks up another scattershot pistol, which was white. Darrell cocks the pistols as they were full of ammunition. "Shotguns, uzis, you name it, I got you covered!" Adrian yells. He walks to the

shotguns and uzis as he pulls out a white shotgun.

The color schemes of the firearms share minor

characteristics with each other. For white firearms, the

bullets either spread out or disperse into fragments. For gray

firearms, bullets have a sharp pointed tip and are heated to

create a burning sensation. As for the black type, they have

the standard characteristics as they had no modifications.

"Guys, come here, you're getting an upgrade," Adrian said.

Darrell and Phoenix walk to Adrian and check out the

shotguns and uzis. "Looks like you've been paying attention

to the way they organize their work. We're going to go with

all white weapons this time. You guys ready for this?" Adrian

said.

"You know the answer, Adrian," Phoenix said.

"That's a wise answer, Phoenix." Adrian cocks one of the

shotguns and throws it to Phoenix as she catches it. "Because we're going to give them one hell of a storm by the time we get there!" He grabs two more shotguns, one to throw at Darrell and one for himself. "Each of you get a pair of Uzis and ammunition, too. There's still plenty left."

They go into the ammunition room and grab shotgun shells and magazines. "After this, we're not hesitating, we're going with full force!" Adrian said.

"I'm with you on that, Adrian," Phoenix said, cocking her shotgun. They walk out of the ammunition room as Darrell and Phoenix stay behind him. "When we get to the garage, I want you guys to wait for me. You guys pull out first, but I'm taking the lead this time," Adrian said.

They walk out of the weapon storage and make their way to the garage. When entering the garage, Darrell and Phoenix walk to the Lamborghini. "Before I open the door, I'll let my vehicle down to avoid suspicion. Even though the city's in the dark right now, they could still be lurking," Adrian said.

He goes to the platform carrying his white Audi and lowers it down by a lever on a wall until it touches the floor. Adrian rushes to the garage door and places his hand on the hand scanner. The door slowly rises open, projecting the clear skies outside.

Darrell backs out of the garage and turns to face the road. "Wait for me," Adrian said through the vehicle's communication system. Adrian backs out and turns until his rear bumper faces Darrell. The garage door slowly lowers until it touches ground. "Let's get out of here, go full throttle."

They accelerate as they make their way to the airport. "What trial is this one?" Adrian said.

"The eighth one," Phoenix said.

Adrian sighed, "I don't know about this one, guys."

"Just keep your eyes peeled on this one. We can't accept failure this time."

"I'll be operating the jet. You'll take the back seats," Darrell said.

"I didn't associate with aerial vehicles in the organization. I trust you with this."

As they head into the airport, Darrell gets in the jet and opens the rear hatch as they pull the vehicles inside its interior. As they all get inside the jet, they get themselves ready for takeoff towards the city of Rome.

Chapter 37: The World Will Soon Know

Rome, Italy, 1931 hours

Darrell and Adrian were roaming through the eloquent streets of Rome. The buildings were historic in appearance as they were irregularly, but neatly layed out. Some buildings were even conjoined. The buildings' signs and lights illuminated the city as the streetlamps added to it. The transportation was mostly made up of sports cars and supercars. Almost every country has that level of transportation. The people walking on the sidewalks looked at their vehicles as they were surprised by the way Darrell's looks. "Just ignore them," Adrian said. "The entire world will soon know about them."

Darrell and Adrian hear vehicles from the commute beep their horns loudly behind them in the distance. Adrian notices two supercars showing their high beams as they weave and cut people off in traffic. "But I would keep your eyes peeled if I were you," Adrian said.

"Why, what's wrong?" Darrell said.

The two supercars accelerate to Darrell and Adrian. They realized they were agents as they shoot a couple rounds from their vehicles' machine guns. The bullets startled Darrell. Phoenix looks in her side mirror and pulls out one of her machine pistols, cocking it. She looks at Darrell, "We have company!"

The agents continue firing as they accelerate closer towards Darrell and Adrian. They all drifted into another street as they left thick trails of smoke. They were already ten feet away from them. Adrian tenses his body and grunts as he hears the bullets impacting his Audi, "Don't fire yet, hold your fire!"

"Why?! They're fucking agents!" Phoenix said.

"Exactly, but we're going to do things differently. Let them pass us." Adrian activates his machine guns and presses a button with arrows carrying a flame behind them. "Because if IFHR's plan is to organize in secrecy, then I've got a few tricks up my sleeve."

The agents pass as they roll down their windows and shoot a few rounds with their assault rifles, almost webbing Adrian's window and barely snowing Darrell's. The agents resume firing as they shoot from the rear. Adrian begins firing his machine guns, but the bullets were buzzing at a blistering rate of speed. Darrell and Phoenix have never encountered that type of machine gun ammunition before. Darrell was in shock, "Phoenix, look!" Phoenix was in awe as she heard the buzzing of Adrian's machine guns. "He must have installed it!"

Adrian yells as he continues to fire at the agent's rear bumper in his lane. "Come on, shoot them, damn it!" he yells. Darrell activates the machine guns with the magnetism and pointed ammunition and fires at the supercar in his lane. Adrian was able to penetrate through the agent's rear bumper and puncture his vehicle's tires. The supercar ignites in flames and flies in the air, hitting the wall of a building as parts and fragments of twisted metal are picked off of the vehicle. Adrian turns his weapons to aim at the supercar Darrell's shooting at. He shoots the supercar at its side as Darrell continues to fire at the rear. The supercar explodes and engulfs in flames as it flies in the air and hits a building. "How the hell did you do that?!" Phoenix said, referring to Adrian's machine guns.

"I modified the vehicle myself. It has different enhancements placed into it," Adrian said. He looks down in his navigation system and finds a red blinking dot that's close

in the distance. "They're not far from here, follow my lead!

I'm picking up a blip nearby." Adrian accelerates past Darrell

as they go after the blip.

Chapter 38: Estrangement

1956 hours

"We're about a couple turns away from the blip. They're not moving," Adrian said. They take a right and then a left to see where the blip is leading them. "No way." Adrian was shocked.

"That's his car," Darrell said, surprised. They see Alex's Mazda parked beside a local bar in the city. The bar was about the height of five stories as it was between two buildings that's three times taller than it.

"Looks like he made it there first. Doesn't look like any

agents are surrounding the bar," Adrian said.

"Why would he be at a bar?" Phoenix said.

"Maybe a place to take a break, but unfortunately, we've been estranged since we escaped from the organization's reach."

"Are you guys close at all? He didn't deliver any bad seeds when he mentioned you. He seems to have a sense of humor."

They park next to Alex's Mazda and get out of their vehicles. They walk up to the entrance of the bar. "Self-deprecating?" Adrian resumed. He had two gun straps to his back, holding his shotgun and machine pistols.

"That would be the correct answer," Phoenix said.

"Well, let's hope he's able to recognize me after a couple years of absence."

Adrian quietly opens the doors as they screech. Inside the bar were rectangular ceiling tiles and chandelier light fixtures. There were three counters. A serving counter to the side, a serving counter in the middle, and a table for socialization. Adrian notices Alex waving a white pistol in the air. He was wearing the traditional IFHR attire. Alex panics and yells as he tries to explain the situation to them. The people around the tables and counters were scared and petrified. "Listen up, people!" Alex yelled. "There's a war coming. They're going to kill us all if nobody does anything!"

"Sir, calm down!" one of the bartenders yell. Alex pauses and quickly turns his head around, walking to the bartender. He points the pistol at him, "Calm down? Calm the fuck down?!" He looks at the bartender in desperation and frustration, talking like a maniac, "I don't fucking know who the hell are you tell me 'to calm down,' sir. You don't even know what you're going up against!" The bartender gets so overwhelmed with fear from the pistol, he actually sheds a tear.

Alex walks around the bar's floor as he makes eye contact with everyone. "There's an organization out there that's been in hiding for over three decades. It has been talked about in all of your mainstream news broadcasting stations. Nobody knew what it really was, until now. It was the organization that was founded by the current president of the United States, Donovan Lavensa. There were two people that fought against the organization since 2019." He suddenly snaps, "That's when it got really out of hand, but for a good cause. In New York City, the police reported the incident of a dangerous car chase and shootout."

"ALEX!" Adrian yelled, startling him to get his attention. Alex turns his head and looks at Adrian, Darrell, and Phoenix standing by the entrance doors. Alex was surprised to see them. "Adrian?" Alex said calmly in relief. He smiled and walked towards Adrian.

"Come here, man. I'm here now," Adrian said, letting his

arms out. Him and Alex embrace to give each other a hug.

"I thought I would never see you alive again," Alex said in relief. They let go as Alex walks back to where he was. "Stand by me, Alex. I want the other two to stand by me as well. The people need to hear this. And lock the doors just in case we get uninvited guests," Adrian said. Adrian locks the doors by the doorknobs as they walk towards Alex and look around the people. They saw that the people were confused and still scared. Alex begins a speech, "I, Alex Wortham, would like to introduce my brother, Adrian. The other two were the targets, Darrell Friegman and Phoenix Leyton. They became the FBI's most wanted for vehicular assault and manslaughter, but they dropped charges soon after doing a deep and thorough investigation. They investigated the government's affiliation with IFHR, the International Foundation of Human Resources. Don't let the friendliness of the company's name fool you! Ever since the Civil War of

2020 broke out, they already decimated the United States' capital and two of the largest cities in the nation, Los Angeles and Miami. They are now both in ruins. They even decimated the city of Dubai, which used to be a peaceful and beautiful paradise!" Alex stomps on the ground and yells, "But they turned it into a FUCKING ruin that melted down in a single instant! And if somebody doesn't do anything now, then YOUR city will be next! They will stop at nothing to kill every single person off in existence!"

Suddenly, everybody was startled from the loud knocking of the entrance doors. They hear yelling from outside as there were also loud whistling engines of supercars pulling up to the bar. Alex wasn't intimidated, but the people were scared. He readies his white pistol as Adrian, Darrell, and Phoenix to the same. "Best find a place to hide, everybody," Alex said. He looks at the group beside him, "Get you weapons ready and find a place to hide. They could go in all directions and shower these people with fucking bullets and kill most of them, if not all. We're going to protect our freedom from this hell!"

The knocking was getting louder as the agents' yells increase in volume. Alex yells at the top of his lungs, "Come on, you motherfuckers! We don't have all day! Come and get us, come fill us with lead like the fucking cowards you are!"

As the agents try budging into the doors, they actually crack and give way to the damage. As the doors grow weaker, they run around to various sections of the bar and hide, readying their weapons. The customers and the bartenders just hide under and beside the tables and counters. They squeeze the triggers of their weapons, awaiting for a standoff with IFHR.

Chapter 39: Kill Zone

2009 hours

The agents budge through the doors and aim their assault rifles in all directions as there were red laser points on their scopes. The agent standing in the middle of the men was Nero Armetta. He had black hair that was slicked back and a black goatee creasing upwards in the center towards his bottom lips. He smiles as he shows an expression of prideful arrogance as he carries a white assault rifle. "Men!" Nero yells with an Italian accent. "Let them have it! Give them everything that you've got!"

The agents fire their assault rifles around the room as they already kill a couple people. The bar already turns into a devastating kill zone. "Light them up, guys!" Alex yelled. The people start getting out of the tables and run around to find ways out of the bar, panicking from the situation. Phoenix and Darrell draw their machine pistols and get out of cover. They grin their teeth with determination as they pick off a few agents by shooting a line from their diaphragm up to their skull.

Alex and Adrian draw their shotguns and get out of cover. They run into the line of fire and shoot them in the head, making their blood and brains splatter on the wall and floor. They both get behind an agent as Adrian presses hard against the agent's back and blows a hole through him about the size of a bowling ball. Alex sneaks up behind an agent and slits a deep cut through his throat. The blood showers out of his neck as it spreads onto the floor. He collapses on the floor and dies as his blood forms a circle around him.

While Phoenix shoots down a couple more agents with her machine pistol, a couple agents run up beside Darrell. She panics, "Darrell, look out!" When Darrell looks beside him, he sees two agents charge and tackle him, pinning him down. He is struggling as the agents grab his arms and legs. One of the agents pulls out a knife and smiles with pride as he puts it by his neck.

Phoenix quickly pulls out her shotgun and aims it at the agents near Darrell. "Hey!" she yells. She fires a shell in each of their foreheads as they blow off of their bodies. Their bodies collapse to the ground. She runs to Darrell's aid and pulls him up, "You alright?"

"We'll see how calm the storm gets," Darrell said.

Darrell stands up and dual wields his pistols. Him and the rest of the group fires at the remaining agents, quickly killing them all except for one. Nero was still alive as there were blood splatters all over his suit and face. The group draw their

weapons and all aim at Nero.

Chapter 40: Standoff

2015 hours

"Well, it seems like you guys came a long way to get this far," Nero taunted. "But there's always something to watch out for."

"Yeah, we have you now, Nero. We've already showered your men with bullets. You're surrounded now!" Adrian said.

Nero turns around and faces Alex and Adrian. He looks at them in mania, "Oh, the smugglers are talking, the people who chose to back out of the organization and fight against them. That's a big infraction in our rule book. Because once you're recruited, you're one of us!"

Alex points his shotgun and aims it at Nero, "We have our reasons, but I hate to break it to you. The more people you kill, the more the media will know about you!"

"But that's what we expect from the public eye to witness. We want them to see a war coming, and it worked in the Civil War of 2020. It has very much exceeded our expectations!"

Adrian cocks his shotgun and aims it at Nero, "Well, you're going to expect a hell of a lot more if you EVER try anything gutsy!"

Nero was numb from Adrian's seriousness, "Do you think I'm scared, Adrian? We've killed so many people since the history of our organization, we're so used to it."

Alex walks up to Nero and throws him back a couple steps with his chest, "Then, why don't you try me, boy? Because I'm more than ready to kick your ass!"

Alex punches Nero in the chest and kicks him in the diaphragm. Nero bends down grunting from Alex's attacks. Nero quickly recovers and stands back up. Alex charges his fist towards Nero's face, but Nero dodges just before Alex could do damage.

Suddenly, Nero draws a switchblade and cuts deeply through Alex's diaphragm. Alex grunts from the cut and thuds to the ground. His action petrified Adrian as he gasped in shock. "ALEX!" Adrian yelled. Nero forcefully pulls out the switchblade and mercilessly stabs Alex through the chest multiple times more. Alex grunts and gags after every stab delivered to his body. Nero laughs nefariously and yells, "Does it feel good to be a smuggler?! It sure feels great when we punish those who break our rules!"

"You motherfucker!" Adrian yells. Adrian charges at Nero and forcefully pulls him off of Alex. He takes Nero and throws him against one of the counters, bruising his arms and legs and temporarily stunning him. He walks up to Nero as he's laying on the ground. Adrian pulls out his shotgun and blows Nero's leg off.

Adrian rushes to Alex's aid and crouches down beside him, brushing his head. Alex was too weak to move as he had his hand pressed against his diaphragm. "Alex, hold on," Adrian panics. "We'll take you to my place in Los Angeles. We just need something to cover the wound."

"Adrian......," Alex said. He voice was hollow from the blood coming out of his mouth. His internal bleeding gets worse as the stinging of the pain grows. "It's..... too late.... for me. You... and the targets...... are the only hope....... to restore peace..... in society... again."

Adrian wails profusely as the tears fall on Alex's body, "Alex, please, don't leave me, we can help you!"

Alex takes his other arm as it shakes from the shock in his body and put it up to his lips, "Shhhh.... Adrian...., it'll be alright. Just.... think about the positives..... in life.... instead of focusing..... on the negatives. You guys can do this. You made it..... this far, but..... you can't... give up.... now."

"I'm so sorry, Alex! I'm sorry that it came down like this!"

"Adrian...., why are you sorry? You didn't.... start the organization...... It was..... the organization.... that messed with us....., not ourselves. Think of it that way."

"I can't do this fight without you!"

Alex was growing weaker, "Yes...... you...... can......, yes...... you...... can. You just have....... to have...... faith.... and be strong...... Show that...... son of a bitch, Arkwright..... where his place.... will be."

Alex passes away as he slowly closes his eyes. Adrian continues to wail as he covers his face with his hands. He hears Nero coughing and grunting from his blown leg as the blood pumps out of the veins. He takes his hands off of his face and stands up. He walks to Nero and pulls out a knife.

"Adrian, what are you doing?!" Phoenix said. Her and Darrell run to Adrian.

Adrian crouches down and looks at Nero with rage.

"Adrian, stop!" Darrell yelled. They stopped running until they were beside Adrian.

"Back off, he's mine to kill!" Adrian said in rage. He takes his knife and stabs a deep cut through Nero's diaphragm. Blood squirts out as it spills off of his suit. He applies more force on the knife and pushes it upward, slowly carving Nero like a pumpkin. Nero starts gagging from the damage Adrian is delivering to him. He looks at Nero with hatred and revenge. "You will pay for what you have DONE!" He pushes the knife with even more force until he cuts up to where his heart is. The knife cuts Nero's heart as he gags one more time until his eyes roll to the back of his head.

Adrian breathes heavily as he carefully pulls the knife out. He stands up and looks down at Nero's body with rage.

Nero has a cut line that opened his body as it goes from his diaphragm to his heart. He wails again and slams the knife on the ground. "You fucking bastards will pay for this!" he yells. He screams in agony as he flails his arms and punches the air.

"Adrian!" Phoenix yelled. She walks up to him and grabs him, trying to calm him down. "Adrian, listen to me!" She looks at him in the eyes. She sheds a tear, "I'm on the same road as you are. They took my family, and then they took yours."

"I'm going to kill them!"

"Adrian, it's hard, I know. I would have tried harder if I could to save them, but I failed them. You have to get through it, Alex will always be in your heart." Phoenix spreads her arms out. "Come here." Adrian and Phoenix embrace to give each other a hug.

"I'm so sorry that this had to happen, Phoenix!"

"Adrian, it's not your fault. He didn't die in vain. At least you fought against them, that's what matters. You got out of there before they could kill you on the spot."

"We've all died in vain, Phoenix. IFHR killed people with no remorse, but they were killed from something that was looking for revenge."

"Did you kill anybody innocent in the organization?"

"No, but I wanted to kill the people that were working there. I never understood them. Everyone in the organization becomes dead once they're initiated, even if they don't realize it. We're walking corpses now."

"You don't have to be, at least you're alive, that's what matters."

"Alex was my only brother, he was the only sibling that I've had. I'm so fucking devastated!"

"I could explain the pain you're going through, but it's too much to bare for me as well."

Adrian lets go of Phoenix and panics, "We have to head to Los Angeles, right now."

"Why Los Angeles?"

"There's something I need to do when I get there. We need to prepare again for the next trial."

"Alright. Darrell, you heard him, let's go!"

They all run out of the bar and go to their vehicles.

"Wait, Adrian!" Darrell said. "What about Alex's car?" Adrian looks at Alex's vehicle, "We're leaving it here, we're creating all of the evidence we can get for the witnesses. This will definitely be the nightly news for the country of Italy. Pretty soon, the world will be flooded with streams of this news."

They get inside their vehicles and start driving to navigate through the city. "Tsk, tsk, that's what you get for breaking the rules, Adrian," Russell said, laughing. Adrian switches to Russell's frequency, "You're going to pay for what you've done! I will make sure that IFHR falls!"

"You're a traitor, Wortham! No matter how hard you guys try to fight and rebel, more will be coming your way, and that's a promise!"

Phoenix said through her communicator and changed her frequency, "How many do you have to bring out to realize that they're going to be killed on the spot?"

"It's a bloodsport, Phoenix. It's a thrill that can't be taken for granted. Since you broke the rules, I will not tell you the target's names. However, I will tell you where it will take place."

"You're just going to keep broadening your deathwish, aren't you?"

"I'm a jack of all trades. For the ninth trial, it'll be in a secluded area in the country of Kosovo. It will be in a forest area," Russell dismisses.

"What the?" Phoenix was surprised. She slams the communicator down on the bottom of the vehicle. "That motherfucker's just asking for it!"

"Guys, let's stay focused on what's currently going on.

Let's get to Los Angeles first and talk about it there. Your car

needs fixed to begin with," Adrian said.

As they enter the airport, they park their vehicles in the

jet and prepare for takeoff, heading back to Los Angeles.

Chapter 41: Running Empty

April 8, 2021

Los Angeles, California, 1056 hours

After resting up from the tragic and devastating passing of Adrian's brother, they all wake up and head into the kitchen. "How did you sleep?" Phoenix asked Adrian.

"Couldn't."

"Now you know how I feel."

"You guys hungry?" Darrell and Phoenix sit down at the table.

"I guess we can eat for once."

"Good, because you need energy for later. Does eggs

sound alright with you guys?"

"It's a simple idea," Phoenix said calmly.

Adrian walks to the refrigerator beside the counters and

opens it slowly. "I can't believe this is FUCKING happening!"

he yelled. Darrell and Phoenix just looked at each other, not

saying a word to respect Adrian's pain.

Adrian pulls out a full carton of white eggs and sets them

on the counter. He opens the doors of a top shelf and grabs

two skillets. He grabs a bowl on the top shelf and a metal

spatula on the bottom shelf. He places the skillets on the

heaters of the stove and turns the temperature to their

highest settings. He cracks four of the eggs on the rim and

lets the yolks fall out of their shell onto the skillets. There

were two yolks on each of them. The eggs started sizzling

once they started to whiten. "Are you going to be eating,

too?" Phoenix asked Adrian.

Adrian hesitated, "I'll eat later. You guys are more

important when it comes to this."

Adrian flips the eggs with the spatula and lets their other sides cook. After a few more minutes, the eggs were done. He goes to the top shelf and grabs two glass plates, setting them on the counter. He grabs two forks on the bottom shelf and a couple towels by the sink, which was beside the stove. He takes the spatula and scoops two eggs on each plate. He grabs the plates, forks, and towels and serves the plates to Darrell and Phoenix. He then sits down with his arms folded. "Make it quick when you eat. We need to find out who this target is," Adrian said. Darrell and Phoenix eat their eggs as they take small bites. "I fear that we'll be running out of options if we don't act fast."

"What makes you say that?" Darrell said.

"Your vehicle's almost at its critical level. After all of the damage it sustained, I don't think it'll last for too much longer if we took it out for combat right now."

"So, what are you trying to say?" Phoenix said.

"I'm saying that I have to fix it."

"How are you going to fix it? Do you even have any spare metal sheets laying around?"

"It's located in the same place where all of the weaponry is around here. I have tons of sheet metal."

"What kind of weapons were in your car?"

"Like I said, I'm a mechanic. I've found ways to modify the vehicles by switching their weapons and the performance of them. The weapon I used was a machine gun that had a very rapid rate of fire. Astounding accuracy, too. It could be at around three thousand rounds a minute. That's about ten times more than what your Lamborghini has."

"And I thought that the Lamborghini itself was powerful enough."

"My Audi's an elite class, but I figured I would modify it in case things get out of hand. You have about a minute to finish eating. We're going up in the computer room to find

out where the target is."

Darrell and Phoenix finish eating as they hand the plates,

towels, and forks to Adrian. He takes the plates and just sets

them inside the sink. "Alright, you guys ready?" Adrian said.

Darrell and Phoenix nodded their heads. They all wash their

hands by the sink and head to the computer room upstairs.

Adrian rushes to the chair by the monitors and sits

down. Darrell and Phoenix walk up to Adrian. "Alright, let's

see what we have here," Adrian said. He zooms in on the

map inside the continent of Europe. "He said it was in

Kosovo." He zooms in on Kosovo. "Looks like a small

country." He zooms in on the natural terrains and locates a

base in the middle of a mountain range. "There's a base

there, but there's a ton of mountains to move around in. It'll

be hard to get there."

"Where's it at?" Phoenix said.

"It's in the Prokletije mountain range, or "Cursed

Mountains" in the Albanian language. It extends from Albania

to Montenegro."

"Does it have the base's establishment number?" Darrell

said.

"Base No. 00003."

Phoenix was shocked, "Wow, it seems that we're getting

closer to the first base that was constructed. I wonder what

could be next after this one."

"I would keep your eyes peeled if I were you." Adrian

notices a red dot that's moving towards the base. He goes

over the dot with his mouse, but it doesn't show the agent's

profile. The text box above the dot projects a texture of static

as it produces white noise. Adrian slams his hand down on

the computer desk, "Shit!"

"What happened?!" Phoenix yelled.

"Arkwright must have known we're tracking the agents

now."

Phoenix gets frustrated, "Oh, that son of a bitch! He doesn't even realize what he's doing. How fucking gutsy of a hubristic hypocritical bastard can he be?!"

"Well, guys, you know what you have to do. Come on, let's get you to Prokletije right now." They run out of the computer room and into the garage. "I want you guys to take my Audi. I need to fix your car."

"What?! Why your car? What else does your car do?!" Phoenix yells.

"Phoenix!" Darrell yells. "It's an elite class just like ours!"

"Exactly, but I'm also going to work on your car. My car doesn't have much damage to it. They only managed to bend the front bumper a little bit, but take mine because you never know what they're capable of doing. My car has been modified to over eight hundred horsepower with enough firepower and armor to get you out of there in one piece."

"That's a lot for a sports car like that," Darrell said.

"It was only for protective reasons. I'll lower the platform so that way you can drive it out of the garage." Adrian lowers the platform until it touches the floor. "Go ahead and get in the Audi. I'll lower the garage door for you. My car drives just the same as yours, just has a different appearance."

Darrell and Phoenix get in the Audi as Adrian rushes to the hand scanner by the garage door. The scanner scans his hand as the garage door slowly opens, revealing the clear daylight skies. Darrell starts the car as Adrian makes gestures for backing out of the garage. Darrell slowly turns and straightens the steering wheel and follows Adrian's gestures. Adrian yells as it's muffled from the closed car windows, "Give it a little gas!"

Darrell gently presses on the gas and reverses towards the end of the garage. Adrian lets out his hand, "Stop!" He walks up to the Audi and points his finger down, telling them to roll the window down. "For the Lamborghini, if I work

quick enough, it'll take about a few days to a week for it to be

repaired and to work on your vehicle."

"What are you going to do to the vehicle?" Phoenix said.

"Trust me on this, guys. Let's just say I'll throw in a few

surprises while you're gone. It'll help you out and prepare for

the last trial."

"I hope you know what you're doing, Adrian."

"If I didn't know what I was doing, the whole world be on

its knees right now." Adrian looks outside as he sees the sun

shine on the buildings and streets, "Now, get out of here, the

more we waste time, the less time we have. Go full throttle

when you get out."

Darrell goes full throttle in reverse and turns his head to

look behind him. He abruptly turns the steering wheel and

faces the road ahead of him. Darrell looks beside him to see

the garage door closing. As he straightens the wheelbase, he floors it in drive and propels into the streets.

As Darrell and Phoenix arrive at the airport, they prepare for takeoff and venture towards the vast mountain range of Prekletije, Kosovo. "It's too close to call, isn't it?" Phoenix said after they ascend to five miles in the air.

"I know how you feel," Darrell said.

The conspiracy keeps unfolding with every brush of death they encounter.

Chapter 42: Prokletije

April 9, 2021

Prokletije, Kosovo, 1158 hours

Darrell and Phoenix are driving around the vast mountain range of Prokletije. The mountain range extends through the territories of Albania, Kosovo, and Montenegro. They were traveling through Kosovo at this time. The sky was covered in white clouds, but it wasn't stormy. Some of the mountains' tops were tipped with ice and snow as there was rich, green grass in scattered regions. They were driving on a road that was surrounded by the plains and terrains of the mountains. "The ninth trial, I can't believe it," Darrell said.

"This isn't a celebration, Darrell. You shouldn't feel comfortable about the end of all of this," Phoenix said.

Darrell slows down and carefully goes up a hill that's steep on its incline. The Audi has the same offroad capabilities as the Lamborghini. "Go fast, Darrell. This is a steep hill," Phoenix said. Darrell accelerates as they feel a jolt of speed, giving himself a head start towards the hill. He quickly switches gears once he drives up the hill. Their bodies pull against the seats as the incline increases. "Go faster, Darrell!"

"I'm trying, haven't drove up a mountain like this before!"

They catch their break as the incline stops increasing and the hill becomes smoother. Their bodies relax as they're not pulling against the seats. "Phew, that was close," Darrell said in relief. He turns and drives on the smooth section of hill. Darrell looks by the window to see the lush green plains below him. He was in awe and shock, "Umm, Phoenix, I think there's a base down there."

Phoenix gets tense as she was surprised, "Really? Where?!"

"Over there," Darrell points down to the ground.

"Let me see!" Phoenix looks to where Darrell is looking. The base was gray and rectangular as there was a large circle of asphalt surrounding its center. "Stop the car!" Darrell presses hard on the brakes. Phoenix brings her head closer to the window to see what's on the outside. "It's the third base, we have to get down there, now!"

Darrell turns and slowly drives down towards the ground. "Why the hell would there be an established base surrounded by a vast mountain range?" Darrell said.

Darrell eventually gets towards the base and looks at its establishment number, 00003 in large size and white characters. "Go around the perimeters in case there's anyone on the sides," Phoenix said. He gets on the asphalt and quickly circles around the base only to find that there was nobody surrounding it. "Hmm, that's strange, usually they have a large party swarming after us. Go back to the entrance, it looks like there's a way in. I saw a pair of silver doors with a security pad next to it."

Darrell circles around until he finds the entrance. The height of the base appeared more than two hundred feet tall. They get out of the Audi and sprint to the double doors. Once they stop running to the doors, Phoenix pulls out her communicator and attempts to override the security pad. She didn't succeed. "Shit!" she yelled. "Guess I'm going to put this on emergency." She sets the communicator into emergency override and resumes to surging the security pad. "Come on, you piece of shit!" she said to the communicator.

After several seconds of circuit distortion, the electrical energy has successfully surged through the base's security system as it emits a bright blue light on one side. The energy

didn't throw her back as she let go immediately after the

system surged. "The doors didn't open," Darrell panicked.

"The organization invested in advanced technology. It'll

probably take a few moments before it recognizes the

actions," Phoenix said.

The doors slowly started opening as they created noise

that's commonly heard from hydraulic machinery. As the

doors reveal the interior of Base No. 00003, Darrell and

Phoenix were in shock and awe from the complex and neat,

but mysterious structure of its layouts. "Wow," Darrell said.

"And this is the third base that's established from this

organization," Phoenix said. She looks at Darrell, "I can tell

we're getting close to something, but what is it? How did this

all start in the first place?"

They enter inside the base as they begin to explore the

mysteries of the foundations of IFHR.

Chapter 43: Too Many, Too Soon

The room they entered in was arranged with windows that were each twenty feet in length and width. The windows were separated by metallic pillars that were silver in color. There was a multitude of windows as they began walking all the way to the end of the room, which was the alleged distance of a thousand yards. The windows were stacked on top of each other as they ranged from the floor to the ceiling.

"Wow, unbelievable," Darrell said as his voice echoes through the acoustics of the room.

"It's pretty dead here. It seems like nobody's around," Phoenix said.

"Maybe it's abandoned. Their secrets could be found anywhere. Just look at the way this room looks. This is unlike any of the other bases we've seen before."

"It's past the thirtieth anniversary of the organization's founding.

"Which makes this year its thirty-first."

"Maybe there's other reasons why this all started," Phoenix said.

"It's a long way from home. It may feel too close to call now, but this is just the beginning."

Darrell was questioning Phoenix's statement, "What are your plans after all of this is over?"

"Right now, I'm afraid I can't tell you. We each have our own war to fight when it comes to standing up for the greater good in society."

"I understand."

"Sometimes you have to fight for what's right instead of what is easy."

"Because in today's world, not much of that is always common. We all get taken for granted even if we don't realize it sometimes," Darrell said.

"We lose too many people in our lives at the wrong times, too many, too soon. Sometimes too soon, it can be more than what we can handle."

"We're capable of so much. That's what scares me the most. The ways we coalesce influence us in whether they're for the good reasons or the bad ones."

"Sometimes you have to focus on yourself if you want to do what's right for you, Darrell. Not what's based on what others say you should do."

"I never really knew what I wanted to do in life. I couldn't understand the meaning of it. Sometimes I wander why I'm still alive after all that has happened."

"It wasn't your fault, Darrell. I was the one that brought you into this. It's mainly my fault that I lost my husband and my parents. I'm still ashamed to this day because I couldn't protect them. Your past doesn't define you, but it helps you learn from your experiences. It doesn't matter on what could have been, but it's what you're going to do about it is what counts. If I listened to what people were trying to tell me, I would've listened. If I was given the chance to fight harder, I would. If I had the opportunity to go back in time and get back what I've lost, I would definitely take that chance. However, what has happened already happened. The past is now history, you can't change what has already happened. I think it would be considered cheating if you try to change what could've been. If you tried, you wouldn't be successful. It'll only just make it worse. You will only let it eat you alive on the inside if you kept going back to what happened and turning back to the memories. Once it's gone, it's gone. There's nothing you can do to bring it back."

"You couldn't have said it any better than that, Phoenix."

"Life is messed up sometimes. Sometimes, so messed up, that you regret doing certain things immediately after it takes place. We've all made mistakes throughout our lives, big and small. Sometimes too costly that we live in nothing but regret. Sometimes, you have to be your own best friend because you're the only one that can truly understand yourself as a person. Trying to make somebody understand what they're going through is like trying to explain to someone what the color, yellow looks like. It's very difficult. We have our own goals and objectives that we strive to accomplish in our lives. But, yet, we're tempted to try to fit in others' shoes, it will feel uncomfortable if you keep walking in their shoes. You have to make difficult choices whenever you come to a fork in the long, curved roads of the cycle of life. You can take a road that will either benefit you or halt you in the process. These are just some of the hard facts taught in the journey of life."

"Not everyone is a ventriloquist, so why make them the puppet?"

"Exactly. In the end, what matters is that you made it through the day realizing that you're alive. When it comes to understanding the borderlines between life and death itself, the choice is ultimately yours for whatever path you take. But don't take life for granted. If you can make anybody's day whenever they're in the dark, then it won't matter how it happens. It could save somebody's life. Just remember that we're all the same. We think the same at some points, we have things in common, and we all have different stories to write with every chapter of our lives we create."

They reach the other side of the room as there was a pair of black double doors with a security pad. Phoenix pulls out her communicator and overrides the security pad. "It's all

on a day's work when you try to change lives for the better,"

Phoenix said.

"I'm with you all the way, Phoenix."

The black double doors open as they reveal a room that

looked different from the entrance. The room appeared to be

from the era of the 1990s.

Chapter 44: How It All Started

1249 hours

The room actually appeared as a workplace of an office building. However, it did show some signs of aging. There were dust particles that were shown by the light rays from windows on the sides of the room. "Wow, didn't know that they were involved with business," Darrell said. There were computers on desks that had bulky monitors and towers. There were beige cabinets on one side that extended to the other end of the room, which was allegedly a couple hundred feet away. There was nobody inside the base as the noise level was close to a dead silence.

"This is probably how it all started," Phoenix said. "But there has to be clues somewhere. Let's try looking in the cabinets."

"What about the computers?" Darrell said. Phoenix glances back at the computers, contemplating, "Actually, you might be up to something."

"Why do you say that?"

"Because if it's said to have technology ahead of their time, then there has to be a clue to how they started the conspiracy in the first place. There's still questions and mysteries that have to be solved, Darrell, and we don't have much time."

"Then let's get moving."

They go to the cabinets and pull the drawers out one by one. "There's nothing but physical documents of everyone's profiles," Phoenix said.

"These look similar from back when we discovered the

Archives. Just one of those moments of déjà vu that hits you when you least expect it."

"I still don't understand how these people could live with themselves with so much hubris."

"They don't even realize how much it has already consumed. It devoured their mentality and all they could do is just perceive life as a series of mechanical functions. We weren't made as machines, nor are we meant to be."

"That's the scary part when it comes to living."

After pulling out and finding nothing but documented profiles, Phoenix pulled out a cabinet drawer and stumbled upon a letter sized paper of four men. The tint of the paper was in sequoia. "Darrell, you might want to come look at this," Phoenix said.

Darrell stops searching in the cabinets and goes to Phoenix. Phoenix continues to study the paper as Darrell glances at it. She suddenly became shocked by the way the men's faces looked, "That's Lavensa, Arkwright and Atkinson!" President Lavensa was sitting at a desk next to Arkwright as they were wearing IFHR attire. They looked at the two men that were standing in front of the desk. Atkinson was standing by a man that had his face out in black marker. The men standing had their arms connected to their backs. "They crossed the guy out standing next to Atkinson. They must already know we're here."

"How can you tell?"

"If it was somebody else, it would probably be different in their case, but they crossed out that specific person for a reason," Phoenix said firmly. "We have to find out where this man is and who he is! There has to be more clues than just in this room!"

They run to the end of the room and come across a steel door with a security pad. Phoenix looks at Darrell and points her finger to the center of his lips, "Shh! We're going to go through quietly in case somebody's here."

Phoenix overrides the door and slowly opens it, peeking her head and quickly scanning her surroundings. There were two hallways that were naturally lit by the light from outside. Both of the hallways had windows stretching to their ends on one side. "Looks like the cost is clear from here," Phoenix whispered. "Come on!"

Darrell and Phoenix go through the door and walk into the hallways. "Looks pretty bland in these hallways," Darrell said quietly.

"It's the third base, what do you expect?"

They turn and walk into one of the hallways' paths as the windows' light shines on their bodies. "Maybe there's something in that room ahead. They always have an intricate way of covering things up," Phoenix said.

"No, shit, why do you think the people call it a conspiracy in the first place?"

They reach the end of the hallway as there was a silver, steel door with a security pad. All of the doors have security pads next to them. Phoenix overrides the door and pushes it open.

After Phoenix opened the door, she revealed a large and long room that has columns of large, black, trapezoidal computers that extended to the end of the room. "Wow," Darrell said in awe.

"Looks like we found one of the technological hubs in this base."

"These are all supercomputers. They're not just like every other computer. These can calculate a hell of a lot more than just a regular home desktop." Darrell realized that there wasn't a company name on the supercomputers, which increased suspicion. "Let's take a look at these computers. These don't look like they belong to any real-world company."

They walk by one of the computers and scan the racks

inside it. There was more than one rack as there were spaces

that separated them to the end of the room. "These appear

modern. They might've been put in here recently," Phoenix

said.

"Yeah, they look up to date." Darrell looks closely at the

racks as there several high-performance processors that were

compressed with one another. "This is pretty alarming,

Phoenix."

"Why?"

"This room may be one of the centers from where they

calculate the next person's cancellation number."

Phoenix panicked, "Oh, shit! We have to find that person

fast! We have to get out of here first! I found a door towards

the end of this room!"

Darrell and Phoenix sprint to the end of the computer

room as she quickly overrides the door and budges through.

There was a stairwell ahead of them as they ran up the stairs.

After getting off the stairs, they see three more hallways with

supercomputers on both sides. "Holy shit," Phoenix said.

"This entire base is a technological hub." She looks at the

ceiling of the hallways to notice security cameras following to

their movement. "Shit, there's security cameras! Somebody is

in this place! They're watching us right now!"

They sprint down the hallway to their right as the lightly

tinted sequoia windows shine down on the floor. "Come on,

they can't be that far!" Phoenix yelled.

As they reach the end of the hallway, Phoenix overrides

the door and budges through, going up the staircase and

revealing more hallways filled with supercomputers. "What

the hell?! There's hundreds of these fucking computers

everywhere!" Phoenix yelled. She looked at the three

hallways and noticed they started to bend. Each of the doors

at the hallways' ends begin to intersect, eventually leading to one section. She looks up at the ceiling, "Looks like we'll be taking the stairs for quite a while. It may look the same for the next couple floors."

They sprint to the hallway straight ahead of them. The hallway they entered was lit by white fluorescent tube lights that stretched down to its end. Instead of walls, the walls were actually made of glass as they can see the two hallways between them. All of the computers they ran past were quietly humming as they were still allegedly in operation. As they reach the end of the hallway, Phoenix overrides the door and budged through. There was a small glass window on the top of each door they went through. They keep running up and into the same center hallway until they reach the door leading to the seventh floor. Phoenix peeks through the door's window, "Looks like this is the last floor. I can only see one hallway."

Phoenix overrides the door and budges through once

more. They sprint at the fast possible speed towards the end

of the hallway.

Chapter 45: The Conspirator

Darrell and Phoenix entered a large room that was bright in color. The room was white as there were computer and television monitors. The monitors showed the cameras' points of view from the hallways of the lower floors. There were security cameras surrounding the ceiling's corners. The cameras and monitors appeared advanced from their time. Everything confining the room was metallic in texture, increasing its shine and brightness.

They see a man in IFHR attire standing in front of the

television monitors while having his hands connected to his back. The man was white in skin color as he was bald. "It took you two a while to get here," the man said. He turned around and looked at them with a cunning smile. Phoenix was surprised as the man looked familiar, "Steele."

"Yeah, that's right, Devin Steele. I told you I would be back."

"So, what brings you here? Did Arkwright send you, or did you just do your own thing?"

"Let's start off with the basics. All of those computers are running on ultra-high speed processors. Each of the racks have a speed of a hundred and thirty-seven petaFLOPS, or FLoating-point Operations Per Second. Peta- is after tera-."

"What are the computers for, Devin? This place looks awfully ancient for a third establishment," Darrell said.

Devin said with arrogance, "Well, judging by your knowledge, the history of IFHR have a favorable pardon for developing advanced technology and modifying its current

age. Therefore, using it to our advantage."

"Why use it on people?" Phoenix said.

"We're called IFHR for a reason. We collect data and

recruit in an attempt to create a top secret organization that

seemed to be beneficial for the greater good, but we decided

to get away from that."

"But why kill innocent people? You're not answering my

fucking question!"

"We have a maniacal appetite for receiving power for

ourselves. Our mission was to eliminate every single person

that was called out on the computers in the vast and

expansive network of our organization."

"What about the start of the conspiracy?" Darrell said.

"I was actually the one who encrypted the complex, yet

intricate code for the Number Conspiracy. A year after its

founding in 1991, the organization decided to get involved

with technology as it grow exponentially over the years. I came up with the idea with the code. It started with just numbers, a system of communications, but a couple years later in 1993, I completely reencrypted the system of numbers. In today's society, we have grown to share data, data that's too much for us to take in. Everyone has their own profile, so we were able to find out the database for everyone's identity from ages twenty-one to fifty years old. Once I hacked into the system without them knowing, it was one of the quietest security breaches that nobody knew about. It was completely harmless."

"But how did you fucking get away with it?!" Phoenix said.

"Once I hacked into the database, there was a series of numbers that were randomizing themselves on the screen. The numbers stopped and revealed a nine-digit code. It displayed the person's portrait and their general background, similar to what you would see on a driver's license."

"Were you able to switch the numbers by yourself?" Phoenix said.

"No, after the system generated the number, it was locked. I couldn't change it, but I didn't want to. So, I came up with the idea of the Cancellation Method. It's the same thing that happened to Francesco Maldonado in 2019. We were successfully able to kill over three hundred people silently just on that method over the course of thirty-one years. You guys are the only ones who were able to fight back against the system, but also the first to become the double targets " Devin laughs nefariously.

"Get real funny, because you're going to be on camera. The whole world will know what you did," Phoenix said.

Devin laughs again, "Do you think I would be sympathetic about what happens after this? We are filled with pride all around." He starts to yell, "I would like to thank my partner in crime, Russell Arkwright, and this is the reality show!"

Devin suddenly pulls out a white remote control from his pocket with a couple buttons on one side. "What the hell is that?" Phoenix panicked.

"This is one of the main controls of the system I encrypted. This base is one of the main control centers of the Cancellation Method. With just one press of the red button, it will activate its full potential. That means that it will control the world's governments' most advanced security networks. And once that takes place, the system will control everything, increasing the cancellation rate of innocent lives."

"You wouldn't dare!" Darrell said. "You don't have the nerve to do it!"

"Why do you say that?" Devin said. "Aren't we supposed to be daring?" He turned around and set the remote by the large desk below the computer and television monitors. After he set the remote down, a hole in the desk started to open and pull the remote down beneath it. The hole then closed afterwards. "But let's not too excited here. You like to fight, right?"

"I don't do it for thrill," Phoenix said. "I do it for a multitude of reasons."

"Good, because I am the ninth trial. We are going to play this game just like how Arkwright organized it." Devin pulls out two large knives and unbuttons his suit jacket, revealing a couple sets of platinum daggers and more knives. "I hope you're ready for your next challenge."

"Oh, we'd be more than obliged to accept it," Phoenix said boldly. She pulls out a couple knives. Darrell reaches into his suit jacket and pulls out a couple knives. "If I die first, the hole will open by the desk. But if you die, the world will be expecting some changes by our standards! Blood for blood!" Devin yelled.

"You're right," Phoenix said. She yelled, "BECAUSE IT WILL BE BLOOD FOR BLOOD WHEN WE'RE DONE WITH YOU!"

They charge at each other and begin the fight as it becomes a race against time. IFHR pushes the envelope of the final countdown towards a global civil war.

Chapter 46: Steele

1324 hours

Devin takes his knife and tries to strike, but Phoenix blocks his attack. Darrell takes his knives and attempts to strike Devin, but Devin blocks him. Devin performs a counter attack on Darrell by punching him in the diaphragm, knocking Darrell backwards by a few feet. Devin dodges Phoenix's attack by ducking below her arm. "Missed me, you bitch!" Devin taunted. Devin quickly gets up and punches Phoenix in the collarbone. Phoenix grunts from Devin's hard knuckles. "I'm just moments away from intensifying the magnitude of my creation!" Devin takes his knife and charges it behind him.

"Don't get your hopes up, buddy!" Phoenix said. She quickly dodges Devin's attack by the skin of her teeth and slightly nicks across his hand. The nick sliced through the thin layer of his hand, making him drop his knife. Devin grunts from the cut as he forcefully clenches his fists. He takes his other hand and pushes on his cut hand, continuing to clench his fist. He whistles with pride and yells, "Woo! That felt better!"

Devin drops his other knife and clenches both of his fists with force. He looks at Darrell and Phoenix with an expression of rage. "Now let's downsize things a little bit!" Devin said. He swiftly pulls out two daggers from inside of his jacket, charging at them immediately. Phoenix quickly pulls out two of her daggers just in time to block Devin. They started swinging at each other in multiple directions.

Devin and Phoenix catch each other in a break as they push against each other by their arms with force. "You should try to kill for the thrill like I do!" Devin yelled.

"There's no thrill in killing. It's not in my blood!" Phoenix yelled.

Phoenix breaks free from Devin and swings at him, slightly cutting his cheek from the thin layer of skin. He grunts as the blood slowly drips down from his cheek. While putting his hand on his cheek, Darrell charges and swings at him with one of his knives. Devin dodges and prepares one of his daggers. He slices a small cut through one of Darrell's palms, making him yell and drop his knives. Devin charges at Darrell and pushes him hard. Darrell was pushed back hard enough to fly back and thud to the ground, stunning him. Devin walks up to him and kicks him hard in the hip two times. "Stay put, go lay down!" Devin yelled, talking to him like a dog.

Devin drops his daggers and is now using only his fists. "Since we can't have a fair fight, we can do things my way, like the way it should be!" Devin yelled. "Drop your fucking daggers!"

Phoenix hesitated, but dropped them to the ground, "I guess we can compromise on this!"

"Finally, you're listening!" Devin and Phoenix charge and swing punches at each other, dodging and blocking each other's attacks. Phoenix dodges one of his hooks and knees him in the pelvic area. Phoenix charges and attempts to punch Devin in the hip, but Devin blocks her. He takes her arm and spins it towards her back. Phoenix was grunting as she was struggling from Devin's hold. "Let go of me, you bastard!" Phoenix yelled. Devin ignored her. He kneed her in the back and punched her hard in the back of her skull, making her fall to the ground and roll over, facing the ceiling.

Devin slowly walks up to Phoenix while expressing rage and clenching his fists. "Now," Devin said. "You're going to do things my way. You should've backed off when you had the chance."

"I don't listen to someone's company that I don't agree with."

Devin pounces on Phoenix and pins her down. He begins punching her in the chest and face. "WELL, YOU'RE GOING TO LISTEN TO ME!" He takes his hands and tightly grips around Phoenix's neck, choking her and making her gag loudly. Devin gets close to her face, "Because once I'm done with you, we will go on with our merry way."

Suddenly, Darrell gets up and charges at Devin. He saw Darrell charging one of his daggers towards his temple, but Devin grabs his arm. Devin gets up and tries to bend his wrist, making him drop his weapon again.

Phoenix was free from Devin, so she rolls over and quickly stands up, getting back in the fight. She prepares two of her daggers and charges at Devin. Devin is startled by her, losing focus on Darrell.

Devin and Phoenix return to swing their blades and

blocking each other as by grunt and yell while attacking.

Phoenix noticed that Devin's chest was in the open. She saw

her chance as she quickly took one of her daggers and stabs

through his diaphragm. Devin grunts and drops his blades,

putting pressure on his chest with both hands and bending

over.

Phoenix knees Devin in the chin and punches him where

his heart is. She grabs a hold of Devin's neck and stabs him a

couple more times in the diaphragm. She takes her hands

and tightly grips on her blades. She starts punching him in

several areas of his body, mainly his chest, face and hips. She

punches him multiple times in the eyes, already giving him

black eyes. She lastly gives him a punishing kick in the chest,

making him fly backwards and fall to the ground.

Devin groans and gags from the bruises and cuts in his

diaphragm. Phoenix walks up to Devin with rage filling her

heart, "You better shut the hell up, Steele."

Phoenix pounces on Steele and pins him down. She grips onto Devin's neck and gets in his face, "And you better listen to me! Once I'm done with you, I'm one step closer to freedom!" Devin was coughing as Phoenix's grip gets tighter around his neck. She takes one of her daggers and stabs through his heart, making Devin's face freeze and head shake vigorously from the pressure of the wound. His head begins to redden as the pressure continues to grow. She pulls out the dagger from his heart and stabs through his neck. Devin stops struggling as he didn't make any movement, dead on the ground. She breathes heavily as she looks down aggressively at Devin's face.

Chapter 47: Surge

1341 hours

Phoenix stands herself up and walks towards the computers and television monitors. "You might want to stand back, Darrell," Phoenix said. "I'm going to override the base's computer network." She takes a few steps back and pulls out her communicator. She presses E and OVERRIDE and begins the surging of the system. The communicator caused the computers to create circuit noise and distorted sounds. The electrical light and energy from the communicator was getting brighter and stronger. The room's main light was quickly being replaced by the communicator's light. The electrical energy kept intensifying as the light's magnitude continues to spread across the room. "Darrell, close your eyes and step back, damn it!" Phoenix said.

Phoenix closed her eyes tightly as she was quickly surrounded by light and large bolts of blue and white static tapping aggressively into the monitors. "This should be it!" Phoenix yelled.

Phoenix released the buttons on the communicator as the lighting of the room returned to normal. She was sweating and breathing heavily from the ordeal. The monitors returned to showing their surveillance screens in the hallways.

The hole in the desk slowly opens as it shows the remote control for the base's computer network. Phoenix runs to the desk and snatches the remote control. "Now, how the hell do you work this thing?" Phoenix said. There was a red button, silver button, and a black button. She observes the silver button that has the words, SHUT DOWN under it. The red button had ACTIVATE and the black button had TERMINATE SYSTEM. "We're going to shut down this base's system," Phoenix said.

"Why?" Darrell said.

"It'll make good evidence. We need all of the evidence we can get." She presses the silver button and watches over the monitors as they witness the halls of supercomputers whistle downward towards dead silence. "Wow, that was easy," Darrell said.

"Now, let's get out of here. There's one more trial we have to complete."

Darrell and Phoenix sprint of the control room and work their way out of the hallways. Phoenix gets into the communicator and goes to Adrian's frequency, "We got the target. It was Steele this time."

Adrian was surprised, "Shit! He's dead, now."

"Who do you think would be the next target?"

"I don't really know since Arkwright decides to be a fucking upstager on things around here!"

"You said you were working on the Lamborghini. How's that coming along?"

"I'm still working on it, it'll take about a week for me to put what I feel would help you on the last trial."

"What are you putting on it?"

"You'll see when you get back to Los Angeles. There's some hotels at Kosovo. It's best if you hide out for a little while, anyways. Try heading out of Kosovo within a few days. I'll pinpoint the nearest hotel and transfer it to the Audi's navigation system."

Darrell and Phoenix sprint back through the entrance of Base No. 00003 and make their way out of the mountain range of Prokletije. After miles of driving, they eventually head towards the Emerald Hotel in the city of Pristina, Kosovo to rest and hide out.

After a few days of resting and brainstorming about the final trial, they drive to the nearest airport and head out of Kosovo.

Chapter 48: A Way Out

April 16, 2021

Darrell and Phoenix roam through the streets of Los

Angeles as they pull up to the auto shop. The sun was bright

as the skies were clear. The garage door opens as Darrell

parks in front of it. They see Adrian standing by the side of

the garage door, signaling them to pull inside. As they pull

inside, Phoenix was curious to see a white tarp covering their

Lamborghini.

Darrell and Phoenix get out of his Audi as they see a

couple bullet holes surrounding the vehicle. "Looks like

you've been busy," Phoenix said.

"Come here, I want to show you something," Adrian said. They both follow Adrian to the covered Lamborghini. Adrian grabs a hold of the tarp by the top. "You guys ready?"

"Show us what you've got," Darrell said.

Adrian pulls off the tarp to reveal the extensive and intricate modifications of the Lamborghini. The vehicle was completely redesigned and restored as the bodywork appeared to come out of the factory. The rims were different in color as they were silver and chrome. They noticed there was a carbon fiber spoiler installed on the rear bumper of the vehicle. Darrell and Phoenix were shocked as they saw the additional weapons and modifications installed on the vehicle, both front and rear. "What the hell have you been doing all this time, Adrian?" Phoenix said in awe.

"I designed your way out. All of these weapons are considered the best and recommended in IFHR's elite classes.

It's not just the weapons I tinkered with, but I gave you a boost specifically for this trial. The elite vehicles already have heavily upgraded engine capabilities. What I've down with your vehicle is a special treat from me. I've tuned and installed parts to the engine already modified by the organization and made it better, faster, and stronger than what it was before."

"How fast does it go? Did you test it?" Phoenix said. Her and Darrell looked down and notice the Lamborghini parked on a dynamometer wheel towards its rear axle. "Yes I did," Adrian said.

Adrian walks around the vehicle and pushes a tile on the wall to reveal a security pad. After he punched in the combination, part of the wall turned around and revealed a complex computer setup, presenting lighted green and red scopes. Beside the scopes displayed multiple measurements such as torque, horsepower, and speed. Adrian showed them the vehicle's specifications by pointing at the numbers on the side of the screen. The scopes displayed a large gap from each other. "Wow! What do the scopes mean?" Phoenix yelled.

"This shows the difference of two dyno tests. These can help determine your vehicle's performance specifications," Adrian said.

"But what about the colors of the scopes? Is this a good thing?"

"The red scope is the previous test. These were high results when I checked the data. It was at nine hundred horsepower, clocked out at about two hundred and eighty miles per hour, it could go faster, but the rate of speed was slowing down by that number." He points to the green scope, "The green scope is when I modified it while you were gone."

"Damn, Adrian. That's a lot of work in a week."

"I was able to get it up to a little over thirteen hundred

horsepower. More than likely can go well over three hundred in a straight shot. Plus the driving range was greatly expanded so you can go longer without running out of gas."

"What about the weapons? Where did you get all of them?" Darrell said.

"The weapons on this vehicle were underground just like where all of the firearms and armory is." Adrian points to the areas of the Lamborghini and explains the types of weapons. "The weapons on the roof are heavy machine guns and missiles, which are capable of ripping through large holes of metal and obliterating any vehicle in the front and back of you. The weapons on the front bumper are light machine guns and automatic shotguns. The weapons on the front were specifically modified for IFHR's military vehicle fleet. That's where the bodywork had to be changed."

"I noticed that the vehicle looks different. What's with the screwed in plates?" Phoenix said.

"I also repaired the first layer of steel. The original bodywork modified by IFHR provides plenty of protection, but I molded pieces of thin, but reliable and durable metal and repainted it as the car's color."

"What's the metal made out of?" Darrell asked.

"I experimented with a multitude of metals while you were gone. There are six thin layers installed on the vehicle. Two of each that are titanium, steel alloy, and tungsten."

"Wow, that's incredible."

"I changed the tires, so that way they can run excellent on all terrains. The metal of the rims were changed to titanium-grade metal for added style and durability."

Adrian continues. "The final two weapons I installed are on the sides of the doors. They're missile ports, but they have to be activated in order to use them. They come out below from the flaps I folded onto them. You will be able to use your previous weapons along with the installed ones. I installed a control system for using the other modified weapons in the vehicle. I'll show you inside."

Adrian pulls out a steel, bulky key from his pocket and unlocks the Lamborghini through its many layers of armor. He opens the door to reveal a dashboard containing several buttons around various sections of the gauges and the passenger seat. By the center console is an added monitor for the extra weapons. Darrell and Phoenix were still in shock and awe. "This looks like this could be enough to start a small war," Darrell said.

"Oh, this isn't small for any reason. The Civil War of 2020 wasn't small. Both sides used every resource they had. Your vehicle's now a moving weapon." Phoenix had a confused look on her face, "Thought it already was."

"If you don't believe me, I can show you how strong the metal is on your car. Follow me, the testing room is beside the hall of firearms and it's underground."

Darrell and Phoenix follow Adrian through the kitchen

and enter through the crack in the hallway to demonstrate

the resistance of the Lamborghini's armor.

Chapter 49: Target Practice

1119 hours

They walk through the hallway of firearms. Adrian picks up a white shotgun and assault rifle towards the end of the hallway. "These weapons should be great for testing out the armor," Adrian said, cocking the shotgun.

"Where's the target practice?" Phoenix said.

"It's by the opposite of the armory. The testing room is large, too. It can stretch to about a twentieth of a mile."

They turn to the left as the hallway lights up from their motion. The hallway's walls and floor were gray as it was clear and translucent. They could partly see their reflections on the walls. "There are security cameras in this place, too," Phoenix said. There was white, chrome surveillance cameras mounted to the corners of the ceiling.

"Security cameras were required to be installed for anything involving the organization's activity. The security cameras here, however, aren't connected. They're now used for protection."

"Well, it backfired for them when they took the time negotiating with investments," Phoenix said.

"We all know it's easy to get carried away with spending money in today's world. Sometimes, we don't realize how much it can affect us personally."

They stop walking as they approach a clear, silver, steel door with a security pad. Adrian takes out his communicator and overrides the security pad.

The door slowly opens as it whistles, revealing a room

with electronic and physical targets containing several objects. The targets were in the distance as a section had a Plexiglas wall with a steel desk. The desk had holes for the guns to go through. By the side of the Plexiglas wall were sheets of titanium, steel alloy, and tungsten. Behind them were hangers and shelves carrying safety goggles and black industrial earmuffs. "Get a pair of safety goggles ready. You'll be testing them with me, too," Adrian said. "I'm going inside the firing range to prepare a couple sheets of each metal."

Adrian takes two large sheets of the three metals and opens the door. Darrell and Phoenix see Adrian walking in the firing range to remove the targets originally set in the hold of the hydraulic robotic arms. He places the sheets of metal as the robotic arms immediately clamp onto them. "Alright, we're set!" Adrian yelled. He made his way out of the firing range.

Adrian opened the door and readied his shotgun. "I'll

demonstrate with the metals. Let's first start off with the titanium," Adrian said.

"How do you know this will work?" Phoenix said.

"These sheets were tested in IFHR." Adrian smiles. "Get your goggles and weapons ready. Each of you will test the other two metals."

They all go to the shelf of the safety goggles and earmuffs and each put a pair on. They go back to the Plexiglas wall and cock their shotguns. There was one lever by each of them. The levers were made to move the targets around the room.

Adrian inserted the shotgun through the hole and crouched down until the butt of the gun was pressed against his shoulder. "This won't hurt a bit," Adrian said. He pulls the lever back until it's in the center of the range.

Adrian slightly pulls the trigger as he anticipates by sweating from his forehead. The shell fires out of the barrel with intense velocity. As the shell came in contact with the sheet of titanium, the metal barely give in, showing no miniscule amount of damage.

Darrell and Phoenix were surprised at the results. "That's some strong ass titanium," Phoenix said.

"Now, you guys shoot a shell at the steel alloy and the tungsten," Adrian said. Darrell has the steel alloy and Phoenix has the tungsten. They carefully insert the shotguns in the holes and crouch down, pressing the butts of the guns against their shoulders. They each fire a round at the metals, showing the same results as the titanium. They were both shocked again. "These aren't regular types of metal used in the public eye, how is this stronger than the regular bonds?" Darrell said.

"These metals were carefully molded to make them stronger and lighter for use by the organization," Adrian said. "Now let's do the assault rifles."

They pull out their assault rifles and cock them, inserting them into the holes and preparing themselves. "Keep firing until you use a full magazine," Adrian said. "It's going to get loud as hell in here." They pull the triggers as they each rapidly fire at the sheets of metal. The bullets echoed from the acoustics of the range.

They run out of their magazines as they look at the results. "There's no minimal damage, but they keep firing at the same spot, the armor will start to dent, but by extremely small amounts. You'll barely see them," Adrian said. "Looks like we're done here."

They head out of the target practice room and enter the translucent hallway. "They're going to be hitting harder than they did before. It's the last trial," Adrian said.

They exit out of the underground weapons storage room and head into the garage. "Do you know where the next target is?" Phoenix said.

"I still have to find the coordinates. I'll try to locate it once you pull out of the garage," Adrian said.

Darrell and Phoenix look at their modified Lamborghini as they were still in awe by its appearance. "I don't know how the hell you do it, Adrian. What are you going to do after all of this is over?" Phoenix said.

"I did this for a reason. We all need heroes sooner or later. Probably after all of this, I'm going to start a new life."

"How?"

"Once IFHR's exposed to the media, I'll walk away silently from all of the events that happened."

Phoenix looks down and said, "Thank you for helping us out after all of this time. At least you have morals and is willing to help mankind be strong again." Phoenix walks up to Adrian and gives him a hug. Adrian takes a deep breath and closes his eyes as he sheds a tear, "Thank you. Both of you are our only hope now."

"We'll do the best we can during the last trial," Phoenix said.

"You have one shot at this. Make it count."

Darrell and Phoenix get in the Lamborghini as Darrell starts the vehicle. While starting the vehicle, it whistles from the engine, which it has never done before. The interior lights up as it illuminates most of the dashboard.

While Adrian fast walks to the garage door, he lets his hands out, telling them not to move. He puts his hand on the hand scanner as the garage door slowly opens, revealing the clear skies from outside. He makes hand gestures to move around the Audi and pull up towards the end of the garage door. The Lamborghini's engine whistle pitch gets higher while moving. He then signals them to stop.

Adrian starts walking to the Lamborghini as Phoenix lets the window down. "I just want to tell you guys good luck. Don't stop, keep going no matter what the obstacles are.

IFHR will use every amount of oppression against you. Don't fall back at any costs."

"Thank you, Adrian," Phoenix said. "It means a lot."

"Hope you guys bring them down. Godspeed."

Darrell pulls out of the garage and propels into the streets with blistering acceleration. "Can't believe it's already here," Darrell said.

"Don't get too comfortable," Phoenix said. She tapped on the navigation system to zoom out, showing the entire world. She notices a red blip on the continent of Africa. "We already have a location."

"Where at?" Darrell said.

"Hold on, let me zoom in." She taps on the navigation system to zoom in closer towards the blip. "It's in the Sahara Desert, but it's pointing at Morocco for some reason."

"Well, that's where we will be heading now."

Suddenly, Phoenix gets a headache as she pictures the

vision from Washington D.C. as she presses both hands on her head. She yells as the pain grows. "What's wrong?!" Darrell panicked.

"We have to get there now! Something's telling me that something important is in the desert. I can feel it."

Darrell accelerates through the streets of Los Angeles until they get to the airport. They make their flight to Morocco as they prepare for the final Trial.

Chapter 50: Omen

April 17, 2021

Sahara Desert, Morocco, 1918 hours

Darrell and Phoenix are driving through a flat section of the Sahara Desert at cruising speed. The sand and dirt creates clouds behind them as they are going smoothly through the terrain. The sky was filled with clouds that are gray in color. It was storming as lightning was coming out, but it didn't rain. Phoenix's head begins to feel pressure again as she places her hand on her forehead. "It's getting closer," Phoenix said.

"How can you tell?" Darrell said.

"I can picture the vision I had. I can sense that it's getting close."

"I don't see it up there."

"It's mostly in the far distance. I feel that it's straight
ahead."

"Did you know that you had-"

"Extrasensory perception? No. It's commonly known as
the sixth sense from what people would call it. The sixth
sense is the ability to foretell the events of a future
occurrence. I'm already starting to think of it as a curse."

"What do you see?"

"The same building I pictured. It's just plain. Doesn't look
like there's anything on it."

"What does it look like?"

"It's very tall, looks tall enough as the Central Plaza in
Shanghai. It looks straight and rectangular and it was in the
same climate we're in now."

"Is there something on it?" Darrell was getting worried.

"I don't know, I can't really see it, it's blurred except for one part. I can partially see one number, but there's no zeros."

"What's the number?"

"I can't really tell."

They hear loud engines coming from behind in the distance. Darrell looks up in his rear-view mirror to see a large fleet of armored supercars, infantry vehicles, and armored Arma tanks. Their armor makeup is similar to the Lamborghini. "We have company," Darrell said.

"Then let's put these weapons to good use."

Darrell looks down at the buttons for all of the weapons and prepares to engage in vehicular combat. The final hour begins as they approach the tower in the distance of the desert.

Chapter 51: Vehicles of War

1926 hours

The fleet of IFHR draws in closer as Darrell scrambles to select a weapon. He looks down at the buttons of the installed weapons. He activates the light machine guns in the rear as the Lamborghini accelerates at blistering speeds. He locks onto two supercars as the bullets fire. They come out at a medium rate due to its heavy weight. The bullets partially shake the Lamborghini's interior. "Keep firing! Give them hell, Darrell!" Phoenix yelled. The bullets eat through the vehicles' armor and destroys their tires completely. They explode and fly in the air.

The rest of the fleet increase their speed and begin to fire warning shots at the Lamborghini. "Get the missiles ready, we're going for the Arma tanks," Phoenix said. Darrell prepares the rear missiles and locks onto two of the Arma tanks. He fires one of the missiles at one of the tanks as it charges and hisses towards its front armor. The missile explodes on impact as it partially breaks through its armor. He aims for the other tank and fires one missile, partially chipping off armor.

The fleet caught up to Darrell as they are now beside them, surrounding him in every direction. "Shit, we are fucked!" Darrell panicked.

"Not if we keep fighting! Go for the smaller targets first, then we'll work our way up to the tanks!"

Darrell accelerates and drives beside a few of the supercars. The supercars begin firing as some bullets deflect off of the armor. He locks onto two of them as he activates the front machine guns. He fires at their rear bumpers, slowly chipping off their plates of armor. He switches to the modified shotguns as he accelerates closer to the supercars. The shells came out with intense velocity as it charged with heat, leaving a white trail of light. The shells ate through the rear bumpers as it cut through their engines, making them explode and perform barrel rolls.

Darrell accelerates and turns the modified weapons towards one of the targets beside him. He constantly fires at their side as the armor chips off. He quickly switches to the shotguns and fires a hole through the passenger's side. The bullet was strong enough to obliterate through the driver's hip, making blood and body parts splatter around the seats and windows. Darrell abruptly turns to ram the supercar beside him. No effect. "Shoot one of their tires and hit him again!" Phoenix yelled. Darrell turns the modified weapons towards the side of the supercar and fires at one of the tires, melting the rubber as the rim snaps off. He takes the steering

wheel and rams the vehicle, making it flip over and perform

barrel rolls as one of the Arma tanks crushes it like a pancake.

Darrell turns from the totaled supercars and prepares

against the rest of the fleet. There were still some supercars

left as the overall width covering the fleet spanned to a half

of a mile. "Damn," Darrell said. "There's a shitload after us."

They both see the infantry vehicles begin to accelerate

towards the Lamborghini. "I've had it with these people! I'm

blowing their fucking asses up this time!" He looks in the rear

view mirror to see the infantry vehicles continuing to

accelerate. "That's it, you just keep getting closer." He

prepares the rear light machine guns. The infantry vehicles

began firing machine guns at the Lamborghini as some bullets

deflected on its armor. Darrell immediately starts firing at

them. The damage was significant as the Lamborghini's

bullets blew off most of the vehicles' fronts. The damage was strong enough to cut large holes through their interior, showing the agents expressing their petrified faces. Darrell switches to the rear high powered shotguns and fires at the drivers, cutting through their bodies as guts and body parts splatter inside the vehicles.

More of the infantry vehicles and supercars, but not all of them, begin to accelerate towards Darrell. Some of them turn and attempt to drive directly into him. "Shit," Phoenix said. "Things just got worse now." The vehicles are dangerously drawing in closer. "Darrell, you're going to have to do a little more movement than going in for a straight shot!"

Suddenly, one of the infantry vehicles without warning fires a missile near the Lamborghini, making Darrell swerve out of its impact. Most of the supercars and infantry vehicles began firing their machine guns as Darrell constantly swerves left and right to dodge the bullets. While swerving, he drifted at some points as he began firing the rear weapons at the agents. The bullets and shotgun shells ripped through their armor as the vehicles exploded in midair. Pieces of twisted metal and armor spreads as it bounces off of the speeding Arma tanks pursuing them. "I'm going after the Arma tanks," Darrell said.

Phoenix panics and snaps, "What?! Take care of the smaller targets first! Don't waste your fucking weapons!"

"I'm not, I'm saving the missiles for the tanks. Because if it's a civil war they want, I'll be more than happy to sabotage their plans. I'm just getting started!"

Phoenix suddenly calmed herself and smiles cunningly, "Good choices of words, Darrell. I was testing you on that."

"Hang on," Darrell said.

"Don't tell me what to expect, I'm ready when you are."

Phoenix tightly grips onto her seat as Darrell slams on the brakes. The deceleration rate was quicker as its modified brakes almost brought the vehicle to a screeching halt. Their bodies were pushed forward from the strong G-force of the deceleration. The Lamborghini stopped in between the narrow gap of the moving Arma tanks as he allowed them to pass with blistering speed. The Arma tanks they were facing were faster and stronger as their top speed was higher, close to one hundred and ninety miles per hour. Their engines were loud as they were pounding against the heavy weight of their structures.

Darrell prepares the side missiles and slams on the throttle, pursuing the tanks. The flaps on the sides of the Lamborghini slowly come out and whistles. The flaps revealed four large, black, triangular missiles with the white IFHR insignia painted on them. Two of the missiles were on each side. They were high-powered ballistic missiles as they were tipped by a chrome silver color on their front ends. "The tanks are faster than before," Darrell said.

"They're heading to the base pretty quickly by the rate that they're going. Best lock on to one right now," Phoenix said. "Tanks don't usually go that fast."

"It's a fucking deathwish if you're pursuing tanks with just a damn car."

Darrell accelerates and turns to one of the tanks in an attempt to tailgate them. As he draws closer, he locks on to the rear of one of the tanks on the screen.

They notice the tanks slowly moving their turrets towards the Lamborghini. "You better come up with a solution, Darrell. They know you're pursuing them."

As Darrell is about a thousand feet away from them, he activates the side missiles. One of the missiles charged off of the flaps with brute force and intense velocity, creating a booming and cracking sound. The missile emits a white light behind it as it leaves a thick trail of smoke. It increases in speed as it follows the path of the tank. "Come on, come on, come on!" Darrell yelled, anticipating the missile's path as sweat pours down his head. "HIT THE TANK, DAMN IT!"

The missile impacted the Arma tank as it created a shockwave from its large blast radius of thirty meters. The missile emitted a white, bright luminescence as it partially destroyed the tank's armor. However, Phoenix noticed it only impacted most of its rear. "FIRE ANOTHER ONE!" she yelled.

Darrell looks at the target screen as he presses a button on the steering wheel to fire another missile. Suddenly, it didn't fire, making Darrell panic, "Shit!"

"What the hell are you doing, Darrell?! Fire the damn missile!"

Darrell looks at the top of the screen as there was a red bar that was almost full, "Shit, the missiles have to recharge!"

The Arma tank beside the damaged tank fires a ballistic missile towards Darrell. Phoenix panics as she sees the bright trail approaching the Lamborghini, "Shit, steer from the missile!"

Darrell accelerates and quickly steers away from the incoming missile. They dodged the missile, but barely as it exploded and created a shattering shock wave behind them. "Shit, that was close!" Darrell yelled in relief.

"Is the missile ready yet?!" Phoenix yelled.

Darrell looks at the screen, "Recharge is at ninety-six percent!"

"Because the other tank has its turret solid on its target!" The other tank fires again. "Shit!"

Darrell accelerates and pushes through as he barely dodges the missile again.

The screen made a fast beep and circuit noise as the side missiles were done recharging and ready for use. He immediately locks on the damaged tank and fires another missile as it propels towards its exposed armor. The missile exploded and destroyed its primary layers of armor, severely weakening its structure. The interior was exposed as black smoke came out and a couple agents' bodies were fried and splattered by the extensive heat signature of the missile. Their blood spilled on the sides of the tank.

Darrell accelerates and activates the missiles on the roof. He fires as the roof fires small, but powerful missiles in an alternating pattern. Each missile created devastation as it weakened its silver dual tracks and turret of the tank. The tank eventually gave in to the missiles as the tank bursts into flames, creating a shock wave by the explosion. Darrell turns away from the destroyed tank to avoid the power of the shock wave. "Same drill with the other one," Phoenix said.

Darrell decelerates and turns towards the second Arma tank as its turret follows him. He notices the rest of the smaller fleet still pushing towards the base located in the distance. The tank fires a couple ballistic missiles as Darrell quickly turns out of its target path.

Darrell switches back to the side missiles and turns the missiles towards the turret. He locks on and fires at the turret. The turret was destroyed as it blew off of the roof, but the tank was still moving in the same rate of speed. He switches back to the roof's missiles and accelerates, driving beside the tank. He turns the weapon until they are aiming at its tracks. He starts firing as the missiles destroy the intricate gears and wheels supporting them. He switches to the side missiles and fire the last one at the side of the track, destroying it as it explodes in flames and creates a large shock wave. "Got that out of the way," Darrell said.

"Now let's take care of these bastards ahead of us before they reach the building!"

Darrell accelerates and pursues the infantry vehicles and supercars.

As he gets close enough, he switches to the light machine guns and shotguns. Him and the rest of the opposing fleet fire machine guns at each other as it becomes

a moving kill zone. "Like you did before, go for their wheels!"

Phoenix yelled. Darrell abruptly rammed some of the

supercars to the sides as he fired the shotguns on both sides,

destroying the vehicles as they explode and fly in the air.

Darrell battled with the rest of the supercars by firing the

machine guns on both the front and rear. Him destroying the

supercars didn't intimidate the infantry vehicles as they kept

pushing through. Bullets from all directions were fired as they

deflected off of the Lamborghini's armor. He rammed the few

of the remaining supercars and fired at their chassis while

they were performing a series of barrel rolls.

Only the infantry vehicles remain. "You ready for this?"

Darrell said.

"That's a stupid question, Darrell," Phoenix said, looking

at him and smiling boldly.

Darrell activates the rear roof missiles and light machine

guns as most of them were behind him. A few were beside him, but in the distance.

Darrell fires a missile and destroys the vehicle behind him, alerting the others as they begin shooting their machine guns at him. He swerves in both directions as the bullets continue to bounce off of the Lamborghini's armor. His and the infantry vehicles' bullets created a shower of devastation as they travel with extreme velocity. The bullets travel fast enough to create yellow lighted trails. Darrell turns and fires the light machine guns at some of the vehicles as they were quickly destroyed.

"There's still more left! Keep fighting!" Phoenix yelled. She noticed that the building was larger as they were getting closer to it. Darrell abruptly turns to the infantry vehicles to the other side and shoots chunks off of their metallic bodies, finishing them off as the explosions create shock waves and slightly shake the ground around him.

Darrell straightens the vehicle as his skin tickled from the large amount of sweat pouring down his head. "I'll be damned, we shot two fucking Arma tanks that were armored, literally destroyed an armored fleet! How the fuck did we get so lucky?!" He yelled.

"You mean *you* shot them down, I didn't shoot anything, I only helped you with what to do. *You're* the one that's lucky," Phoenix said.

They focus their attention on the building as they look up at the lighted roof. The building was tall, even from a couple miles. Phoenix was shocked as the vision of D.C. revealed to be in exact detail in her head, "Oh, wow. That's the building."

"Are you serious?" Darrell said in panic.

"Does it look like I would make that up?" Phoenix looked at him. Darrell saw the seriousness in her eyes. "This must be the first base ever established from IFHR."

They notice something on the top of the building that's

painted in dark tan and gray. "That's the name number 1 in the vision," Phoenix said, petrified.

The building didn't have zeros following the number 1, but had the mysterious coincidence of letters following the number. The top of the building showed the name, CATA1.

Chapter 52: The Catalyst

1957 hours

"The Catalyst," Phoenix said quietly in shock.

"The Catalyst?" Darrell questioned.

"Below the roof shows CATA1. CATA for Catalyst. 1 means the organization's first establishment."

The building has a large, pointed needle that has a cyan light fluctuating from the tip of it. They both get out of the Lamborghini and look up to where it says CATA1. The building was black as its exterior reflected and was arched on its sides. Behind them was a square fence that surrounded the perimeter of the building. Around the building was asphalt.

Phoenix was calm, but angered, "Wow, we've came this far. It all comes down to this. This is exactly what I have envisioned."

"I can't believe this marks the end of the road."

"Let's go inside. They're definitely waiting for us. Get your weapons. They're going to fight harder than ever before."

They walk up to the entrance of the black double doors ahead of them. They can feel the breeze of the winds blow against them. As they reach the doors, Phoenix prepares her communicator and overrides its security pad. "It ends here, it ends now," Phoenix said.

"It was a crazy ride along the way, Phoenix."

"Best count your blessings because this marks the end."

The double doors clicked and slowly open as it reveals the interior. Darrell and Phoenix enter into the first establishment as they await for the final battle between

humanity and a lust for power.

Chapter 53: The Darkness

2001 hours

Ahead of Darrell and Phoenix was a dark, narrow, and confined hallway with lights that were all flickering. Around them were transparent walls as they saw their reflections on both sides. They look around as they were petrified from the atmosphere. "Doesn't get more serious than this," Phoenix said. They notice the surveillance cameras moving towards their point of the view in the ceiling's sides.

"This will definitely fill the United States' evidence rooms," Darrell said, referring to the cameras.

Phoenix overrides the door ahead of her as they enter another hallway. This hallway had a stairwell ahead of them. "Looks like we're going to do a lot of walking in order to reach the top from here," Phoenix said. As they reach the top of the stairwell, they see the number, 2 engraved by the side of the door. They go through a massive series of corridors and stairwells several floors later. There are one hundred and seventeen floors.

While reaching the sixty-seventh floor, they step foot on a steep platform as the ground below them appeared to have a deep pit. The floor was massive as it had the range of a football field. The room was dark as it was dimly lit in all corners. There were several machines and small rooms that were scattered across the floor, reenacting a small town. The walls were dark gray as there were red lines slowly moving towards the ground.

Darrell and Phoenix look down on the floor's ground to

see what looks like people laying on the ground. Phoenix

started hyperventilating when she saw puddles of blood

around their bodies. There were also agents walking around

in a formation of a V. They were marching as Darrell and

Phoenix heard their foot steps. Darrell grabs a hold of

Phoenix and covers her mouth as she started panicking, "Shh!

They'll know we're up here if you yell. Let's get off of this

floor and go up!"

They start sprinting towards the door ahead of them and

get away from the sixty-seventh floor.

As they enter the one hundred and tenth floor, a loud

alarm sounds as the halls had red lights fluctuating around

them. "Shit, we have to reach the top fast!" Phoenix

panicked.

They reach the one hundred and fourteenth floor. In

front of them were steel platforms and a pair of staircases in

a large room. The room was lighted well as it illuminated all areas of the room. There were advanced computers and cameras in front of them and in all directions.

Suddenly, they see lines of agents budge through the doors on the platforms as some run over the platforms and some run down to the floor. Most of the agents were carrying knives and daggers with the exception of a few carrying various firearms such as pistols and assault rifles. "It's the end of the road!" one of the agents yell. All of them draw their weapons as they see red laser reticles dancing on Darrell and Phoenix's bodies.

"We know," Phoenix said while smiling boldly. Her and Darrell pull out their assault rifles and aim at the agents. "We just want to give one last thanks to the welcoming committee before it's time for them to go!"

Darrell and Phoenix prepare to get engaged and fight through the obstacles the agents bring them.

Chapter 54: The Welcoming Committee

2014 hours

Darrell and Phoenix charge and yell at the agents. "Go for the ones with the guns first!" Phoenix yelled. They both start firing at the agents with the firearms as they kill most of them with headshots. They both kick a couple agents out of their way and fire at the remaining agents carrying firearms.

Darrell and Phoenix pull out their knives and daggers and charge at the other agents, slicing them in the necks and chest. They drop their blades and begin to punch and kick them. After every agent gets knocked down and bruised,

Darrell and Phoenix grab their blades and execute them. The agents' blood splatters onto their faces and chest as they pull out the blades pushed into their heart.

Phoenix jerks her head towards the platform, "That's one set down. We have three more floors to go. I know there's more. Come on, Darrell!"

They pick up their blades and sprint up the platform and budge through one of the doors. They run through a transparent hallway as more agents budge through the door ahead of them. Darrell and Phoenix fire at some of the agents as the bullets travel through their skulls, causing brain matter and blood to splatter out of their heads. Phoenix draws her pistols and wall runs. She shoots down a couple agents in the heads as Darrell continues to kill the agents with his assault rifle. Phoenix jumps off of the wall and kicks the two remaining agents in the heads.

The agents pull out their daggers as Phoenix prepares

herself with her blades. Darrell pulls out one of his knives and charges at one of the agents. They start swinging at each other as they all deliver punches and kicks. The agents were open in the chest, giving Darrell and Phoenix the chances to strike. They grab the agents' necks and stab them in the heart as their blood oozes out of their chest.

After Darrell and Phoenix enter through the door, they see a large, bright room with walls that are made of glass with sections. Behind the glass walls were agents on mounts that carried white modified rifles. Phoenix looks around at the agents angrily, "Come on, you motherfuckers! Why don't you step out of your cubby holes and-"

One of the agents fire a loud warning shot as the bullet disintegrates on the floor. Darrell and Phoenix became shocked and petrified. "SHIT! THEY'RE FUCKING SNIPER RIFLES!" Phoenix panicked. "LET'S GET TO HIGHER LEVEL NOW!"

Darrell and Phoenix begin sprinting towards the raised

platform ahead of them. The rest of the agents start firing

their sniper rifles as some bullets ricochet on both sides of

the walls. "FUCK THIS! WE WEREN'T PREPARED FOR SNIPERS

AT ALL!" Phoenix yelled. Phoenix activates the emergency

override on her communicator and budges through the door,

sprinting through the hallway and up the staircase ahead of

them.

As Darrell and Phoenix enter through the one hundredth

and sixteenth floor, they see only a few agents with their

back turned. They charge at the agents as they pull out their

knives. The agents slowly turned their heads as they heard

their footsteps, but it was too late. Darrell and Phoenix

grabbed a hold of two of the agents, twisting and slicing their

neck. They pounced on the last agent and cut him up on

several areas of his chest, arms, and face. "Ahead of us is the

last floor," Phoenix said.

They sprint to the door ahead of them as Phoenix overrides it. They budge through the door and run through the hallway and staircase that leads to the top floor of the base. They stop at the door as Phoenix cautiously readies her communicator, "This is it, Darrell."

"The tenth trial," Darrell said.

Phoenix overrides the door and budges through. They enter a room that's intricate in design as there were a few platforms on both sides. There was a pillar ahead of them as there was an agent standing in front of it with his hands connected to his back. The pillar had several advanced computers showing databases of agents and live surveillance footage streaming throughout CATA1. "It's over for you," Darrell yelled. "Turn yourself around, you coward!"

The agent lets his head down, "I knew you guys would make it this far." The agent turns around and looks at Darrell and Phoenix nefariously. "Because I'm just a moment away from getting what I've always wanted."

Both of them were shocked to see that it was Russell

Arkwright.

Chapter 55: Arkwright

2029 hours

"Arkwright," Phoenix said in anger and disgust.

"PHOENIX! So good to see you guys again!" Russell

yelled as he smiles with malicious tendencies.

Phoenix was growing with rage, "I guess we found what

what we were looking for all of this time."

"I *am* the tenth trial! You made through the other nine

circles, but this is only the beginning for you and me."

"How does this have to deal with the Inferno? You're still

a fucking idiot just like before. Your pride has pretty much

495

consumed you. You can't even tell what's real or not."

"BUT I CAN SEE YOU AND DARRELL! That's the FUCKING reality! You're finally here to get your punishment for foiling our plans for world domination!"

"You're welcome, Russell. We don't support groups that engage in omnicidal practices."

"But the pride, it feels *really* good. That feeling in my heart." Russell takes a slow and deep breath and breathes out, feeling his body going through a release of energy. "It just keep growing if you give it a chance. It takes only one person to realize the gift of its power."

"And what benefits does pride have for a person?" Darrell said.

"Anything you can afford, it's only a matter of how you use it."

"Why don't you shut your fucking mouth before I shut it for you?" Phoenix said.

"Sorry, I don't partake in caring for widows."

Phoenix's anger grew after Russell made his statement and yelled, "YOU KILLED MY HUSBAND AND PARENTS! You think I would let it slide if that happened?! I FUCKING warned you what would happen!"

"You don't scare me, Phoenix. You may have killed every agent that blocked your path, but it's my turn to take control of things around here."

"Just as the world needs to make things worse," Darrell said, angrily. "You're such a damn coward."

"If I was a coward, then why am I not scared to look at you confidently with arrogance?"

"You let vehicles and weapons do the killing instead of killing people yourselves. That's what cowards do, they have to take control in order to keep things in line," Darrell said.

"You're still standing away from us," Phoenix said. "It makes me think that you're afraid to be confronted by my standards of taking care of things."

Russell slowly walks up to them as he stomps until he's at the center of the room, "I'm getting closer, Phoenix. COME ON, DO SOMETHING!"

"If you try anything else on me, I'll kill you right now."

Russell walks up to Phoenix and breathes in her face, "You're going to kill me anyway."

"Exactly."

Russell yells at the top of his lungs, "SO DO SOMETHING, YOU BRAZEN LITTLE BITCH! I'M IN YOUR FACE RIGHT NOW! YOU SEEM PRETTY DAMN CALM WHEN I'M STANDING FACE TO FACE WITH YOU!"

"I'm still waiting."

Russell breathes heavily on her face and walks towards the pillar with the computers. He gives a thumbs up as he types on one of the keyboards. "I like the spunk that you two have," he said. "But I'm going to introduce you to the way I do things." He presses a neon white key on the side of the keyboard. The key displayed a holographic screen as it started generating series of randomizing numbers. "You see these numbers?! These numbers aren't just a network of the world that's continuously collecting and expanding, but it's also the entire network of supercomputers connected to every single base that's been established in our organization's history!"

Russell quickly turns around and looks at them like a maniac, "These computers have ALL of the power to control every single stream of electronic data around the world. That means that I will have full control over what we call our species, humanity! Our blind pursuit of technology just keeps growing and becoming more advanced, which is perfect for my plans! Pretty damn exciting in my point of view!"

"Celebrations are short lived if you take things for granted," Phoenix said. She pulls out two of her knifes as their shine reflects on the floor.

"Oh," Russell said, not intimidated. "You really want to finish this game, do you?" He says in flattery, "Because I would just love to fight my enemy until their down on their knees, begging for mercy." He points to the computers behind him, "You see those computers over there? The white key activates our organization's full potential. The red key in the middle deactivates our supercomputers permanently. This is the main control system of our foundation thanks to the help of President Lavensa himself." Russell laughs nefariously.

"Get yourself ready, Darrell. Hope you can fight with just knives in your hands. Our score settles here," Phoenix said.

"Let's end this with a bang. A loud bang," Darrell said.

"I CERTAINLY CAN'T WAIT FOR MY HAPPY ENDING!" Russell yelled.

Darrell and Phoenix embark on their last battle as they

prepare for the final hour towards deciding the fate of

humanity.

Chapter 56: The Last Stand

2041 hours

Darrell and Phoenix throw punches and attempt to strike

Russell with their knives, but they end up blocking each other

instead. Phoenix and Russell push against each other with

brute force as they try to break each other's attacks. "Better

make that choice quick before you develop that fork in the

road!" Russell taunted.

"I've dealt with trial and tribulation among this for far

too long! It's time for you pay for what you've done to not

just my DAMN family, but also to the innocent people you

got involved!" Phoenix said.

"Oh, we pay good money for what we have!" Russell laughs with no remorse. Russell breaks Phoenix's hold and swing fists at each other. Bruises were starting to be felt on Phoenix's body. "Oh, boy, doesn't it feel good when you're close to something you want?"

"I already know what I want. I want avengement." Phoenix knees Russell in the groin and gives him an uppercut, but he recovers from the adrenaline flowing through his body. "Oh, you're going to pay for that, you little bitch!" Russell taunted.

Russell charged at Phoenix and tackled her to the floor, making her drop her knives. He takes his arms and tightly presses down on her face. Phoenix stretches her arm out with all of her might to reach for one of her knives, but Russell caught her. He takes his other arm and pushes it away from her. Russell laughs as he looks down on Phoenix while she's struggling. He takes his other arm and presses down on her arm with brute force.

Phoenix was grunting in pain, "DARRELL, NOW!"

Darrell charges at Russell and tackles him off of Phoenix. They both roll on the floor as they deliver hard punches. Darrell punches Russell in the chest and face.

Russell saw his chance as Darrell was about to punch him again. He tightly grabbed Darrell's neck and punches him in the face, knocking Darrell off balance. Russell picks him up and grabs him by his dress shirt and suit jacket. "Now it's your turn, Darrell!" Russell said, cracking his neck. "Time for you to get an appointment with death!"

Russell picks Darrell up and throws him to the ground, bruising his back and arm. He walks up to Darrell and pins him down, delivering hard and unforgiving punches to his chest, diaphragm, and face. "You're the target! You should've just gave up in the past before you made it worst on yourself!" Darrell was coughing from the blood and bruises around his body. Russell takes both of his arms and tightly grips around his neck. He gets close to Darrell's face and looks at him menacingly, "Now, doesn't it feel good to accomplish something that you've always wanted to achieve?!"

Phoenix notices Darrell struggling and tries to stand up. She grunts as she attempts to get on her feet and grabs her knives. She quietly walks up to Russell as she notices Darrell gagging and his face turning red from his grip.

Phoenix saw her chance and violent pushes Russell off of Darrell. Darrell breathes heavily and coughs as he catches his breath. Russell regains his balance and prepares his knives. They resume to swinging at each other and block. "Fooled you, didn't I?" Phoenix said.

"You didn't fool me at all," Russell said. He takes his knife and slashes a small cut on Phoenix's hip. Phoenix grunts from the burning of the cut, temporarily stunning her from attacking.

Russell charges at Phoenix, "Prepare to meet death at the door of fate, Phoenix! WELCOME TO YOUR END!"

Phoenix quickly recovers in time and punches Russell in the jaw, knocking him off balance. She charges at him and starts punching and kicking him in several areas of his body. Her fighting skills causes Russell to move backwards towards the pillar.

Phoenix unsheathes one of her swords and spins around, slashing through his chest as blood spills on his suit. She grabs Russell and ferociously throws him onto the pillar, dislocating one of his collarbones. She drops her sword and grabs her knives. She stabs through both of the palms of his hands, causing him to yell from the burns of the cuts.

Phoenix pulls out the knives in Russell's palms and stabs him through his heart. Russell starts gagging from the pressure and sting of the pain. She gets close to his face,

"You're right, it ends here, it ends now. The evidence is clear

to what the world will soon know. Maybe you should've

thought about investing in security instead of twisted

espionage. Especially, your morals."

Phoenix pulls out the knives and stabbed through

Russell's heart. Blood splatters as it hits Phoenix's body.

Russell was gagging from the internal bleeding spreading

through his body. She throws one of her knives and prepares

the other, moving it towards his forehead. "YOUR NUMBER'S

UP!" she yells. She charges the knife and stabs through

Russell's forehead. His eyes roll back as the blood from his

forehead drips down to his suit.

Phoenix breathes heavily as she carefully pulls the knife

out of Russell's forehead. Blood spreads around his body

while she stands up and looks down at him. She grunts as she

presses her hand against the cut on her hip. She looks at the computer screens with determination.

Darrell pushes himself up from the ground as he's still coughing from the pressure in his neck. He walks up to Phoenix while brushing himself off from the ordeal. He breathes heavily as he puts his hand on her shoulder. "It's finally over, Phoenix. The world can feel peace again," Darrell said.

Phoenix looks down at the keyboards, "It's not over yet. There's still one more thing to do." She presses the red key on the keyboard.

An alarm sounded throughout the building, startling Darrell and Phoenix. Suddenly, the computer screens display timers in bright red. The timer read as forty minutes and started counting down. "What?!" Phoenix yelled, surprised. She punched the keyboards in frustration, "It's a self-destruct sequence, that motherfucker!"

"Then what are we waiting for, Phoenix?! We have to

get out of here! Let's go!"

Darrell tries to grab Phoenix, but she pushes him aside.

He was surprised, "Phoenix, you can't just sit there! We'll

make it out in time! We have to go!"

"I'm sorry, but I can't go with you this time," Phoenix

said calmly.

Darrell was astonished by what Phoenix said. He realizes

that Phoenix has a different objective set in stone.

Chapter 57: Letting Go

"What? Why? Why are you staying here?!" Darrell yelled.

"Because I was the one that brought you in this mess," Phoenix said.

"We brought ourselves in this mess together! We have to get out-"

"THERE'S NOT ENOUGH TIME FOR BOTH OF US! I have a different set of priorities than you!"

"Phoenix, please don't do this!" Darrell started crying.

"I have to. I need to do the right thing." Phoenix walks up to Darrell and gives him a hug. "You have to get out of here. I know there's more of them coming up here. Things will be alright." They let go of each other. "I'll let you take some of my weapons to fend them off." Phoenix pulls out her shotgun and one of her assault rifles and throws them at Darrell. He catches them. "Maybe you can help change the world for the better one day."

Darrell stops crying. "How can I? We both killed several people in the organization."

"There's always two sides to every story. Your side is different, but we worked together. The evidence is clear and it will be released to the public once this is over."

"Good thing there's security cameras in every base."

"This will be a reminder to the President of the United States for after what he did to our world. Now go, they'll be coming any minute."

Darrell starts sprinting towards the door, but turns around. "But what about you? What's next for you?" he yells.

Phoenix yells, "Don't worry about me. You have a message to spread. The evidence is all you need."

"It's been a pleasure meeting you, Phoenix."

"You, too, Darrell. You seem to have a lot of potential. Remember what I have told you from all of this time. We may come from different paths and have different goals, but we're all connected in one way or another."

Darrell nods in affirmation and sprints out of the room as he races against the clock to escape the complex structure of CATA1.

Chapter 58: Escape Plan

2055 hours

Thirty-six minutes remain in the self-destruct sequence

as Darrell begins to make his way down to the first floor.

Phoenix looks around in the computer room with rage.

Twenty-eight minutes remain on the sequence. "IFHR will fall

to its breaking point along with its legions," she said. "And I'm

on the brink towards achieving what I was hoping for." She

pulls out her weapons and shoots at everything she sees,

destroying everything in her view.

As Darrell reaches the forty-seventh floor, he enters a

large room with metallic platforms and barriers scattered around. All of the agents in the room aimed at him as the red laser reticles danced vigorously around his chest. Darrell crouches just before all of the agents started firing at the barrier he's taking cover in. "They just don't know when to stop, even on self-detruct," Darrell said to himself. The agents stopped firing for a brief moment. "But I've done my fair share with cheating death."

Darrell quickly gets out of cover and fires at the agents below them, counting them to be all headshots. He quickly draws his white pistol and shoots at the few remaining agents with his scatter shot ammunition. They thud to the ground as their blood spills out of their skulls. "They're still out of their fucking league," Darrell said. He leaps over the barrier and drops down, sprinting to the door ahead of him to enter the next lower floor.

Seventeen minutes remain on the sequence as Phoenix

stays by the pillar, patiently waiting while watching the door ahead of her. "Come on, you bastards. I know you're all there coming to get me," Phoenix said to herself.

While Darrell reaches the tenth floor, he runs through a hallway as he sees agents charging at him with daggers and knives. They constantly swing at each other until Darrell eventually counter attacks them. He stabs them in the neck by performing uppercuts and kicks them out of his way. He resumes sprinting down the floors as the sequence continues to drop.

Nine minutes remain on the sequence. "I hope you're there soon, Darrell. You don't have much time," Phoenix said to herself.

Darrell finally reaches the first floor as he stops to look around. He then looks back to the door that leads to the second floor, "There's no turning back now. I've done all that I can on this journey. It's time to put this to rest once and for all." He sprints and budges through the door ahead of him, witnessing the thundering skies outside. The clouds displayed bright, purple, and distorted lightning as it danced in the skies. However, it wasn't raining.

Darrell runs up to the Lamborghini and begins to turn around. He slams on the throttle and accelerates at a blistering rate as he drives away from CATA1. The terrain was flat enough for him to make a straight shot through the desert's landscape. He constantly shifts gears as he feels his body get lighter from the fastly growing amount of speed throughout the vehicle. "Come on, go faster!" Darrell yelled. The vehicle was going strong as at already reached a speed of two hundred miles per hour.

Two minutes remain on the sequence. Phoenix hears agents' footsteps and voices as they yell. "It's time," Phoenix said. She looks behind her to see the live surveillance from outside as she saw the dust clouds created from the

Lamborghini. "You're free to go, Darrell."

The agents kick open the door and aim at Phoenix with their modified assault rifles. They wore black ops suits with helmets showing heads up displays. Phoenix just looked at them, showing no intimidation. She lets her head down in despair and relief. She starts to think about flashbacks that constantly switch between her parents, Warren, and Darrell. She starts crying as she becomes overwhelmed from the memories. She slowly looks up to the agents and smiles, "It's finally over."

After the last three seconds pass, the room becomes illuminated by a light that's blinding as the sun. The end of the sequence creates a loud and deafening blast that quickly decimates the building's interior. The blast takes the lives of the agents inside the building as well as Phoenix.

Darrell continues to drive away from the building as he sees its floors being destroyed. "PHOENIX!" he yells. "NO!"

The building collapses as the blast was strong enough to create a massive shock wave that travels at an extreme velocity of speed. He noticed that the shock wave was traveling towards him, making him panic. "Come on, car, go faster!"

The shock wave keeps getting closer as it was about a half of a mile away, but that isn't much distance for Darrell. He was going at about two hundred and fifty miles per hour. "I have to activate the nitrous systems!" he said.

He activates the nitrous and feels a sudden jolt of acceleration coursing through the vehicle. The vehicle pushed him back on his seat as he was being chased by the shock wave. The top speed was drastically increasing as it reached over three hundred miles per hour. He hyperventilates and breathes heavily as he looks straight ahead to keep from losing control of the vehicle. "Wow, Phoenix, you've got some nerve in you to pull something off like that!" Darrell said.

The shock wave was disappearing as it was losing distance with Darrell. He kept his foot on the throttle as he watched carefully at the digital speedometer. The vehicle has reached its top speed, three hundred and sixty-seven miles per hour.

The shock wave disappears. Darrell slowly presses on the brakes and gradually decelerates. After decelerating for about thirty seconds, the vehicle comes to a complete stop. His breathing calms down as he feels relief and looks down on the steering wheel. "Phoenix, you did it again," Darrell said to himself.

Chapter 59: The Evidence Is Clear

2133 hours

Darrell gets out of the car to look around the vast, desert landscape. He notices a bright blue light ascending to the skies in the distance. He was in awe and shock by the phenomena of the light, "Phoenix? Is that really you?" The blue light becomes brighter as it gets closer to the clouds.

As the light comes in contact with the clouds, the blue light turns into a bright white. "May you find the peace that will mend your heart forever," Darrell said. "Goodbye, Phoenix."

After the bright light disappears in the skies, Darrell suddenly hears helicopters chopping air behind him. He turned around and saw searchlights coming his way. He started jumping to get their attention. "I'm here! I'm here! It's over! It's finally over!" Darrell cried in joy. The three helicopters landed on the ground. They were not ordinary helicopters. These were helicopters that held large cargo. They were black as they had red, white and blue decal stripes on both of their sides. They had the letters, U.S.A. on each of them. Their cargo was enough to hold four vehicles at a time. "One of you open the hatch to the cargo!" one of the soldiers said as his voice sounded muffled inside the helicopter. The helicopter in the middle opened the back hatch as it whistled from its hydraulics. "Get in your vehicle and pull inside. After you're done, get out. We will speak with you!"

Darrell runs back into the Lamborghini and pulls up towards the helicopters. He turns and pulls inside the cargo area as it was illuminated by orange lighting. After he parks, he gets out of the car and exits the cargo area.

Soldiers in camouflage suits open the front hatches of the helicopters and get out, walking up to Darrell. "Mr. Friegman," one of the soldiers said in a bold, mature voice. "My name is Lieutenant Oliver Harrison." Harrison was tan in skin color and had black, short hair.

"Am I going home?" Darrell questioned.

"Yes, but you need to stay with us for this one."

"What?! What are you talking about?! The ordeal's over! IFHR's no longer in operation!"

"That's the thing, you're coming with us. We're questioning you about the incidents."

"You can't do that!"

"Watch us! Soldiers, apprehend him!" The six soldiers including Harrison run up to him. Darrell yells, "Wait, what is the meaning of-" One of the soldiers tazes him in the hip, causing him to scream in pain. A million volts of electricity

was coursing through his body. Another one of the soldiers

pulls out his baton and strikes him in the head, knocking him

out cold. "Put him inside the back of the helicopter, we're

taking him back to the White House," Harrison said.

Two of the soldiers drag Darrell to the helicopter and

throw him inside the back seats. There were four seats in

each of them. They buckle him down and get up in the front

seats. They start up the helicopters and prepare to depart

from the Sahara Desert. "Wow, I don't know how they did it,"

one of the soldiers said. "IFHR almost took over the White

House and eventually the world, but thankfully the national

capital is still standing in one piece unscathed."

"Mr. Friegman will have to speak to President Lavensa

and see what he has to say," Harrison said.

"I just can't believe it's finally over. We counted the

death toll to be over twelve million. There were over five

million members working in IFHR. About three thousand agents were killed to date."

"All of the evidence is clear. They've documented everything over the course of thirty-one years. These helicopters also have cameras, so it's a good thing that they recorded the collapse of CATA1 to get a glimpse of what really happened. We will be releasing every single of piece of information sooner than expected. We will find the profiles of each IFHR member and send them in for death row after what they did to our country and everyone else. The penitentiaries will be filled up by the time we start."

The soldiers fly away from the decimated remains of CATA1 as they take a deep breath from the relief of the end of the civil war. The duration of the Civil War of 2020 is no more. They begin their way to the White House as they start to fly through the North Atlantic Ocean.

Chapter 60: Questions

April 26, 2021

Washington, D.C., United States, 0922 hours

Darrell is sitting face to face with President Lavensa in

the Oval Office located in the West Wing of the White House.

He still has bruises from the fighting with Russell. Most of his

blood marks were healed as they were never there on his

face. Lieutenant Harrison was standing next to Darrell. The

President was old as he ranged in his sixties. He was white in

skin color. His skin was smooth as it reflected from the sun

shining behind him. He has white hair all slicked back on the

top of his skull as he only had a few gray hairs on his stubby goatee. "Mr. President," Darrell said with a frustrated tone. "It's nice to see you relaxing from this beautiful weather."

"You must be Mr. Friegman," the president said with his strong and mature voice. "I hear that you want to ask some questions about the events leading up to the Civil War of 2020."

"Your soldiers sent me in. They knocked me out along the ride for a good purpose, that way I wouldn't go crazy. I'm one of the key people that was involved in it. I know exactly what happened."

"Alright, but before we start getting into your questioning, I'm going to ask you about some things." He pulls out a pen and pulls a notepad closer to him and prepares for writing.

"Then you better make it quick, because you don't have all day to mess around anymore," Darrell said.

President Lavensa looks at him in disgust, "What gives

you the right to talk back to the President? You do realize your talking to a high profile of authority, right?"

"Did you hear what I just said? Do not waste my time, sir. I have some things to take care of after today."

President Lavensa looks at Darrell in anger, "So, what started all of this, Mr. Friegman?

"They started chasing me down for no reason. It was a conspiracy at start, but it started unraveling from there."

"How long ago was this?"

"2019. Maybe you should check the evidence."

"How do you know so much about the organization?"

"I did my fair amount of research over the past two years. I thought *long and hard* about it, but then they started going into a rampage and committing mass murder across multiple nations."

"Was there anybody with you at the time?"

"One of the boldest woman that ever walked on this planet."

The doors open behind them as their conversation was interrupted. Harrison looks at the doors to see two soldiers coming in. "We have a visitor," one of the soldiers said.

"Is he considered a threat?" Harrison said.

"He doesn't have any weapons on him."

"Alright." One of the soldiers walks out and says, "You can come in, sir."

Adrian steps inside the Oval Office as he walks up to Darrell. "Thank you," Adrian said to the soldiers. He said to the president, "Looks like you have a lot of explaining to do."

President Lavensa was surprised as the soldiers allowed Adrian in. "What the hell is the meaning of this?" Lavensa said. "You can't just invite citizens in there, Harrison! This is top secret!"

"But he's also one of the key people that was involved,"

Darrell said. "Now, time for my questions." He looks at

Harrison, "Hope you don't mind if I express how I feel to the

President. Might get physical with him in a minute."

"Take as long as you like, Mr. Friegman. The President's

days are about to come to a close here, anyways," Harrison

said.

"Thank you. So, Mr. President, how were you able to get

away with creating an organization that eventually commits

omnicide at a critical level? You didn't control the way they

did things."

The president was shocked as his breaths were shallow.

He has no response. "No answer, huh?" Darrell said.

"Alright." He stands up from his chair and walks around the

desk to stand beside Lavensa. "If you can't answer that

question, then maybe this one will bring some light to what's

going to happen to you. How are you going to explain the

evidence that's spilled all over the media?"

"It's a conspiracy, Darrell."

"It was a conspiracy until we did something about it."

Darrell walks up to the President and pushes him violently onto the front of the desk. He takes the President's head and presses it against the desk. "I may be bruised and scarred, but I can still fight and defend myself! So, why did you do it? Did you think it was going to be a bad idea?! Huh?!" He lets go of Lavensa's head as the president presses his hand against his head. There was a bruise on the side of his forehead. "You know what?! Stand the hell up!"

Darrell pulls the president out of his chair and forcefully pushes him back. He walks up to Lavensa and pushes him against the windows. "Not only does this day mark the end of your presidency, but I also have the opportunity of kicking your ass!" He bashes the president against the windows as he grabs him by his dress shirt. Darrell gets in his face, "It's no longer a conspiracy if it's spilled out in the media, because with every single camera recording the video, the evidence is clear. So, go ahead, keep spilling lies and trying to make the world think that there's nothing to worry about. In a few minutes, you have to go outside and speak to the people and officials standing in front of the White House. They want the truth, Lavensa, and you'll have to pay the consequences for what you did. The live cameras are waiting to hear about the Civil War and your future as a president. And if they decide to organize another election, they better not pick me because *I know* I'm not fit to be the president."

Darrell lets go of the President as him and Adrian make their way out of the Oval Office. "Meet us outside, we want you to see him speak as well. The cameras might capture you in the audience, so the world may want to see you as well," Harrison said to Adrian and Darrell. No response. "You just lost your title as the President. Get ready, Donovan, the people want to see you." Lavensa looks at the window once more in disgust. "No matter how hard it seems, get up, dress up, and show up."

Lavensa looks out the window to see citizens, officials, news vehicles, and live video equipment scattered around the gardens of the White House. He sighs and walks away from the desk and exits the room. The soldiers follow him out as he prepares for his last speech to address to not just the United States, but for the world's nations to witness.

Chapter 61: The President's Last Address

0934 hours

The skies were clear as there were no clouds to be seen. The crowd was loud as people talked over each other, anticipating the president's speech. The crowd was silenced and shocked as they see Darrell and Adrian walk outside, joining them. Both of them noticed that the gardens weren't covered with dead bodies, vehicles, and twisted metal. It was clean as it almost looked like the beautiful rose gardens and plentiful glass it contained before the Civil War of 2020.

"Wow, they did a good job cleaning up," Darrell said referring to the gardens.

"Thinking about cleaning up the place doesn't apply to us right now, Darrell," Adrian said.

A few minutes later, Lavensa along with Harrison and the other soldiers open the doors of the front entrance and walk up to the podium ahead of him. People were taking pictures as Lavensa stands by the podium, looking numb and motionless. There were several microphones that showed the names of popular news stations from around the world. "Yeah, you better look innocent, you hypocrite," Darrell said. The crowd didn't cheer, they didn't speak, they are about to become witnesses of what is about to become a pivotal event on the planet's history.

Lavensa clears his throat, "Good morning, America." He connects his hands behind his back and looks around at the people as he sees the video equipment recording his every action. He takes a deep breath before continuing to speak again. "The world is no longer engaging in the Civil War of

2020. We can now exist in peace and independence again.

IFHR is no longer in operation as of April 17, 2021, ending its

run of thirty-one years. But don't get too comfortable as I

have something to tell all of you." Lavensa notices Darrell and

Adrian staring him down, waiting for him to continue

speaking. "I've made promises that were kept and granted to

our country, but I've also failed you as a president."

Lavensa takes a deep breath and starts to get nervous.

He calms down, "I was originally the start of IFHR, which

stands for the International Foundation for Human

Resources. Do not let the name fool you, however, as I am

responsible for all of the deaths of people's loved ones and

the people affiliated with the organization. It was spiraling

out of control and I have never done anything to control it.

There was a total of over eight million people and ten

thousand agents were deceased over the course of thirty-one

years, starting with 1990. I've failed to protect not just the people of my nation, but people from other nations as well.

The organization recruited people from different countries as

the four key founders including me sparked its objective. I am

ashamed of this creation. The key people that founded the

organization included I, Donovan Lavensa, Devin Steele,

Russell Arkwright, and Barrett Atkinson. Three of them are

dead with no chance recovery of their bodies. And I know

nothing can be paid back after what has happened to our

world as the organization corrupted our societal views on

ourselves."

Adrian mouths the words, "You better say it now."

Donovan calmly looks at Adrian and takes a deep breath,

looking down at the microphones with shame, "As of today, I

hereby announce the resignation of my title as the President

of the United States. It's all in the media, now. The damage

and scars that IFHR left behind are no longer a conspiracy.

The world is in a safer place now. Thank you."

Lavensa walks away from the podium and returns back
into the White House. While he's walking straight, a woman
working in the White House said, "Hope you're happy with
what you did." Lavensa ignores the woman and walks on with
his shame.

Chapter 62: Like Phoenix Said

0946 hours

Darrell and Adrian turn away from the crowd and walk through the White House South Lawn and the President's Park. "It all ends here. We did it. We can finally put all of this to rest," Adrian said.

"It's over for you, but not for me. I have one more thing to take care of after today," Darrell said.

"What's next for you?"

"It'll be in the media soon." They stop walking and look face to face with each other. "Maybe we'll see each other again in due time." They give each other a hug as a sign of departure. "Look on the bright side, we saved the world from a massive civil downfall. This is not a goodbye, but a temporary farewell. I give you my thanks for helping me out to fighting against them in times of trouble. You're one hell of a mechanic."

They let go as Adrian chuckles. "I guess you could say," Adrian said.

"Hey, you fought against their objective for a long time and succeeded. Phoenix was right, you're not like them. You're no longer one of them. All of our freedom has been restored, but the media and news will be releasing details about IFHR soon. We're winning this fight now, and it's the greatest feeling I've ever experienced in a long time. This journey was a roller coaster, but all of us made it through."

"I guess I'll see you around, Darrell. It was a pleasure working with you," Adrian said. "May we meet again."

"In due time, Adrian. In due time."

Darrell and Adrian walk away from each other and depart. They never saw each other again.

After Darrell exits the President's Park, he finds the modified Lamborghini and starts the vehicle. He drives away from the White House as he thoroughly contemplates about the events leading up to the start. He said while entering a highway, "I may be lucky to survive today, but my escape was just the start of it. I still have a story to tell in the end."

Chapter 63: The Count

April 28, 2021

The newspapers were flooded with topics involving IFHR.

A sample of text came from one of the articles:

APRIL 28, 2021

Donovan Lavensa has announced his resignation as the President of the United States earlier this Monday after mentioning his affiliation with the newly, but overly anticipated organization, the IFHR. (International Foundation for Human Resources) Crime scene investigation and forensic

groups traveled around the world to find out more about the

conspiracies leading up to the Civil War of 2020. All groups

have found evidence that were associated with advanced

technology that appeared ahead of today's current

technological levels. Every base contained several cameras

which recorded live video over the course of its founding in

1990. Physical documents such as profiles of agents and

citizens' profiles have been taken for investigation.

The groups counted the amount to be over 2.8 billion

pieces as of April 27, 2021. The evidence ranged from

physical to digital documents, with video footage spanning to

over eighty years and counting from all bases established

from the organization. The organization had a total of

thirteen thousand, five hundred and sixty-seven bases. Stay

tuned on your local news channels to watch an interview

with Darrell Friegman, which was one of the people involved

with terminating the organization. The interview will take

place on June 12, 2021. Further information will be revealed

when possible.

Chapter 64: The Last Laugh

June 12, 2021

Darrell is sitting in a lounging chair beside the host of a talk show. There was a glass table in the middle of a beige carpet floor. There were glass windows behind them as they appeared to be at a high altitude due to the cityscape in the background. The skies appeared to be in the daytime. Darrell and the host wore attire that was composed of all black except for their dress shirt, which is white. They both wore a black tie.

The event was an interview with an interviewee by the

name of Xavier O'Brien. O'Brien had short black hair and was tan in skin color. The dialogue for the airing of the O'Brien Show is as follows:

O'BRIEN: Hey, everyone, welcome to today's episode of the O'Brien Show. Today, we'll be talking to one of the survivors of the Civil War of 2020, Darrell Friegman. How are you doing today, Mr. Friegman?

FRIEGMAN: I've seen better days, O'Brien.

O'BRIEN: So, how did this all start?

FRIEGMAN: Well, first things first, it started out with just a conspiracy. Everybody was talking about it even before I was involved in any way.

O'BRIEN: Give me an example of what people were saying.

FRIEGMAN: Everybody had a different opinion on it. They either chose to walk away and go on with their lives, and others wouldn't stop talking about it. It's like they were attached to trying to find out what the conspiracy was coming from.

O'BRIEN: What do you think were one of the warning signs that caused it to spiral out of control?

FRIEGMAN: I was actually reading a newspaper article when I got off work one day in 2019. The article said that there was a man named Francesco Maldonado that went missing. It said that the witnesses claimed to see people dressed in business attire to be the captors.

O'BRIEN: What happened to you when it comes to your situation?

FRIEGMAN: It's honestly a long story to tell. It was a mix of emotions, a treacherous roller coaster in my point of view.

O'BRIEN: Then tell me the basics. I'm not going to force you to say things you're not comfortable with.

FRIEGMAN: I was getting off work one day. They suddenly decided to go after me. I didn't know what to do, they drove high-performance vehicles most of the time just like almost

everybody else did.

O'BRIEN: How did Phoenix get in the picture?

FRIEGMAN: She thought I was one of them until I explained

my side of the story. She definitely had more nerves than me.

She's one bold woman, I've got to tell you.

O'BRIEN: What was her affiliation?

FRIEGMAN: She wasn't one of them. IFHR had her husband,

but a man named Barrett Atkinson killed him off. She killed

Barrett off soon after.

O'BRIEN: According to the released footage, they're planning

on displaying all of it for the world to see. It's still growing by

the amount they find.

FRIEGMAN: That's what I was hoping for.

O'BRIEN: In 2020, about three weeks before the Civil War on

August 18 of that year, what was the difference between that

incident and the incident a year before?

FRIEGMAN: They don't compare. The first encounter was a trial run. The incident in 2020 was far worse than what I experienced. The threat level was beyond my control, but we had more of a fighting chance. I went through two vehicles until Phoenix hijacked one of their elite vehicles. I was the driver.

O'BRIEN: What make was it?

FRIEGMAN: It was a late-model orange Lamborghini.

O'BRIEN: Do you still have it today? I heard it was modified by a mechanic that used to work in IFHR.

FRIEGMAN: Yes, I still have it, but I only use it if I ever need to for good causes. The mechanic's no longer affiliated with them. He quit working for them because he realized their objective.

O'BRIEN: What was their objective?

FRIEGMAN: To commit omnicide on a catastrophic level, which basically means the intentional destruction of the human species.

O'BRIEN: That's some pretty scary stuff to think about. How about the third encounter, what was that like?

FRIEGMAN: Like I said before, the first encounter was a taste of what the organization was like. The second encounter is when we gathered information from them. The third encounter is when we realized our differences and objectives. The third one was the worst of them all.

O'BRIEN: What was your experience with Russell Arkwright?

FRIEGMAN: He screwed us over during the second encounter. The third encounter was when he started to mess with our heads a little bit. That's when he went rogue.

O'BRIEN: What was his plans during the third encounter?

FRIEGMAN: The Game of Trials is what it was called. We had to travel to different countries to kill off certain members in the organization in order to regain our freedom.

O'BRIEN: What were the consequences and tribulations

during that experience?

FRIEGMAN: It was a bloodbath, something that will stick with me for a long time. It will never go away. We suffered through deaths that were painful to some. Sometimes I wonder why I'm still alive today. If you were in my situation, you would not look at yourself straight in the mirror.

O'BRIEN: What happened towards the end of the third encounter?

FRIEGMAN: The collapse of CATA1 is a tough event for me to discuss, but I'll manage to talk about it. Phoenix was able to kill off all of the agents including herself inside the building. It was the main control of the computers spanning across all of the bases that were ever established.

O'BRIEN: How did Phoenix's death make you feel?

FRIEGMAN: It took me by surprise, she lost her husband, Warren, as well as her parents. The damage was physically and mentally overbearing. The shock wave was so powerful, I wasn't sure if I was going to make it out alive from the speed

that I was going. I was lucky that day.

O'BRIEN: When the helicopters arrived at Morocco, you saw

something by CATA1, what did you think it was?

FRIEGMAN: It was a blue light that was ascending into the

sky. It was the most brightest and beautiful shade of blue

that I've seen. After the blue light hits the clouds, it turned

white and disappeared. It made me think about Phoenix.

She's not in pain anymore. She's with her parents and

husband. She has a chance to be free again and find peace.

O'BRIEN: Let's talk about the resignation of President

Lavensa. Has that impacted you in any way?

FRIEGMAN: Yes and no, no being the primary factor. He was

the one that started the organization from what I learned

during my experiences while fighting against IFHR. I'll admit

that I put my hands on him because of what he did. He

deserved it. Even though he confessed on national television,

I still don't give him credit. Over twelve million innocent people died because of his careless actions.

O'BRIEN: How many members do you know of were killed in action during the encounters?

FRIEGMAN: There were over ten thousand confirmed deaths that I know of.

O'BRIEN: The news in previous times leading to the events stated that the penitentiaries from around the world were being filled up with all of the members of IFHR. There were over five million members affiliated with the organization, is that correct?

FRIEGMAN: Yes, O'Brien.

O'BRIEN: Lavensa was arrested two days after his resignation. He's currently serving time in the penitentiaries. What's your opinion on that?

FRIEGMAN: That's one less person we have to worry about. Our world needs to find peace again instead of worrying about losing things. We tend to love things more than people.

O'BRIEN: What were your plans during your encounters with IFHR?

FRIEGMAN: I wanted to help change the world for the better, hopefully make a difference to people.

O'BRIEN: It seems that your plans are working. Do you have any other plans?

FRIEGMAN: Nothing else, they will stay the same.

O'BRIEN: Alright, that's all of the time we have for today's show. Thank you for coming up to New York City to talk to us today.

FRIEGMAN: Pleasure doing business with you, Mr. O'Brien.

O'BRIEN: Is there anything else you want to say?

FRIEGMAN: I have nothing left to say.

O'BRIEN: Is there any other experiences you want to share with us?

FRIEGMAN: You have the whole world to look up if you're

interested. You can't miss it. It's all in the media.

END OF THE SERIES

Writer's Note

The final installment of this series talks about sacrifice,

tribulation, struggles, and hardships. Sometimes in our

darkest moments, we realize our own goals in life. They will

differ from others as nobody has the same goals. We all have

our own personal struggles we face from time to time. No

matter much you try to explain your struggles, it will never

turn out in perfect form. Sometimes, you have to be your

own best friend to fight through whatever you are going

through on your own. Life is an emotional roller coaster and events turn up when we least expect it.

There comes a time for when you feel like you are going deep into the downward spiral, you need to release your emotions. It is not worth bottling up your feelings, it will only make matters worse.

If you feel something is out of the ordinary, take a step back and think about the situation. Follow your dreams and heart however you can, but be careful in doing so as it also involves taking risks with your life. Unfortunately for some, they do not make it out alive as some have a high level of potential.

If there is something that is holding you back, fight against it however you can and let your emotions out. That is where the term, catharsis comes in, the emotional cleansing through various practices of art. There are points where you have to hurt in order to see success. Your past does not define you, it helps you learn lessons. Your future is yet to be written.

Make a difference today, it may mean the world to someone else.

Hello, everyone! My name is Travis Heeter and I am a musician and a writer that grew up in the small town of Vienna, Ohio. I am the author of The Number Conspiracy series as well as the director of the web series, Codename: Project Space. The series serves as a documentary platform for my second album. As the final installment of the Number Conspiracy closes, I would like to thank the audience for giving me the chance to share my vision with you. However, my journey is just beginning. As the next chapter of this incredible journey opens, I invite you to join me as I adapt to the next platform of my works through the ever-evolving age of technology as we know of today. Thank you to everyone that has made this vision become a reality.

"We are the network, the database, the framework, the collective, and lastly, we are one."

Follow me on the official Travis Heeter and The Number Conspiracy pages on Facebook as well as my YouTube channel:

www.facebook.com/OfficialTravisHeeter

www.facebook.com/TheNumberConspiracy

www.youtube.com/user/TravisHMusic